"Get away from Wheeler City," the sheriff warned.

"I ain't partial to running," the Duke said.

A heavy Colt glided into his hand. The sheriff reached for his weapon. Too late. The Duke's revolver blazed six times in succession.

All the Duke wanted was a chance. But now he had to run—away from the sleepless men who were ready to shoot him down on sight.

Books by Max Brand

Published by POCKET BOOKS

Most Pocket Books are available at special quantity discounts for bulk purchases for sales promotions, premiums or fund raising. Special books or book excerpts can also be created to fit specific needs.

For details write the office of the Vice President of Special Markets, Pocket Books, 1230 Avenue of the Americas, New York, New York 10020.

MAX BRAND

THE BANDIT
OF THE BLACK HILLS

PUBLISHED BY POCKET BOOKS NEW YORK

POCKET BOOKS, a division of Simon & Schuster, Inc.
1230 Avenue of the Americas, New York, N.Y. 10020

ISBN: 0-671-47432-4

First Pocket Books printing October, 1950

12   11   10   9   8   7

CONTENTS

THE BANDIT
OF THE BLACK HILLS

Back to Wheeler City

WHEN THEY HEARD that The Duke was coming back, they gathered from all quarters. Charlie Barr dropped into Wheeler City from Northern Montana. Old man Minter came in from New Mexico near the line. Bill Thunder, of Big Bend fame, got off the train in time to shake hands with Harry Matthews from Spokane. The four were perhaps the most famous of those who came to Wheeler City, but there were others who arrived, one by one, unheralded and unsung, grim-faced men with guns in working order and a sacred purpose of ridding the earth of that celebrated encumbrance, The Duke.

They filled Wheeler City with sleepless nights. Not that they went about proclaiming their intentions from the housetops or at midnight. That was by no means true of them, for they were, on the whole, quiet-spoken, gentle-acting men. And they had come on such a serious mission that much noise was not in order. Men needed quiet so that nerves and brains would be prepared for the sudden test.

And the result was that a terrible silence fell upon Wheeler City. Even during the day men moved about with soft footfalls, and when Sam Curtin, the huge butcher, came in to gossip with old Jake Deland, the hotel proprietor, he talked in a whisper, glancing secretly about him and over his shoulder while he talked.

What was the sheriff's opinion? The sheriff was an old man and a wise man. He bore the weird and unsavory name of Onion. And the cunning of Tom Onion was celebrated afar.

Of course he was consulted by timorous townsfolk. He was asked what he would do. His response was to ask the townsfolk what he could do. And when they went on to say that, if something were not done, there would be a killing when The Duke returned to town, he replied that they were perfectly right, saying that the word "killing" should be put into the plural. Men were certain to die.

The logic of the sheriff was unimpeachable. His attitude might have seemed more questionable. Sheriffs were supposed to do their best to prevent crime, and Tom Onion seemed to be shirking his sworn duty. To balance that opinion there were ten years of fearless and diligent service of the public to the credit of the sheriff. No matter how he talked it was known that his actions would be greater than his words.

But what the sheriff said, most briefly reported, was simply this: The Duke is a killer. We all admit that he is. The longer he lives, the more people he'll kill. He has the taste, the style, the speed and the surety of a natural man-slayer. Sooner or later he must be removed for the safety of society. And the sooner he is removed, the better. I myself am willing to face this celebrated fighter, but I confess I am very glad to have such support. Here we have expert guntoters from the far corners of the fighting West. What could be better? All of these men realize that sooner or later The Duke must be removed from the books— wiped out—erased. They are willing to do the erasing. And if one of them meets The Duke there will be an explosion. It is true that The Duke is just out of prison, and that his name is supposed to be clear at the present moment; but we all know that that's supposing a great deal too much!

Such was the reasoning of the wily sheriff. And more than one other man in Wheeler City agreed with him. The Duke was known to be heading home, and it was well to meet him at the entrance to his old home town with guns well oiled and minds resolved on action.

And The Duke himself?

He detached himself from beneath a freight car when the train slowed to a crawl at the steep grade three miles out of town. From that point The Duke walked in. Why should The Duke, who hated physical exertion of all kinds, and walking above all the rest—why should The Duke walk into Wheeler City?

A foreboding had come to him through the empty air that it would be well to enter Wheeler City softly and without a blare of brass to herald his coming. So The Duke walked in. Neither did he aim straight for the heart of town, though his very vitals had ached with desire to see that place during the three years of his absence. But rather he chose to stalk along the outskirts. He listened at windows and near open doors. He picked up a word here and another there in the broken conversations he overheard, and with the matchless shuttle of suspicion he wove them in a solid cloth. In half an hour of lurking here and there he knew that Wheeler City was filled with armed men who were bent on shooting him down at sight.

When he had made out this information The Duke retired to a dark corner where a tall fence walled him away on three sides with shadow. Here he rolled a cigarette and lighted it and smoked it. It would have been well had his enemies been near by to study his face feature by feature. He was smiling. They would have noted that first.

He had always been a great smiler in the old days. And the prison had not changed him. It had rubbed away his tan; it had rubbed away his clear and healthy color. Instead, his face was chalk-white, so that the straight black brows were the more pronounced. They met like a deep marking of soot straight across his forehead. And beneath them the eyes glittered and went out from time to time like a covered lantern behind its shutter.

And the young men of Wheeler City would have noticed that The Duke was not less good-looking, just as the old men of Wheeler City would have noticed that three years of hard labor in the State penitentiary had not given him a hangdog manner. His spirit was not broken. That, after all, was to be expected. For they had actually cut short his term on account of good behavior.

Good behavior on the part of The Duke!

However, the world could not be expected to know The Duke as Wheeler City knew him. And when the glow of the cigarette illumined The Duke's smile, the world could not be expected to know that Wheeler City dreaded that particular sort of smile, with the white teeth showing, more than it dreaded The Duke's frown.

He finished the cigarette down to a small butt. Then he dropped it, ground it carefully under his heel, rose and stretched every muscle in his six-feet-one of length. In this fashion a cat, which has been drowsing by the fire through the evening, rises, stretches, makes sure of its strength, and then, with silent footfalls, steals out into the black night to hunt. And as it unsheathes its claws from their cushions of silk, so The Duke unsheathed his six-shooter, weighed it lightly in his long fingers and then stowed it away again.

Having done this, he went straight to the sheriff's house. He went there because the town would least expect to find him in that place, and therefore it would be safest. He went there also because, of all things, The Duke most dearly loved to do the unexpected.

When he reached the dwelling, a brief survey through the windows convinced him that the sheriff was not at home. The sheriff's wife and his two daughters were finishing the supper dishes in the kitchen. So The Duke went around to the veranda and opened the window of the sheriff's office. He stepped inside, sat down in a comfortable chair in the corner behind the filing cabinet, folded his hands in his lap, leaned his head against the wall, and closed his eyes. For he knew that with the eyes shut one's senses are far more alert and acute in the blackness of night. Also, he wanted to think.

His thoughts were a swift survey of his life. He began with the time when he had been a nameless, fatherless, motherless foundling, drifting here and there, picking up a living at the age of eight by doing chores. He followed the course of his life until, a little past adolescence, he had discovered two things: First, that work was mortally distasteful; second, that he had qualities which set him apart from his fellow men.

It is dangerous enough at any period of life for a man to learn that he is more blessed in certain God-given essentials than are his companions. But it is trebly dangerous when the discovery is made in childhood. And at the green age of fourteen, The Duke acquired both his strange nickname and his reputation. He got his name on account of his careless scorn of even the most formidable ruffians on the wide cattle range where formidable and freedom-loving men are apt to gather. And he got his reputation through his uncanny ability with a gun.

It was not that The Duke was vain of his accomplishment or that he boasted of it or that he cherished his attainment with constant practice. But when he drew forth a gun it seemed that a tightened string ran from its muzzle to the target he wished to strike. Just as some men are born with great speed in their legs and others are born with a keen taste for sweets and sours, so The Duke was born with an eye which looked straight and with nerves which could not tremble. One is not vain of such inborn accomplishments any more than one is vain of a gold mine which one has stumbled upon by chance. But just as one is sure to dig out the gold and spend it, so The Duke could not avoid exploiting his powers.

There followed three years of riotous adventure and wild living. He roamed from Alaska to the City of Mexico, and wherever he went he stayed only long enough to build up a fame which caused brave men to avoid him. Then he went on to fresh fields and pastures new to find untried foemen. He did not cling to gunwork only. If it were a matter of fisticuffs, at sixteen he had the strength of a grown man and the natural speed of a wildcat. In the winter of his seventeenth year he lived in lumber camps in Canada and passed through a graduate school in rough-and-tumble fighting. And the following spring and summer he was initiated into the intricate mysteries of a profession of which he already knew the ABC's and the simple grammar—knife play.

And still, no matter where he went and no matter what he did, he was forgiven. For he was "only a boy." And if a boy wanted to fight grown men it was the fault of the men if they were injured. Surely no jury could convict him.

There was a sudden change, however, in his eighteenth year. He had had his full height now for two years, and for two years he had been broadening and hardening into the full strength and the full bearing of manhood. At seventeen he had looked nineteen or twenty. At eighteen, a scant year later, he looked all of twenty-four.

And in the West a man is a man at twenty-four. The

Duke discovered it to his cost on a day in New Mexico when he fell into an argument with three stalwart Mexicans and settled the dispute with his gun. It did not matter afterward that he offered to pay the funeral expenses of the dead man and the hospital bills of the other two. He was led to a jail. They starved him on meager fare for a week, and then the sheriff, a mild man, came to him and said he believed the thing might have been mere self-defense, that a jury, however, would hang him, and that he had better get out. So that night he dug a hole through the wall and escaped.

The next lesson was in the State of Washington. For a little exercise one evening he found that he had all the grown men of the town riding hard on his heels. He managed to square that account by hunting down that notorious man-killer and robber, Nicolo Baccigalupi, better known by the awful title of "Black Nick." He found Black Nick, challenged him, shot a gun out of his hand and brought the wounded captive into town. And for that deed he was pardoned the wounds he had dealt two days before and allowed to go on his way.

But after those first two exploits he came to realize that the world was looking upon him through different eyes. However, it is sometimes easier to see danger than to avoid it. And to The Duke it had been bread and meat. He could not keep his hands out of trouble. He had kicked up ructions for three years and more. And now the horned gentleman was his bunky, so to speak.

What The Duke did in his eighteenth year would have filled several books, until at last, on a hurried excursion back to Wheeler City, he saw the sweet face of Linda Murray. From that moment he decided that he would make Wheeler City his home both in name and in fact. He would settle down. He would no longer strive to get rich at the card table, but by honest labor he would make honest wages, save them, and so earn the means of establishing a home for Linda. And all was smooth before him. Linda was swept from her feet by this hero of eighteen who looked a man full grown, and had about him the aroma of strange deeds and strange lands. If she were a year or two his senior, it did not matter. All went on well enough.

And then came that Saturday night trip to town from old man Carter's ranch where he was working, the meeting with Springer, the interplay of jests, the sudden hard words, the shooting.

The thoughts of The Duke vanished. The front door of the sheriff's house had opened, and footfalls and voices were sounding in the hall.

2

◉

Guthrie's Madman

THIS WAS ALL extremely awkward. He had planned on meeting the sheriff alone. But if he encountered two men they were both apt to start shooting without asking for explanations of why he was waiting for them there in that darkened room. He would have tried to slip away through the window, but if they opened the door and saw the silhouette of a man escaping through the window they would unquestionably fill him full of lead. So he got up from his chair, backed into the corner behind the filing cabinet, and saw that his revolver was in readiness. Then he waited.

The door to the office opened. The two voices mumbled to a pause as the speakers stepped into the blackness. Then a match was scratched, and The Duke saw the pale light waver across the ceiling with its network of deep cracks and fissures. A lamp was lighted, and the glow of it, as the flame settled in the circular burner, seemed to The Duke as bright as the sun of midday. Where would they sit down? No matter where, one of them was sure to see him. And then the explosion!

But: "I ain't going to sit down, Sheriff," said the voice of the stranger.

"All right, Mr. Guthrie. If you're pressed for time—"

"I'm making it back to the ranch tonight."

"Tonight!"

"Yes, sir."

"Thirty miles by buckboard in the dark on those roads?"

"If the hosses will stand it, I'll stand it, Sheriff Onion."

"You know your own business, Mr. Guthrie."

"I don't know my own business. Otherwise I wouldn't be here. All I know is that some murdering hound up in the Black Hills has been using my ranch as a sort of general merchandise store for the past two years, and when I got tired of having things stole out of my saddle room or out of my pantry, and when I started to get my punchers together and send 'em out to trail him down, he pays me back by slipping down out of his hills and trying to murder me!"

"The devil!" said the sheriff.

"That's putting it mild!"

"I've heard that yarn about the man in the Black Hills. Matter of fact, we've all heard about him. And I have my explanation. When you told me about it first, I tried to explain—"

"I know," broke in Guthrie impatiently. "You tried to explain by saying that there wasn't any one man in the Black Hills, but that it was a sort of stopping place for long riders and scamps of one sort and another on their way across country, and that the reason they all picked on me was because my ranch was the only one near to the hills. That's the way you talked then."

"And I still say the same thing. I'll tell you why I know. If there were one man living all the time in the Black Hills, I'd of come across his sign when I was hunting him there, and I've hunted the Black Hills four times to get at this ghost robber of yours, Guthrie."

"That proves nothing."

The sheriff flushed. He was a known trailer. "Maybe not. Maybe it don't mean much. But I've spent a solid month in the Black Hills. I've trailed 'em from bottom to the top. I've gone over 'em with a microscope, you might say. And I ain't seen signs that are more than just here and there. There ain't any trails of the kind a man would make if he was living there all the time. Another thing, Guthrie. If he was up there regular, wouldn't he be riding down here all the time and cleaning up in Wheeler City and all the other towns around the Black Hills?"

There was a grunt from Guthrie.

"I dunno about that," he said. "All I know is that the same gent is the one that's doing the work out to my ranch."

"What proof have you got?" asked the sheriff wearily.

"The way he does things."

"Well?"

"And the fact that he's been seen!"

"You saw him two years ago." The sheriff yawned, manifestly weary of this profitless and stubborn talk. "You got on the trail of somebody that had stole a side of bacon, and you and your boys rode till you come in sight of a gent on a pinto. You see that gent about half a mile away, I figure!"

"Closer'n that."

"Not close enough for shooting."

"Close enough to see his long hair and to see that it was black and that he was not more'n twenty-five. Nope, he was a pile younger'n that."

"Well," said the sheriff, suppressing a chuckle, "you figure that this same gent is still doing the raiding?"

"I do that."

"What's your evidence?"

"I seen him yesterday not a hundred feet away!"

"The devil!" gasped the sheriff, his indifference quite gone.

"It was worse'n the devil."

"A hundred feet away?"

"With light in his face!"

"Guthrie, this is important. What did he look like?"

"Like he hadn't got no older in these two years. He had the same long black hair. Didn't look much older'n a kid. Fine-looking, sort of. But good looks don't make a good man!"

"Not by some miles they don't! Ain't The Duke the handsomest boy you ever seen?"

"He was before my time, but this young mountain rat has the nerve of the devil himself. Lemme tell you what

happened! He came down a couple of days ago and tried
to raid me, but one of my punchers seen him. He raised a
yell and he started after this gent. The man from the Black
Hills lighted out for the Black Hills. They got close enough
to him to see that he could ride like the devil, but he
ducked away from them, and they lost the trail. Which I
got sort of mad and had a talk with my nephew Steve.
Steve and me figured it would be pretty good to lay for
this robber. We done it yesterday, and we pretty near
caught him coming down out of the hills about twilight.
If there'd been bright sun we'd of filled him full of lead
and salted him away for keeps. But the dull light bothered
us, and this outlaw rode his pinto like a snipe flying. He
dodged across country, and when we seen we'd missed
him and tried to ride him down, he had enough of a lead.
He cut back into the hills and seemed to just melt away
into the solid rock.

"But it must of sort of riled him to have me follow him
up that way. He came down last night and shot at me
through the window. The slug chipped off a chunk of
hair above my ear!"

"The murdering hound!" growled the sheriff. "There
ought to be a law to burn a sneak alive."

"I grabbed a gun and cut for the outside. When I come
out I seen the young hound standing—where would you
think?"

"Can't guess, Guthrie."

"Right by the window of the bunkhouse. That was how
I seen him so clear. The lamplight was shining through on
him—and he was laughing!"

"But didn't you have a gun?"

"I did, but I ain't the champion shot in the world, and
he must have knowed it. He was rolling a cigarette, I
think. I ups with my gun and blazes away. Hanged if he
didn't keep standing there a second right in the light—to
finish his cigarette, I guess—and finally he just strolled
around the corner of the bunkhouse!"

"Where were your punchers?"

"They came tearing out of the bunkhouse. I tried to
holler to them to run around behind the bunkhouse and
they'd catch the man I wanted. But they had heard the
shooting. The slugs I'd fired at the thief had whacked right

through the walls of the house. They all were shouting to one another, and they didn't hear me. Doggone me if the fools didn't start running to get hosses—like as if they couldn't even think till they'd got into saddles. And by the time they got all ready and on their hosses, of course the killer was clean gone. We trailed him this morning, though. He'd come right up behind the bunkhouse. He'd left his hoss there. Then he'd gone exploring. We follered his sign clear back to the Black Hills, but we lost the trail in the rocks there. And that's why I'm here, Sheriff. I'll be a dead man inside of a week if I don't get some sort of protection!"

"Guthrie," said the sheriff, "this is sure a queer yarn, but you're going to get protection. Kind of gives me the creeps just to think of this! There's only one explanation —you're right and I'm wrong. And there's only one kind of gent that would fire through a window at you and then stand off and laugh at you and your gun as you come out."

"What do you mean?"

"Don't you understand? The fellow's insane!"

"A crazy man!" gasped Guthrie. "By the Lord, Sheriff, you're right. But it's sure going to take all the nerve out of me to go back and face that sort of music!"

"How about the punchers?"

"They're getting plumb nervous. An old hand quit and come in with me in the buckboard this morning. And after he'd told his story around I couldn't get nobody to take his place."

"That's hard luck, Guthrie. How about your nephew?"

"He stands it fine. There ain't such a thing as fear in Steve. When I was young I had a pretty steady nerve myself, but it sort of oozes out of a man when he gets along in years. But Steve will stay by me through thick and thin. Pray Heaven this crazy man-killer don't get Steve instead of me!"

His voice shook with emotion.

"Guthrie," said the sheriff gently, "I'd like to go out and stay on your ranch myself, but you know the trouble I'm going to have with The Duke. I'm needed here on the firing line. But I'll get some sort of protection out to you."

"The sooner the quicker, Sheriff."

"The sooner the quicker. Keep your head up. Maybe you'll never see the young rat again, anyhow."

There was a dubious groan from the rancher, and his heavy footfall left the room. The sheriff closed the door behind him. Already the problem of the rancher had left his mind. So accustomed was he to dealing with the terrors and the sorrows of other men that he was actually humming as he stepped back toward his desk. And this was the moment The Duke chose to step out from his place of concealment.

3

◉

The Duke Dispels a Doubt

IT WAS A RUDE shock for the sheriff. His eyes rolled wildly, as though he were unable to choose between earthly or ghostly fear and identify his visitor. But presently, gray of face, shaky of voice, he said: "The Duke!"

"That same," said The Duke cheerfully.

The sheriff shrugged his shoulders to gather his nerve. He advanced with hand outstretched. He forced a wan smile to curve his lips.

"John Morrow," he said, "'no matter what men have held against you, you are now a clean man in the eyes of the law. I'm glad to welcome you back, and I only hope that you stay here in peace."

His unregarded hand fell to his side. The Duke was looking him in the eyes with that strangely mortifying scorn and quiet contempt which had won him his name. The sheriff drew back a little with a troubled frown.

"I'm wrong about your intentions then, Morrow?"

The Duke smiled upon him and displayed an even line of teeth, flashing white—as scrupulously cared for as the tapering tips of The Duke's fingers, with which he made his living at cards.

"Never wrong about me, Sheriff," said The Duke. "I ain't here looking for no disturbance. I'm a peace-keeper."

The sheriff maintained as solemn a face as possible and nodded.

"No matter how hard I try," said The Duke, "there's going to be somebody around to spoil the sleep for me and the rest of the town. Don't it look that way?"

The sheriff avoided answer by making a cigarette.

"Sit down," he said when The Duke had refused the "makings."

The Duke took the suggested chair and drew it into the farther corner. There he sat down, with no possibility of anything coming behind him or of anyone looking in upon him through the window. The sheriff had observed these maneuvers with the keenest attention. And suddenly he said, as he sank into a chair facing that of The Duke, "Morrow, how old are you?"

"It doesn't peeve me none to have folks call me Duke," said the latter carelessly. "You don't have to think up that Morrow name. How old am I? I'm old enough to vote."

"I guess you're that old," and the sheriff grinned.

"I was twenty-one last May," said The Duke.

The sheriff thought a moment. "By heavens, it's true!"

"That's sort of mild cussing for you, Sheriff," said The Duke.

"It is," said the other. "But—Duke, how many lifetimes have you crammed into the past seven years?"

"Into the past four years, you mean," said The Duke. "These three just behind me I haven't been living."

He smiled upon the sheriff in such a way that the latter hastily puffed on his cigarette and threw up a smoke screen between himself and his companion. He felt a little more easy behind that false shelter.

"As bad as that?" he said. "Why, I thought that they treated you pretty good down yonder. Didn't they chop a whole year of your term?"

"Sure. The warden got me pardoned," said The Duke. "But you can't be treated well inside of a prison. Stones ain't got the sort of conversation that cheers a man up."

The sheriff shrugged himself into a more comfortable position.

"I guess that's right," he said. "And on you, after being free all your life more'n the average man was free, I guess it was a mite extra hard."

"I boiled down thirty years inside the three," said The Duke calmly. "That's all it meant."

He leaned forward. He took off his hat.

"Look at me," he said as his head came close into the bright circle of the lamplight.

The sheriff looked, and what he saw amazed him. There was a thick sprinkling of gray in the black hair of The Duke. And now that his face was so close to the light he could see that many years had been stamped into the features and the expression. It was enough to make him shudder. And then, sitting back in his chair once more, he drew a great breath and cleared his throat. This interview was beginning to get on his nerves. What did The Duke want with him? Why this continued gentleness? Where was the old insolent, high-handed manner? Where was the flashing eye, the ready sneer, the cutting words? Truly The Duke had changed miraculously. Only his smile was the same—mirthless, cruel, slow.

"I wanted you to see that," said The Duke, "so's you could understand something."

"I'm listening, Duke."

"I want to quit."

"Eh?"

"I'm through with the game, Sheriff. I want to start in being plumb peaceful."

The sheriff nodded.

"I hope you have luck, Duke."

"You don't think I mean it then? Or you think I can't stick to the resolution? Sheriff, I'm more changed inside than I show in the face, even!"

"You are?"

Here the sheriff sat up with a little more assurance and looked at his terrible visitor more closely. Was it not possible, indeed, that the claws of the lion had been clipped and his teeth drawn?

"I'm all changed," said The Duke.

"I sure hope so. Are you going back to the Carter ranch?"

"I'm going to see Linda first," said the man from prison. He raised his head and smiled. "I sure want to see Linda!" He looked down at the sheriff. "I'll let her tell me what's next best to do."

He found that the sheriff was rubbing his jaw and looking vacantly at him.

"You ain't stopped being fond of that girl, eh?"

"Of course not." He rose suddenly from his chair. His voice changed. "Why should I be?" he demanded.

"No reason," breathed the sheriff as though a gun had been shoved under his nose. "No reason at all—I guess!"

"Partner," said The Duke, all his nonchalance completely gone and his face white and drawn with emotion, "you got something to tell me!"

"Nothing, Duke," said the wretched sheriff, wrung by both pity and dread.

"Sheriff, I've got to have it out of you!"

"You were away too long, Duke."

"And she's married another man!"

"Not that."

"She's engaged then?"

The sheriff nodded, and The Duke stepped back from him, back into the shadow near the wall. Whether he was more struck to the heart by true disappointment such as any lover might feel, or whether he was more tortured by a sense of injured vanity, the sheriff could not decide. But when The Duke stepped a little closer again so that his face could be seen quite clearly, he had controlled his expression. The half-cynical, half-contemptuous smile which was now habitual on his face was playing there again.

"I might of known," he said. "Which a girl is sure to get lonely inside of three years. But who's the man, Sheriff?"

No matter how smooth and purring the voice of The Duke, the sheriff knew that there was danger ahead.

"Don't make much difference, does it? Nobody tried to knife you while your back was turned, Duke."

"No?"

That drawling, queried monosyllable made the sheriff

shiver as though ice had been trailed up and down his spine.

"It just happened. Time makes a lot of difference with a young girl, Duke. Besides—"

"Besides, it would have been sort of hard on her to have anything to do with a jailbird."

"I didn't say that."

"Then I read your mind, Sheriff. But who's the man?"

"Duke, you ain't going to start on his trail?"

"And get back inside the prison again?" The Duke laughed in a singular and mirthless manner. "I ain't a fool. If I ever do anything from this time on, it'll be things that the law can't lay a hand on me for. Oh, I've learned my lesson. But I'm curious. Who's the man that got pretty Linda Murray?"

Something in his way of saying "pretty Linda Murray" was proof that in the past ten seconds he had thrust all thought of the girl—at least all hope of her—out of his life forever. And the thought of the cruelly controlled will power which must have been used to bring about such a result made the sheriff sweat with wonder.

"You'd find out sooner or later. It's a gent that you already ain't got much use for. It's Bud Springer, Duke!"

He waited anxiously. But presently The Duke broke into hearty laughter. The sound of that laughter was not audible beyond the room in which they were sitting, but the force of it shook his body.

"That's what I call a pretty good joke," said The Duke. "The gent that I get sent to jail for shooting is the same gent that gets my girl while I'm away!"

And he smiled again, but his face was a sickly color.

"Linda must have been sure fond of me," he commented, "to pick up with that—"

"She was sorry for Bud. You—see—"

"Let's stop talking about her," said The Duke dryly. "If I left a hoss behind me it would have mourned for me a longer time then she done. And if it was so plumb easy for her to forget all about me I reckon that it will be plumb easy for me to forget all about her. But what I want to know about now is this here reception committee that's so doggone anxious to say 'Welcome Home' to me!"

The sheriff smiled in spite of himself.

"The town ain't exactly full of friends of yours, Duke."

"No, it ain't," agreed The Duke. "Some of 'em have come quite a ways looking for me. What's the meaning of it, Sheriff?"

"Can't you guess?"

"Sure. I know that they've come to sink a chunk of lead in me if they can. But once upon a time they wouldn't't've been so anxious—" He hesitated, at a loss for words.

"Once upon a time," translated the sheriff, "they would just as soon have put a noose around their necks as come out hunting The Duke. I know, Duke; but while you been away some of the boys have been practicing with their guns. I suppose they figure that they've got a better chance at you."

"It's open season on me, eh? They can any of 'em go for their gats and try to drop me the minute I'm in sight. And him that gets me will only be cheered. No arrest for him! They'd give him a vote of thanks, most like!"

"In the old days," said the sheriff, "didn't you declare open season on everybody else? Did you hold back to think and ponder any? No, Duke, you went out to get into trouble, and you sure enough got there. Who you hurt didn't make no difference to you. Well, when they hear that you're out of prison, everybody that you've ever injured comes up here loaded for bear. There's Bill Thunder—Billy Hancock, you know. He comes up from Big Bend. He allows that when you dropped his brother, young Hal Hancock, four years back, you done it by taking advantage. And there's Charlie Barr come out of Montana way, saying that you done him dirt a long time ago. And there's others come from every direction. Before, they kept still. They sort of figured that there wasn't no hope in trying to stand up agin' you. But now—"

"But now they figure that I'm out of practice?"

"Something like that."

"So they're stepping out and roaring around pretty loud?"

"Duke, the thing for you to do is to forget that you ever lived in this town. Get away from Wheeler City and stay away! There's too many of 'em here!"

"Get away and stay away?" murmured the ex-convict.

"And once I'm gone, have it known all over the ranges that I've showed the white feather?"

"Running from a whole crowd ain't showing the white feather, Duke!"

The Duke stiffened to his full height, and he seemed a giant to the sheriff as the latter looked up at him.

"I ain't particular partial to running, Sheriff!" he said.

The sheriff swallowed and said nothing. He had picked up a box of fishhooks and was juggling them in his hand. Suddenly the ex-convict took the little box from the hand of Tom Onion, crossed the room and stuck a row of six hooks from the lowest rim of the window sash. He crossed the room to the farthest side again, walking slowly, very slowly. And the sheriff, amazed and worried, stared from his guest to the hooks in the window. They were tiny, glimmering points of light as the rays from the lamps touched on the gilt. And as The Duke crossed the room he was talking deliberately to the sheriff.

"I'm not leaving the town, Sheriff," he said. "I've come back to Wheeler City plumb peaceable, but not anxious to move. No, sir, I ain't running from town to get away from nobody! The main reason is something that may surprise you to hear. Sheriff, the yarn I told at my trial, and that everybody laughed at, was a true yarn. I didn't shoot Bud Springer in the back. It's true that we had an argument. It's true that we were pretty close to a gun play. But we stayed on the safe side of one. And the reason was that Bud didn't want none of my medicine. But while we was still talking pretty loud somebody fired through the window and dropped Bud. It was some dirty sneak that knew I'd be blamed for what had happened. I picked Bud up. You remember that he didn't accuse me till the next morning? And I tell you that that night somebody had got to Bud and bribed him or persuaded him to put the blame on me. Or maybe Bud had worked it out that if he got rid of me in jail he'd have a better chance with Linda—"

As he spoke these words he whirled on his heel. As he spun, a heavy Colt had glided into his hand. The sheriff made a futile gesture toward his own weapon, then saw it was far too late and sat quiet. But he was not the target for The Duke. The revolver blazed six times in swift succession—reports crowded as close together as the staccato beat of a typewriter.

And all in a second the firing was ended, and the shriek of the sheriff's wife from the kitchen came to them.

"I'm not leaving Wheeler City," said the ex-convict. "I'm here to stay. If any of the boys that have traveled so far to see me are plumb set on finding me, you tell them that I'm going to have a good sleep tonight, and that to-morrow night I'm going to be out to the big dance at Warner's Springs. If they want to see me bad they can find me there. You can give these six fishhooks to the six that want to find me the most!"

So saying, he stepped out of the window just as the opposite door flew open and the sheriff's wife ran in.

4

◉

The Stamp of the Lawbreaker

IT WAS, OF COURSE, impossible for the sheriff to do anything for a time but attempt to soothe and quiet his wife and assure her that he was not suffering from a mortal injury dealt by the gun of an assassin. And when his wife was off his hands there were eager neighbors who flocked in, drawn by the sound of the fusillade.

To the latter the sheriff showed the demonstration. He went to the window sill. He found in it six heads of fishhooks which had been sunk into the wood just at the edge of the sill. But the parts which projected downward, namely, the eye and the slender shaft of the hook, had been blown away, the metal being clipped off cleanly. And in no instance, saving one only, had the bullet touched the wood. In that case there was a light graze funneling the lower surface of the sill.

The sheriff did not draw out the hooks. Instead, he called his good friends to behold the sight. He held the lamp so that they could see better.

"And all six shots fired by lamplight," he explained calmly, "and all the time used up in getting out his gun and firing them six shots was just about the time that it would take an average good hand with a Colt to get out his gat and pump in one placed shot. Yes, friends, I got to admit that The Duke has fallen down in his shooting so's he can't do better than this. Look how he actually cut the wood with one of them six shots!"

The irony of the sheriff was not needed to drive home the point. The crowd saw, understood, and went away abashed to tell the tale to others. And others heard and came to see for themselves. Big Bill Thunder heard the tale and laughed heartily in derision and came to see for himself. And Big Bill Thunder saw, swore reverently under his breath, and retired with a thoughtful look. And others came to behold it. There was Charlie Barr, and Harry Matthews, who had ridden in all the way from Spokane to "get" his man. And old man Minter came and looked and said nothing and departed in silence. And the others came. They rose out of their beds in the hotel and made a hurried pilgrimage.

It was not until midnight that the sheriff's house was silent again. The rest of Wheeler City, meantime, was murmuring. A faint buzz of conversation did not go out with the lamps, and there was a strain of talk here and there until the dawn came and wakened the rest of the town.

Once well awakened, the town heard new tidings passed around, and with the news went great laughter. Terrible old man Minter was gone from Wheeler City for parts unknown. Harry Matthews, who had come all the way from Spokane, had presumably started all the way back again. Charlie Barr was nowhere to be found, and Bill Thunder had presumably felt a sudden passion to see once more the muddy waters of the Rio Grande.

All, all the heroes were gone! And on the field of battle there was left only the solitary form of The Duke. Yes, in the drowsy latter half of the warm July morning The Duke appeared, strolling with the utmost leisure down the street.

And, with his accustomed courtesy, he was seen raising his hat to the ladies and bowing to the men.

Who had taught The Duke these strangely formal manners? Perhaps he had learned them from some old Mexican gentleman who had about him more of the Spanish than a mere name. Perhaps something was born into The Duke, something of which he himself knew nothing. But at least there was no example for that stately courtesy, that formalism of manners, in Wheeler City or in any of its environs.

So down the street went The Duke, and it seemed to matter nothing to him that the men he encountered stared and grunted in answer to his salutations, and that the women, whether old or young, stared and did not answer at all.

"They been telling yarns about me," said The Duke calmly. "Doggone if they ain't been telling stories about me all the time. They got me eating raw meat by this time."

The thought pleased him so much and seemed so apt that he paused in the middle of a stride and laughed heartily, albeit in silence. That laughter was noted by a little boy who, clinging to the calico skirts of his mother, was passing on the farther side of the street. And he gasped in terror and excitement. That fear in the child was not unnoticed by The Duke. It made his brow black with anger—but in an instant he had smoothed his expression again and had gone smiling on his way.

He reached the hotel. On the veranda he lingered and looked up and down its length as he stood on the middle step, leading in from the street. But not one of the half dozen loungers cared to meet his eye. He strolled to the door of the musty old room which served as a lobby. And there was no violent and sudden stir of angry and courageous men jumping to their feet to open fire on him.

The Duke looked them over one by one with that famous smile of his. Then he turned, paused on the veranda to roll a cigarette, and, finally, with smoke curling above his head, stepped down to the street and continued on his way.

It was even worse than he had imagined. He had fondly thought that a term served for an offense wipes out the balance against a wrongdoer. Now he saw that society is apt to use a penitentiary merely as a means of putting a brand upon a man by which he may be set apart from the law-abiding during the rest of his mortal days. He had done the spectacular thing. He had routed his enemies before they had a chance to strike a blow at him, but the victory remained with the hostile forces!

He paused in front of the blacksmith shop which Bud Springer operated. He stepped to the door. Instantly there was confusion within. A door opened hastily at the rear of the shop, and a shadowy form, screened by the smoke from the forge, disappeared. And Bud's three helpers stood around silently, waiting, staring at the newcomer.

"Is Bud here?" asked The Duke quietly.

There was no answer—nothing save those staring eyes fixed solemnly upon his face; and no one spoke. If things had come to such a pass as this, it was very bad indeed. He went on down the street with a faint smile still on his lips, but with desolation in his heart. They were all turned against him, every man of them, and the odds were crushing.

He went on without heeding where his footsteps were leading him until he stopped short with a start. Without his conscious volition he had turned from the main street and gone up a by-alley. Now he found himself squarely in front of the Murray house, and yonder was Mrs. Deacon, watering her hedge of sweet peas and watching— watching eagerly to see what he would do. And there was Mrs. Seth Murphy standing at her kitchen window and peering out. What should he do? He could not retreat now that he had come as far as this. So he turned in at the Murray gate. He climbed the steps. He tapped at the front door.

"Is that you, Bud?" called the voice of Linda from within.

He did not answer. There was a scurry of footsteps. The door was jerked open, and he found himself standing before the smiling, expectant girl. The smile went out at sight of him. She even jerked the door almost shut, but she opened it again on a crack and peered at him, a colorless and frightened face.

The Duke, removing his wide-brimmed sombrero,

studied that face carefully. No matter how he himself had changed, the girl had altered even more. Or was he seeing the truth about her for the first time? It had never occurred to him in the old days that her eyes were a little close together or that her forehead was unnecessarily low or that her mouth was too generously wide. And certainly in three years the bloom was gone from her cheeks. She was the same—and yet she was entirely different. This was Linda, but he noted curiously that she did not affect him as he had expected she would. There was no sudden wrench and tearing at his heartstrings. It was as though he had picked a rose and raised it and found that the fragrance of the blossom was gone.

"Have you—have you—have you come to see me?" stammered Linda faintly.

"If you ain't too busy," said The Duke and smiled upon her.

Linda opened the door. She hesitated another moment.

"Will you come in—John?"

She had been almost the only person in the mountains who called him by his real name. The sound of it came sweetly home to him.

"I guess I'll stay here, Linda," he answered. "I just dropped around to give you a message."

"From whom?"

"From myself. I've come to tell you that Bud don't have to worry none about me. I went to see him and tell him the same thing, but I couldn't find him at his shop. I guess he had business some other place."

In spite of himself a faint sneer crept into his voice, and Linda colored hotly to the eyes.

"Bud ain't told me that he was worrying," she said.

"Is he keeping secrets from you already?" The Duke laughed.

He saw her wince under the acid of his irony.

"And, finally," he said, "I've come to wish you and Bud good luck."

He held out his hand. Slowly she put her own forth to meet it. He felt the tremor of her body as their fingers closed together, then fell apart.

"Oh, John," she was saying faintly, "it was such a long time, and people were saying such a lot of things—"

"Of course," said The Duke. "You couldn't wait forever."

"And we were so young," said Linda, half sobbing.

"We're older now," said The Duke. "We can see how foolish we were, Linda."

"I—yes," murmured Linda faintly

Certainly there was no joy in her voice. There was even a shade of wistfulness. Or so it seemed to The Duke.

He stepped back to the edge of the veranda.

"Good-bye, Linda."

"Good-bye, John."

He went down the street. He turned again at the gate and raised his hat to her once more. And was it not possible that the presence of the watchful ladies across the street made his smile even brighter than there was need as he turned away?

5

◉

"Raised for an Outlaw"

BUT HE KNEW one thing with perfect surety as he went down the street again. Being free of Linda was like being free from deep sand when one wishes to ride fast. Being free from Linda was like coming from a hot lowland onto a breezy plateau. He put behind him the awakening from that old dream. If only he could have seen the truth about her three years before, how much happier that prison life would have been! As for Bud Springer, let him have all joy and happiness!

He went on to the verge of the town. It was not the same outer verge which he had known. Wheeler City had had a new lease of life and had spread outward rapidly during the past few years. But even the newcomers had heard of him. Doubtless the town paper had carried his picture during the past few days. Everyone was familiarized with the face of the "bad man." Yonder a stocky, dark-skinned little man who was hoeing in a vegetable garden stopped at his work and straightened to look at him with the wide and staring eyes to which The Duke was growing accustomed. He had heard all about the manslayer, and a faint dread of death was what made him stare so fixedly. And yonder was another he had never seen before, a buxom dame shrilling to her children and calling them in from the yard where they played. Now she gathered her two boys close to her and stared defiantly at the tall man in the street.

What did they take him to be—an ogre?

And yet there was an odd thrill about this. Better to be dreaded even by women and children than to be despised. Better to be like this than like Bud Springer, for instance, dodging out through the rear door of his shop when danger approached from the front. There was something fated about it. He had come home determined to live the life of a quiet and law-abiding man. But who could be quiet and law-abiding in such a murderous atmosphere of suspicion? If all their hands were to be against him, let his hand, then, be against all other men! There was a charm in that dark and fatal future which fascinated him. In a little while, perhaps today or perhaps tomorrow, there was sure to be a crash. And afterward he would be an outlaw. As an outlaw he might maintain the battle for a few months, a few years, of skulking hither and thither, chilled by every rain and burned by every sun, wretched, lonely, supported in a desire to live only by the fierce joy of maintaining a single hand against the united force of society. And then a death, hunted down by numbers—a fighting death with his boots on!

Such was the force of these gloomy and exciting thoughts that he had slowed his walk and finally had halted with his head bowed. He did not raise it again until he heard the loud creaking of a heavy wagon in the near distance—and the jarring rattle of an empty wagonbed. He looked up in time to see the lead pair of a long team turn the corner, and span after span with nodding heads and the sagging traces which betokened an easy load or no load at all.

It was a huge freighter capable of supporting a burden of twenty thousand pounds over all the jarring rocks and the twisting ruts of the mountain roads. Its iron-spoked wheels rose as tall as a man. In front of it straggled seven couples of horses controlled by a jerkline from the driver on the lofty seat. The wrath of this driver was now aroused by the off horse in the sixes, a tall gray which must have stood a full sixteen two, and which was bucking and dancing and hurling itself from side to side with all its might. But it was helpless. Behind was the ponderous wagon on which, if necessary, the driver could jam the great brakes. And as for stepping to one side or the other, the weight and the strength of the horse ahead of him and of the horse beside him or the one behind him prevented. Yet he struggled like a mad creature, striving to draw back his head through the collar, then hurling himself forward as though bent on ripping his harness to bits. His gray coat was blackened with sweat, and bits of foam covered him.

The driver had been thrown into a paroxysm of fury, no doubt by the long continuance of the performance. Now he stood up in his place and swung the six-horse whip. In an amateur's hands that long stalk and that cumbersome, braided lash were worse than useless, and the lash was generally swung only to be curled around the neck of him who wielded it. But Tony Samatti was a man of another ilk. With all that length of stalk and lash it was said of Tony that he could swing and cut in two the horsefly on the hip of a horse without touching the hide of the horse. This was doubtless an exaggeration, but certain it was that he could wield his tremendous weapon with such force that it sliced through the hide as though there were a knife blade at work.

And he was plying the whip now, not with oaths but in a dreadful silence, his jaws locked, and the crack of the whip sending shivers through the rest of the team. They crouched and leaned anxiously into the collars, in dread lest their turn to taste fire should come next. And The Duke, lifting his fine head, walked around the leaders to get a better view of the punished horse.

He had had only a glimpse before. Now he could make sure that he had been right. The gray horse was far spent with exhaustion, but he was fighting with unabated vigor. In ten minutes more he would kill himself, and the dark-faced foreigner who drove would probably be glad to see him die.

Plainly this animal was a misfit. Aside from that one exception it was a splendidly balanced team. The leaders, well muscled but rangy enough for speed which leaders of a long team must have to keep the chain taut on a turn, might weigh twelve hundred or a shade less. The wheelers, solidly built, were a full fifteen hundred pounds apiece. And the spans between leaders and wheelers were carefully tapered. Yes, it was an ideal team—with the sole exception of this leggy gray stallion which was fighting against man and overruling destiny there ahead of the pointers. And what a horse that was! He had the agility of a panther and apparently the same savage temper. His legs were slenderly made; they were the legs of a runner, not a draft horse. His head short, small-muzzled, deep, from the eye to the point of the jaw, told of good blood. What was he doing in such a team as this?

The Duke held up his hand and Tony Samatti jammed on the brakes. They screamed, grated, and the wagon stopped. The team stood still, trembling even now in dread of the whip as Tony scrambled down from his seat. He abandoned the long whip. He came with a limber blacksnake in his hand.

The tall gray had stopped fighting and now stood shaking with nervous excitement and weariness—until the driver passed him. Then instantly there was another outbreak.

"Will you look at that long-legged fool?" queried Tony Samatti to the stranger, as the gray lunged and kicked and twisted against the harness. "I've handled hosses twenty years. I never seen the like of that—"

He finished the sentence with a rich profusion of oaths such as only a teamster has on the tip of his tongue for an emergency.

"Looks to me," said The Duke, "that the gray ain't up to the rest of your team, partner. Where'd you get him?"

"Up to the rest of the team? He ain't anywhere. He's crazy. How come I ain't taken him out of the traces and shot him to put him out of pain, I dunno. I got him in the foothills. Old Mike was my off hoss in the sixes. Never was a truer puller than Mike. He got took sudden with colic or something, gave about ten kicks and died on me. I hauled him downhill and stopped at the next ranch to get something to fill out that span. There was nobody but a widder woman at the ranch house. She showed me a pile of broncs about as high as my shoulder. Then she gave me a look at this gray off in a pasture by himself. Said her husband that had died a couple of months before had raised that hoss like a pet for four years and never had give him no work under anything but a saddle. Well, looked to me like he could fill out the team till we got to Wheeler City, and then I could sell him for something on account of his style. I gave her a hundred dollars cash and hitched him up. We went along a couple of miles till I started to make him pull, and then this here dance started and didn't come to no end. Raised for a pet? Raised for an outlaw, that's what he was raised for! Look out, stranger!"

The Duke had gone straight to the wild horse. The gray reared, plunged, strove to catch the newcomer with his teeth—and then suddenly was standing still and had nibbled something out of the outstretched palm of John Morrow.

"Now what in time have you got there?" asked the teamster in wonder, coming close.

"Sugar," said The Duke, and stepped back with that odd smile of his which had no mirth in it.

"Sugar?" echoed the driver, and he stared in utter bewilderment, for as The Duke turned his back the terrible gray stallion had crowded as close as he could get to him and now stared about his shoulder in defiance at Tony Samatti. It was like a miracle to the teamster.

"You say you're going to sell this horse?" asked The Duke.

"If I can get his price."

"I've got forty dollars," said The Duke truthfully, and he took the money out in his hand. "That's all I can give you, and I'll give you my note or my promise for the other sixty."

"Your note or your promise?" Tony Samatti grinned. "I don't know you, stranger."

"My name is John Morrow," said The Duke.

"John—" began the teamster, then gasped and opened his eyes like a child seeing a blaze of light. "The Duke!" he breathed.

"Some call me that."

Tony Samatti was backing away, looking anxiously at the holster which hung at The Duke's hip. The latter swallowed a smile.

"I figure your promise to pay would be as good as gold," said Tony faintly. "But if you try to work that hoss and he turns into chain lightning and blows up under you—remember that I warned you."

"Thanks," said The Duke. "I'll remember. And here's the coin."

6

◉

For Forty a Month and Found

HE KNEW THAT the credit he had received had been earned by the dread he inspired rather than by any personal confidence. But what mattered was that when the great wagon creaked away he had the gray—a naked horse and a halter with which to lead him.

The Duke stood back and regarded his new property with professional interest. It had been half pity and half admiration which had made him strike that bargain for the horse with his last cent of money. But now that the stallion was loosed from the harness The Duke found that he more than lived up to the best of his expectations. The gray horse had seemed too leggy and lean in contrast with the solid frames of the work horses, but now, considered by himself, that fault disappeared. How Tony Samatti had ever been allowed to buy such an animal for a scant hundred dollars was more than he could see, saving that the stallion was painfully lean and his coat dull from underfeeding. A week of good fare would change him almost beyond recognition.

And as for the tigerish temper of the stallion, the poor creature was fairly stepping over the donor of sugar and kind words in his eagerness to make friends. The Duke walked him for an hour across the fields. He got some wisps of dead, dry grass and rubbed him down. He gave the gray a short drink of water from a stream, let him roll in a delectable bit of gravel, and then browse on a selected pasture.

The hour worked a marvelous change in the stallion. The hysteria of trembling was quite forgotten. His eyes brightened and grew more trustful. He pricked his ears, and his whole manner changed to that sort of boyish cheerfulness which tells of a happy horse and a sound-tempered horse.

For a name The Duke picked out Monday. He chose that name simply because he wished to change his luck. Monday had always been his day of misfortune. On Monday he had had that fracas with Bud Springer, for instance. On the Monday following that affair he had been arrested. And on Monday he had entered prison. On Monday, again, he had returned to Wheeler City expecting a cordial welcome and perfect forgiveness, only to find a town in arms against him. So he called the handsome gray "Monday" and grinned as he chose the name. If it were ever possible to reverse luck, it should be possible by this maneuver.

An end came to that happy hour. He looked up from the business of teaching Monday to answer his whistle, and down the road he saw a cowpuncher riding in. It was a man from the desert, to be told by the absence of tapaderas and by the smaller size of the horse he rode. He might even have come from that far southern district where men rode little broncos as big as two men, and swung thirty-six foot ropes. Around Wheeler City and that district of knee-high grass, many watercourses and shrubbery everywhere, men sat the saddle on animals up to twelve hundred pounds and used a fifty-foot rope—even a sixty-foot rope on occasion, as The Duke had once seen! But yonder jogged a man from the desert to the West and the South, a man whose hat and shoulders were still gray with the desert dust.

And The Duke gave off playing with Monday to stare guiltily after the thin cloud of dust which blew up behind the solitary horseman. He represented the world of conscientious labor. And The Duke shivered as he watched. For he knew in his heart of hearts that his sin against society was after all not that of violence but of idleness.

He twitched the halter rope of the gray and started gloomily back toward Wheeler City. For an hour he had been wandering in dreamland. Now the world of facts confronted him, saddened him. In the first place he must find sixty dollars to complete his payment for the gray. In the second he must secure a bridle and a saddle. In the third place he must have money enough to support him until he could look about and find work.

Work! Again he shuddered and grew sick at heart. There was no pain of the long trail, no ardor of hunting, no pangs of short rations and long marches which, in the eyes of The Duke, compared with the horror of physical effort. In order that he might think over his problems the more clearly, he dropped a hand upon the withers of Monday and pitched himself onto the back of the stallion. And in this fashion, guiding the horse on in leisurely manner with an occasional pull at the rope and not at all minding it when Monday lingered by the road to nibble at a tempting bunch of grass, they returned to Wheeler City.

Still he could come to no conclusion. Mining or cowpunching were equally unattractive. Moreover, he knew little or nothing about either branch of labor. His gold mine and his cattle ranch had always lain within the compass of a table with a circle of lamplight falling upon it, and with the slipping and whispering of the cards. How his fingertips itched for the silk-smooth touch of them! And how his heart yearned for that circle of players and their intent strained faces as the hours wore on and their nerves wore out! For he, The Duke, never tired. He could have made himself rich by a careful following of the cards, he knew. But something had always held him back when he had a victim cornered—some unpleasant touch of pity, some biting qualm of conscience. And so the big stakes had not come his way.

But to leave cards and take up a cowpuncher's rope! He groaned at the bare thought. What else remained? Perhaps he had been a fool to buy the gray horse. He should have saved that forty dollars. If he had, his back would not have been pressed to the wall. Or suppose he solved his difficulties of the moment by simply cornering some wealthy townsman with a leveled revolver?

He shook his head. But because that thought had come to him he was saddened and uneasy. He knew how hard it was to fight off such insidious suggestions. And he knew how easily such thoughts recur, once they have found a way into the mind. Now that he had sworn to himself that he would make a living by honest work, where was he to turn?

That gloomy burden weighed down his mind by the time he reached Wheeler City again. He dismounted from the bare back of the gray and put him up in the livery stable. Even as he stepped into the street he received strong testimony of how perfectly public opinion was against him. As he rounded the corner of the stable he nearly ran into young Pete Murray, Linda's brother. There was no reason why Pete should be hostile. The Duke had never harmed him. But when he saw The Duke coming he let out a shout and reached for a gun.

He would have died had not his gun lodged for a second in its holster. Even in spite of that delay an ordinary gun-fighter would have killed him. But the brain of The Duke, working like lightning, noted that the weapon of Murray had stuck halfway out of the holster. He checked the pressure of his forefinger as it was curling around the trigger. Instead of driving a bullet through the heart of Pete, he reached out and with the long, heavy barrel of his Colt struck Linda's brother across his forearm. The nerves were numbed, the muscles paralyzed by that stroke. And with a shout of desperate anger Pete Murray leaped in at his foe and struck with his left fist.

Fast as he struck, the reaction of The Duke was fast enough to put him on guard. Still he refused to use his gun. He merely bent his head to one side. The driving arm of Murray flashed past and over his shoulder. His shoulder, as he crouched a little, rapped hard against Pete's ribs. An instant later Pete was turned about facing the street, with his arms twisted up behind his back and cramped so that with the smallest effort The Duke could have broken either or both of them.

He himself was standing behind, of course, between his assailant and the wall of the stable. And it was well that he had secured this position, for a dozen men had gathered with uncanny speed. They had poured across the street. Others were running in the distance, and all carried drawn guns. There was Sylvester, the druggist, standing at the door of his store with his old shotgun hooked at a balance across his arm and ready to shoot when he saw an opening. They were calling to one another. They were urging one another to stand fast and shoot straight, and The Duke would go down once and for all.

The Duke regarded them calmly. These were not professional gun-fighters such as those his exhibition of fancy shooting the night before had scared out of town. These were ordinary, sober, everyday citizens. And The Duke knew that they were more to be dreaded than a whole mob of celebrated desperadoes. For these law-abiding citizens, seeking for no trouble, were worse than hornets once they were aroused. They could not be beaten. They were like the fabled Hydra. If one head fell, two sprang out in its place. These dozen gathering in the street with guns were not all. It was not beyond the bounds of possibility that The Duke could dispose even of that number of good fighters. But beyond these there were more. The town was full of them. And the State was full of them. And there were countless millions beyond and beyond. In the name of the law and in the strength of the law they represented a power with which The Duke could not even hope to compete. And he was wise enough to know it. All he wanted to do was to prove that his intentions were pacific.

"Pete, you idiot!" he growled at Pete's ear. "What made you start to jump me?"

"Somebody said that you and Linda—" gasped out Pete. "I dunno. I figured that you'd be out trying to get anybody related to Linda and—and I figured I'd better hit first if I could!"

"Have you seen Linda this morning?"

"No."

"Then go find her. She'll tell you that everything's hunky-dory between her and me!"

"Duke," groaned out Pete, "I've been a fool. You'd ought to have blowed my head off."

"Thank Heaven I didn't. Now tell those gents out yonder that are champing and raving and tearing to get at me that you picked the start of this fight, will you?"

And Pete Murray obeyed. While he was still held before his conqueror, sheltering the latter with his body, he explained to the gathering crowd that there was no cause for jumping at the throat of The Duke—that he, Pete Murray, had been at fault, and that he apologized to everyone for the disturbance.

When he had said all of this The Duke let him go. But still, for an instant, he was in a critical situation as he faced the semicircle of weapons held ready for action. Had his own gun been in his hand when Pete stepped away, or had he shown the slightest fear or doubt, beyond a question a dozen guns would have roared at him at once. But as it was, The Duke leaned his shoulders against the wall of the stable, folded his arms and smiled genially upon the townsfolk. And the latter regarded him sourly, as though they regretted that they could not finish today a work which would have to be done sooner or later.

Here came a little fellow, bowlegged, pale-eyed, with a scraggly mustache. It was "Pop" Field, who played the violin in the dance orchestra and had done nothing else since his boyhood. But the old man came straight up to The Duke with his revolver weighing down his skinny hand. He confronted the man of might.

"Maybe you get off this time, Duke," he informed the returned convict, "but the next time you ain't going to be so lucky. We're watching you, understand? And at the first slip you make we'll be all over you. This here is a plumb peaceful town and we figure on keeping it peaceful! You tie to that and step soft around these parts or we'll be giving you a free lodging in the cemetery!"

And he turned on his heel and walked off. But The Duke was neither amused nor angry. There had been an air of dignity about old Pop. And there had been strength in him, also. The power of public opinion made him as great as a giant. His words were like loaded guns held under the nose of The Duke.

In the meantime, the little crowd was breaking up. The men who had come out of the livery stable to watch— perhaps to open fire on The Duke from the side if the crisis came—returned to their work. And The Duke wandered slowly up the street, very thoughtful.

It was even worse than he had expected. He was a public nuisance. He was a public enemy. No wonder that, with every step he took, his temper rose closer and closer to a white heat. By the time he came to the hotel he was ready for an explosion.

It was while in this mood that he heard someone on the veranda of the hotel call out "So long, Guthrie!" He turned and saw Guthrie coming down the steps. By the voice with which the latter answered the farewell he knew that this was the same man who had been in the sheriff's room last night. He had stayed in town, then, after all. And at the sight of him there came to the mind of The Duke a hope that, after all, the qualities for which he was known might bring him a steady place of work. He stepped up to Guthrie as the latter reached the ground.

"Guthrie," he said, "my name is John Morrow."

Guthrie was a square-built man with a square-built face which was lined with trouble and experience. He might be fifty years old when he smiled. When his face was in repose he looked sixty. He regarded The Duke without emotion as one who is so wrapped in his own inner problems that lesser causes of excitement mean nothing.

"I know," he said. "You're The Duke as they call you."

"I've come to talk business."

"There's no business you can talk to me."

"Guthrie," said The Duke, swallowing his resentment at this curtness of speech, "I was in the sheriff's office last night. I heard you talk to him. And from what I gathered, the thing you need most is a bodyguard. Am I right?"

The rancher blinked at him.

"I need the killing of that murdering skunk of an outlaw that hangs out in the Black Hills," he said with more interest. "Bodyguard? I never thought of that!"

"Start thinking now. I want the job."

"You? Want a job?"

"I'm going straight, Guthrie," said The Duke. "And I want to work. But I'm no hand with cows, and I don't know much about mining. My job that I've been following has been gambling and—fighting." He smiled mirthlessly. "I'm dropping the gambling. That leaves one thing that I'm trained for. Guthrie, can you use me?"

The quizzical expression of the rancher was much the same as that with which he would have greeted a serious proposal to turn a nest of rattlesnakes into a commercial proposition.

"I ain't carrying no insurance on my punchers out on my place," he said at last, and grinned as he spoke.

"You won't need none."

"You'd come out to take up the trailing of this gent I'm after—and that's after me?"

"I'd do that."

"Can you handle dogs?"

"What sort?"

"A pack of hounds that have been used on lions and bears, and some bloodhounds mixed in."

"I can handle dogs," said The Duke, praying that luck would enable him to carry through the bluff.

"What pay?"

"Regular cowpuncher's. That's all."

Guthrie lifted his brows with surprise. "Forty bucks and found?"

"That'll do," said The Duke, making a grimace. "That'll do," he added, "if I get three months' pay in advance."

"Eh?"

"I've got a hoss half paid for."

The rancher hesitated. To trust an ex-criminal with three months' pay in advance was somewhat of a tax upon the most good-natured and trustful of men. And Guthrie would not have qualified in either capacity. But at length he nodded.

"When do you start work?"

"Tomorrow," said The Duke, remembering the promise he had delivered to the sheriff that he would appear at the dance that evening. "Tomorrow morning, Guthrie."

The rancher shrugged his shoulders.

"Come inside," he said. "We'll make a contract out of this."

7
⊙

Rage and Fury

HALF OF THAT three months in advanced pay went straight into the pocket of Tony Samatti to complete the payment for The Duke's horse, Monday. And there was another section of the money which had to be sunk in the purchase of a saddle—a secondhand saddle, at that, and a bridle to go with it. And by the time The Duke swung onto the back of Monday that evening to take the trail which led to Warner's Springs and the dance, his available cash was at a perilously low ebb.

But he had something more than cash. Some long hours of rest, a feed of grain and the soothing hand and voice of The Duke had made a new horse of Monday. When he swung into a canter down the main street of Wheeler City, The Duke felt as though he were riding out a high sea in a small boat, so great was the sweep and swing of that stride compared to the rocking-chair lope of the average cow pony. A real runner was working under him and fighting for his head to make more speed. The Duke could have sung aloud in his joy.

He swung Monday away from the main street of the little town. It would not do for the men of Wheeler City to know the prowess of this horse in advance. But if, in the turn of the wheel of fortune, it should be necessary for him to flee while they pursued, then they would make a discovery!

Quickly he wound out from the cow town, climbed the first hill beyond the town and headed into the wind. Here was a true test for the stallion. And he met it like a hero. The wind had grown into a half-gale since the setting of the sun. Now and again a gust of raindrops fell with stinging force, and The Duke put on his slicker. But still the stallion went on at an even gait, that gallop which devoured the miles, never slackening. At last, three miles from the start and nearly halfway to the Springs, The Duke halted his mount and leaned over to listen to the breathing. There was no harshness in the sound of the drawn breaths. Monday was as fresh as a daisy and literally filled with running. And this after such a morning as he had spent in the team of Tony Samatti!

It meant as much to The Duke as wings mean to a bird. It made him free, this speed which he had at his command. And in the war against society which he had postponed to the best of his ability, but which he felt to be inevitable in the near future, Monday would be a better ally than a score of armed men sworn to die in his interest.

He rode on again, more slowly. He was in no hurry to get to the dance hall. What his reception there would be, he could not guess with any pretense of accuracy. For he knew that the men would be cold and hostile. But how about the women? Certainly, in all his past no one could find the least cruelty or discourtesy to old women or young. And in the days before he went to jail he had been actually popular among them. The wild stories which were told about him, and which were largely known to be true, seemed merely to give poignancy to the name of John Morrow, alias The Duke! And since, from the days of his boyhood, he had loved dancing next only to fighting, he had begun to feel that it did not matter how men frowned upon him so long as he could pick and choose among the prettiest girls the most graceful dancers for his dancing partners.

But, now that he came back from the penitentiary, a marked man in the eyes of all the men, how would the women regard him? He shrugged his shoulders and laughed away his doubts. Unless the young men had greatly changed, there was not one among them who could compare with him as a dancer. Unless they had greatly changed, there was not one among them who had the same poise, the same personal dignity. If he could not find partners at this dance he was very much mistaken!

He rode boldly up to the shed where the horses had been tethered, since the rain was falling more and more heavily. Then he turned to the pavilion. It was built of timber but it was shaped like a great tent, with adjustable sides which were always raised in hot weather and which were lowered at such rainy seasons as this. Inside, the music was in full sway. He picked out the brazen thundering of the slide trombone. He heard the shrilling of the cornet, the rattling of the piano, the beating of the drums and one desperate violin on which poor Pop Field was sawing with all his might to make his voice heard through the uproar.

The thought of Pop Field and how the little man had bearded him that day gave The Duke a pause. But he frowned, shrugged his shoulder again and forced himself on. Inside the front door he paused and looked about him. There were a dozen men smoking in the little reception room, and there were two or three girls and their escorts, just arrived, hanging up their wraps. The buzz and chatter of talk had been almost as loud, in the anteroom, as the roar of the music beyond. But at his coming, as he stripped off his slicker and knocked the raindrops from his boots, the noise of the voices fell away. There remained only the music and the loud whispering of the dancers' feet.

The Duke looked around him. No, they were not strangers. There were five of the group whom he knew. He spoke to them one by one, smiling his most gracious smile. They answered him as he addressed them, one by one, stiffly. As for the girls, they apparently did not see him. They were busy adjusting their clothes, patting their hair, or talking in whispers to one another. They brushed past him and went on to the door with their companions.

And it seemed to The Duke that there was a faint smile of gratification on the faces of the young men who stood about, drawing hard at their cigarettes and apparently seeing nothing but the floor. It could not be said that they were smiling at The Duke. But he knew perfectly the meaning behind their wisely interchanged glances. He had been coldly snubbed by those girls, and it was a delight to the hearts of these young swains.

To The Duke it was a blow of staggering force. He wished with all his soul that he could withdraw. But here he was, committed to the acid test, with people from three great counties ready to look on and to hear the story of his discomfiture! He grew pale at the thought of the shame. Heavens be praised that he had no family to be shamed by his actions!

He stepped to the door. Yonder came blue-eyed Janetta Miller, bubbling over with talk and laughter, as usual, but dancing wonderfully. She had not changed. She had actually grown younger. He caught her eye as she whirled past, and nodded and smiled at her. But Janetta went on without a glance or a sign.

She had not failed to see him. Their glances had struck together with a shock as distinct as though hands met. But there she was, gone by, still laughing and talking with big, heavy-footed Hal Jackson, her partner.

It was a second shock to The Duke. No matter that he drew himself up as straight as ever. No matter that his head tilted back a little and that he smiled his own old smile. His white face had grown ghastly pale—whiter than the pallor of prison. And behind him, was it not a growing mutter of half-choked laughter? Yes, those young men in the anteroom were watching as they smoked and missed nothing of his discomfiture.

And yet it could not be! But yonder was a true test. There came the flaming red hair which must belong to happy-hearted, gentle-hearted Ruth Boyer. A thousand times they had danced together. A thousand times they had laughed and talked together. They had been better friends than men are to men. They had been inseparable pals at dances hitherto.

She came past. The music slowed, stopped. The couples swung to a stop and began walking. But there was no clapping for an encore. That was strange. And strange, too, that all eyes were looking straight at him!

He spoke to Ruth Boyer, but there was no answering acknowledgment of his words in her face. She looked him through and through, calmly, carefully. Then she turned and continued her talk with her companion.

It was too much for The Duke. He fell back from the doorway with an agony of shame in his heart. He looked about him on the men who were idling. And under his glance every vestige of their smiles went out. Heaven be praised that his nerve had not failed him even in this cruel emergency, but no one would ever dream what the effort at self-control was costing him. If only there were something which he could seize and break! But he must endure and smile—and smile—while he wanted to unlimber his gun and hunt battle.

Since he had turned away from the door, he must do something. What could it be? He could not enter the great dance hall with its garish festoons of flags and ribbons twisted to the peak of the ceiling, and its countless lights and its myriad faces and the deep, soft whisper which, he knew, was speaking of him.

And it seemed to The Duke, even in the midst of his agony, that it was a strange thing indeed that he should have been so completely turned back and discomfited by the eyes of two girls. Twenty men could not have done so much, he assured himself bitterly.

He crossed the waiting room. He wandered to the end of it, rolling a cigarette, and as he passed to a little distance he heard the confusion of quick, delighted chuckling from the men behind him. They had been delighted beyond measure by his shame. Oh, to go back and take them by the throats!

Stairs appeared before him. He went up them without realizing where they led. It was not until he came to the top that he remembered. Along this side of the hall there was a gallery for spectators, a gallery which was never used, for at a Western dance there are no spectators—everyone steps out on the floor. It was a place, therefore, as dusty and deserted as an old attic. Only one smoky lantern, hanging in a corner, illumined it, or rather filled it with shadows. And so, secure in the mercy of the dark, he peered over the railing and down to the floor.

Already the word of his discomfiture had been spread around. All eyes were seeking the gallery in which he was concealed. Those fellows in the anteroom had lost no time in spreading the tidings of his retreat. And now, down on the floor of the hall, they were laughing. The merriment tingled to the ceiling. They were laughing at John Morrow—at The Duke himself!

He closed his eyes. He reeled, drunk with rage and shame. He threw up his hands to register an oath of vengeance. As he did so, there was a slight stir in a corner of the balcony.

This was too much. That there should have been a hidden spectator of his writhings under punishment was a goad too deeply biting. He whirled and hurried to the place. Yes, there was a shadow jerking at a closed door, a shadow swathed in a glistening slicker. He remembered, now, that there was an outer stairway leading up to this gallery. But why should anyone wish to come or go by that murderously dangerous old flight of steps? In the meantime, the rain had swollen the door. It had been opened with ease and shut, but it could not be opened again.

"What's wrong?" asked The Duke.

The efforts of the other to open the door redoubled.

"Nothing!" gasped a voice.

It was a woman's voice and The Duke halted in his approach. Even now he must be gentle.

"Do you wish me to open the door?" he asked.

"Please!"

She shrank away as he stepped up. What devil was in the heads of all these girls so that, if they did not openly insult him and snub him before his fellows, they shrank from him as though he were a wife-beater? It was the crowning touch in his humiliation. He laid his hand on the knob of the door, only wishing that he might tear it crashing to pieces. It gave easily under his pull and he turned to the girl. She had murmured a word of thanks. She hardly waited for him to withdraw before she tried to slip past him. And suddenly, in a burst of fury, The Duke thrust his arm across the doorway and blocked her exit.

8

Sally Smith

"LADY," HE SAID, "I sure got to ask you to forgive me for holding you up, but why in thunder are you scairt of me?"

The instant his arm appeared in her path she had started back. In the suddenness of her move the big folds of the slicker fell apart, and he saw the shimmer of a rosy gauze gown. He looked down at her feet. In spite of the shadowy light in that gallery he could make out that they were encased in rose satin, bright as a reflection in water. She had raised her head, too, so that the shadow of the great sombrero no longer veiled her face; and what The Duke saw made him lean closer, staring to make out more.

"I'm not scairt," said the girl scornfully. "I'm not scairt of you nor no man."

"Oh," said The Duke, smiling in spite of himself, "that makes it a pile different. But a minute back it looked to me like you were working pretty fast to climb through this here wall and get clean of me."

"I was going outside," she answered. "Why should I be scairt of you?"

"There ain't no reason, I guess. Unless," he added as a disagreeable thought came to him, "unless you don't know me, lady!"

"I ain't had that pleasure yet," said the girl, her voice growing calmer. "But I guess I'm in the way of knowing you now."

"My name is John Morrow," he said at last and added honestly, "and some folks know me better by the name of The Duke."

There was a little pause.

"My name is Salvina Gertrude Smith," she said at last, "and some folks know me better by the name of Sally."

They laughed together. And The Duke was enchanted. He had not dreamed that, within the girth of the mountain ranges, there existed a human being who had not heard his name—his nickname at the least! What a delight it was to be freed from the heavy chains of that reputation. He closed the door.

"Did I say I wanted to stay here?" asked Sally Smith.

"The stairway ain't safe," said The Duke.

"Why, it didn't creak once when I came up."

"The wind must of drowned the noise," said The Duke. "It's the most treacherous stairway in these parts. You must be a stranger not to of heard about it."

"I am a stranger," said Sally.

"Which we can sit up here plumb comfortable and hear the music," said The Duke. "How might you have come to climb up here from the outside, though?"

She hesitated.

"I wanted to take a look at things before I went downstairs," she said.

"Not a half bad idea," The Duke commented, wishing with all his soul that he had thought of doing the same thing.

He stared more closely than before. The shadows were maddening. They were like hands pushing him away from the discovery of the truth. But in spite of them he saw that she was very pretty. Her eyes were two great walls of darkness. But when she turned her head the profile showed an outline as smooth and easy as marble. She was looking over the railing at the crowd which swarmed on the dance floor. The Duke saw her lips part with delight and interest. And he himself yearned to be down there, moving with the beat of the music.

The girls wore very simple dresses on the whole. Something light in weight with a touch of color was all they wanted. The men, however, were attired in various array. A great many came just as they might have stopped the day's work on the range, except that they had scoured their faces and hands. There were even some of the punchers from the brush-covered foothills who were wearing their chaps. Others, again, wore their riding boots, though these were now burnished to unbelievable brilliance; and the trousers were worn outside of the boots. Gentlemen equipped with the boots as a rule were accoutered in celluloid collars without neckties. But nearly half of the dancers were dressed in ordinary "store clothes." There was just a sprinkling of the others— enough to give the whole assemblage a cowpuncher flavor.

And The Duke saw that his companion was fascinated. He watched her curiously. After all, the annual Warner's Springs dance was a big affair, but not enough to excite a girl in this fashion—certainly not a girl as pretty as Sally. For The Duke knew that pretty girls are the most blasé of the blasé. From infancy they are surrounded by idolaters. Their will is law. They command with gestures and faint smiles. They torture with a frown; they wound with laughter. Indeed, there was only one thing to which The Duke would habitually compare a pretty girl, and that was a handsome six-shooter, well balanced, straight shooting, wielded in an expert hand. Though, as a matter of fact, he was certain that a pretty girl was much more deadly than any gun.

As such was the dread with which The Duke looked upon beauty in women, it might well be wondered why he paid so much attention to a good-looking girl. But The Duke did not pretend to be logical. That which he dreaded most was apt to attract him most. And, though he went in constant apprehension that sooner or later a woman would make a fool of him, yet he enjoyed the sunshine of the moment to the full. And now a new hope had risen in him. Since by some miracle this girl did not know him, why could he not go down to the floor with her, dance with a beauty far outshining any of the others, and then disappear before she learned the blasting truth about him? It would be a pleasant revenge. It would completely upset the plans of his enemies—and in the category of enemies must be included all who were dancing on that floor.

After that one dance, after he was gone, then they could tell her what they pleased. They could let her know that she had appeared with a social leper, an exile.

"Shall we dance?" he asked.

"I—if you wish," said the girl with a strange breath-lessness. "I—"

Why she should be so excited, he could not understand. But he was not hunting for a mystery. It sufficed that here she was going down the steps from the gallery on his arm! As they stepped into the anteroom the music for the next dance began, a swinging rhythm of a waltz. And Sally twitched away her slicker and threw it over a peg on the wall. He looked down at her eagerly. And what the light showed him was better than the brightest hopes he had dared to keep.

She was a beauty of the Irish type, with blue-black, waving hair which, whenever it was free, twisted at once into a curl; and her eyes were blue—not that pale sky blue, but an intense color, dark and yet lustrous like the deep sea. She had a half-boyish, jaunty fashion of carrying herself, with her head high and her eyes straight and a smile playing in and out on her lips—very much like a boy, indeed—a boy bent on mischief which lay just ahead, thought The Duke. If her features were not as perfect as he had guessed them in the shadow of the gallery, yet they were exquisitely proportioned. One could not criticize feature by feature. But there was about her a sort of aroma of loveliness.

She had lived out-of-doors most of her life. That was apparent at a glance. It was no summer's tan which she wore. There was an ineradicable stain of the clearest olive tint which many and many a year in all winds and weathers had painted her cheeks and the backs of her hands. And that brown skin made the blue of her eyes and the black of her hair the more intense.

Such was the girl upon whom The Duke looked with a deep and sudden interest. The faces of Linda Murray and all those other pretty girls whom he had known before or who were dancing in the hall became an obscure blur. They mattered not! There was only one trouble. Sally was young, very young. She could not be more than eighteen or nineteen. And would these people accuse him of having deceived and outwitted a poor child who knew no better than to appear in public with an outcast? He drew her suddenly back against the wall where the deep shadow sheltered them from the eyes of the idlers in the anteroom.

"Sally," he said, "I have to tell you who I am. You've never heard of The Duke. But everyone else around here has. And they know that I've just come out of the penitentiary. They've turned the cold shoulder on me. The girls I used to dance with can't see me at all. Sally, if you go into that room and start in dancing with me, everybody'll stare at you—they'll—pity you—"

"They don't dare!" cried Sally. "Pity me!" She stamped and raised her head high. "Dance with you?" she cried. "Of course I'll dance with you!"

"Without even knowing why I was sent to jail?"

"I don't care why. I figure I can see that you're good enough for me to dance with."

"I was sent up for shooting—a gent—"

"His own fault for not shooting you first," said this strange mocker of the law.

"They accused me of shooting him in the back!"

Sally lifted her head again, and those dark eyes burned into his. Suddenly she shook her head.

"I reckon they're just plain fools," she said.

"Thanks," said The Duke. "And I reckon it's time to dance. And—Heaven bless you, Sally!"

He led her forward again. There was a new set of loungers gathered near the door of the dance hall, puffing forth rapid clouds of smoke, eager as pawing horses to get back into the dance as soon as their lungs were sufficiently soaked with tobacco smoke again. But they forgot the dance and the cigarettes as The Duke went by with Sally. There was that blankness about the eyes which comes when men are truly astonished. They could not even speak to one another until she had passed. But behind her the murmurs rose like the foam in the wake of a ship.

And now they were through the door! Ah, what a shock to the good, law-abiding citizens from Wheeler City to the Black Hills! What a shock to those girls who had vindicated the power of law and order by snubbing the returned criminal so cruelly the moment before. No matter how pretty, a cloud passed over them. And the harder they peered at her the more impregnable she seemed.

There was only one flaw, and that was that she had come in with the outcast.

"They're breaking their hearts about you," said The Duke. "They can't even find fault with your dress, and they're sick because they're beaten."

She turned her head. She swept the maze of faces around her with careless eyes. Then she looked back at The Duke.

"What do I care about them?" she asked him half fiercely. "All that I want to think about is the dance!"

And from that moment it was as though an intense light burned above them, followed them around the hall as they danced. He saw nothing else besides her face. It was a lucky moment, for the gentleman who wielded the slide trombone with such ear-crushing effect had grown wearied by his early efforts. He was now relaxing, only thundering forth an occasional flourish. And the drummer, too, was growing sleepy; he omitted some of those crashes of cymbals and soul-stirring thumps on the bass drum with which he usually enlivened each dance. The very cornetist was not making his horn shriek as usual. And for the first time in the evening the piano and the violin became truly audible. The sway of the waltz became something more than a musical throb of rhythm. The dance slipped into the pulse.

And then it swung to a pause, stopped. People were scurrying for chairs at the side of the hall. And here were Sally and The Duke far from the door through which they had entered. As the floor cleared, more and more attention was focusing upon them.

Like a blow fell the voice of the girl on The Duke.

"Now take me away!"

"Not yet. We ain't more'n begun."

"If you don't take me, I'll have to go by myself."

"I'll go then, but—"

They started across the floor.

"If you keep frowning," she said, laughing up at him, "they'll think that we've had a quarrel. And that'll please them, I guess!"

He nodded. She was certainly a staunch ally, even if for only a moment.

"They're grinding their teeth," he assured her. "If you

could only stay, these girls would wish you dead, and me dead for bringing you here. And—"

"I can't stay," she said.

"Is someone waiting for you?"

"No. But if I stayed too long someone would know—"

"What?" he asked.

There was a touch of panic in her expression as she looked up at him.

"Nothing," she said.

The Duke was so excited that he hardly knew how they reached the anteroom, or how he folded her in her wrap and put the slicker over it, or how, afterward, he went outside with her. What was it she was afraid that "they" would come to know?

"Where shall I take you?" he asked when they were out in the teeth of the wind again.

"Just leave me where I am and turn your back till I've got around the corner—"

"Till you're out of sight?"

"Yes."

"But when do I see you again, Sally?"

"Never."

"You don't mean that?"

"I do."

"Sally, I've got to see you. Why—"

"I have no time!" she said suddenly.

"But when you're out of sight may I follow then?"

"Catch me if you can," Sally said.

"Good night, then," said The Duke.

"Good-bye," called Sally as he turned.

9

◉

At Guthrie's Place

THE WIND covered the sound of her retreat, but The Duke knew—he felt—that she had run to the left and turned the corner of the house. So, after he had waited long enough for her to round the first corner, no matter in what direction she had gone, he whirled and raced in pursuit. He darted around the corner. She was nowhere before him down that side of the building!

He jerked himself about and rushed along the front of the dance hall to the other corner. But that side was equally blank. He completed the circuit of the dance hall, but she was nowhere before him. Either she had vanished into thin air, gone back into the dance hall, or else raced away from him with the speed of a man.

But he shook his head at all three of those possibilities. He was no amateur athlete. And, no matter how strong a runner she might have been, she could not have made such swift headway, he felt, in those absurd satin dancing pumps and with skirts to impede her. As for going back into the dance hall, he was certain that she had been full of a real anxiety to get away. She would rather have faced a gun than stayed longer in the hall.

And that brief stay went hand in hand with the fact that she had been looking on the dance secretly from above. Only what under heaven could have made her dread appearing in public? What was it that she was afraid that they might come to know if she lingered too long?

He hurried to the shed and saddled Monday. And as he drew up the cinches on the tall gray he was telling himself that in this encounter with the powers of the law he

had been the conqueror. He had invaded them, and on
their own land he had beaten them. He had endured their
sneers and their coldness, and he had left them triumphant.

It was enough to warm his heart. And if at one blow
he saw wiped out all the friendships he had ever formed,
still he was able to endure. He could shrug his shoulders
and bid the entire lot go hang. For, in the meantime, there
was this fascinating puzzle of Sally to take up his attention.

In another moment he was in the saddle, and he swept
out around the buildings. If she were to decide to go into
hiding—whatever her reason—in one of the buildings,
for instance in the hotel itself, he must give her up. But
something told him that she was not there. That sun-
colored skin, that recklessly defiant manner, those straight-
looking eyes—all spoke of one who came from the open
places beyond. And something told him that what had
called her so suddenly from the dance hall had been a
summons back to the wilderness from which she had
come.

So he skirted around to the outer edge of Warner's
Springs with its clusters of hotels, houses, barns, stables.
He cut in between the town and the road which ran out
toward the northern hills, for something told him that she
could not have come from the desert to the west and
south, or from the grass lowlands around Wheeler City.
For desert suns wither and wrinkle the skin and sap its
color. And the dull life in the lowlands could never have
put that glimmer of wilderness in her eyes.

But, though he waited on the road until half an hour
had passed, there was no sign of the girl; not a single
horseman came out from the Springs. There were others
riding in, to be sure, belated men driving ahead at reckless speed to get to the dance. But he saw, finally, that
the girl had given him the slip. And he gritted his teeth
at the thought. Swiftly as he had saddled, she had beaten
him. There was no doubt in his mind that she had taken
this road. In some manner, she had managed to get away
from him at the dance hall—slipped away toward the
place where her horse had been tethered and waiting for
her with the saddle still on its back—and then she had

ridden very swiftly to the north. Nothing but a fast horse and a determined rider could have distanced the gray even with the slight handicap of time.

He turned Monday gloomily up the road, therefore; and, leaning into the wind with his slicker drawn tight about him, he prepared for the long journey through the storm. But Monday made long journeys short. It would have been folly to maintain a canter in the face of such a gale, but The Duke kept his horse at a steady trot, and the long, swift step of Monday wore out the miles with amazing speed. About an hour after the start, as if to reward the constant effort, the wind began to fall away. Then it swung to the east and presently began to break the sheeting of storm clouds and to roll them away in towering masses illumined by a half-moon which, from time to time, plowed its way down and gave an intermittent light to the hills. For they had left the plain long before and were now traveling through ground lifted into long and gradual swells like the big waves which still travel the seas the day after the storm.

It was a fitting night for the thoughts which were storming through the brain of The Duke. He had never been in such a devilish mood—not since that first unlucky day when he had discovered that his hand was steadier than the hands of other men on the butt of a gun, his eye straighter, his fingers more deft.

He had been deliberately scorned and put aside by organized society. And he had been insulted in such a fashion that his hands had been tied. Ah, he said to himself, if only the insults had been winged and driven home by the men of Wheeler City! If only one—yes, or a dozen —of the men at the dance had dared to cross him! But instead they had left the women to do the work as only women can.

Even to this moment it was incredible that the girls he had known so many years could have turned on him at the last moment. He could not know that it had been the result of a most careful conspiracy in which the elders of the town had put their heads together after it was made known by the sheriff that The Duke intended to present himself at the dance at Warner's Springs. He could not know how they had schemed to show him that he was no longer wanted in their midst, and that they had decided to deliver the blow with a silk glove instead of a club. Neither could he tell how girl after girl had been reluctantly pledged to play her part for the sake of the town as a whole. All The Duke knew was that they had denied him, and the thought was maddening!

There had been sweet comfort in Sally and that brief opportunity to dazzle their eyes with her. But the beauty of Sally was gone. She had flashed before him for a tantalizing instant, and then she had vanished. The loss of her was more than all the insults. But he rolled the two pains together and made of them a consuming desire to vent his rage on grown men, strong men, men who were willing to fight. He wanted to take on heavy odds and then destroy them with that consummate magic of guncraft of which he was master. He groaned aloud in his desire, and Monday started ahead with a snort of fear as he heard the strange sound of his rider's voice.

In the meantime, here he was tied down to three months of stupid labor on an isolated farm! Pat upon the thought, Monday paused on the top of a hill which was somewhat loftier than those around it. From the crest The Duke looked down upon the Guthrie place. It was long since he had ridden in that direction, but he remembered well enough. In the old days, before he had been sent away to serve his term, the Blackwaters had owned that ranch. And it was not greatly changed under the domination of the Guthries.

By this time the wind had scoured a clean place in the center of the heavens, and the moon rode high and free in the midst. It showed the group of weather-beaten buildings which represented the ranch headquarters. And everywhere there were huge stacks of winter feed already assembled, even though this was July! Winter must be bitterly cold at this altitude. The warm, strong fall of rain that evening, if it had been January, would have fallen in the guise of a terrible blizzard.

It was not an unpleasant place for a ranch house to be situated, as The Duke admitted even in his black humor of the moment. The Lindsay River, which afterward grew to such a strong current, tearing the hearts out of mountains, was here in its infancy, a mere casually winding stream which flooded in and out through the undulations of the valley. Yonder a rock slide had dammed it and backed the waters into a long, narrow lake. And, by the foot of the lake, where the rocks of the dam had spread to a broad shoulder, the ranch house itself was placed, its white walls dimly visible by moonlight through the screen of pines. Behind it, the ranch buildings and the stacks of hay spread back over a considerable reach of ground from which the trees had been cleared, save for an occasional sapling which had sprung up in the rich soil.

The gloom gradually lifted from the mind of The Duke. If he were condemned to spend his next three months here, at least he could not have chosen a more pleasant single spot. All that was wrong was his conclusion that he had only one way to exist, and this in defiance of the world and its laws and its lawkeepers. They had thrown down the glove to him at the dance, and he would show them that he was not slow in picking up a challenge.

He smiled again, when he thought of it, that slow and mirthless smile, with the white flash of teeth behind it. Then he started down the hillside for the house.

When he reached it he found all in blackness. It was a full hour past midnight. And, since he did not wish to disturb anyone at that time of the night, he went out to the stable to find a place for the gray and perhaps for himself as well. He was successful in both respects. They thought enough of their horses even at this season of the year to put them in stalls, and in one of these, at the end of a long line of cowpunchers' mounts, he put Monday.

He saw that the stallion was well supplied with a feed of hay—he was too hot for grain—and then left his horse and crawled up into the mow. He found a section of hay which had been newly cut and newly stowed in the barn. It was still filled with the clean fragrances of the outdoors, scents of dried wild flowers and the overpowering sweetness of the clean hay itself. Here he wriggled himself into a comfortable place and was instantly asleep.

10

The Duke Is Doubted

HE WAKENED out of a strange dream. He had been struggling up a strange trail through mountains he had never seen before. Enemies pursued him. He bestrode a wounded horse whose strength ebbed with every step. And so he came to a river, twisting a rough course through a valley. On the bank he left his fagged horse. He plunged into the stream. He swam boldly and well until he was within twenty feet of the farther shore.

There the rushing of the current stopped him and threw him back. In vain he pushed forward against it. It was like hands holding him away. And so, choked and exhausted, with the enemy running rapidly up the trail behind him, he had abandoned hope of success when he saw the figure of Sally standing on the shore before him. He called to her with a voice hoarse with labor and hope. And Sally saw him and waved. He begged her to throw the rope which she held. But Sally, laughing as though at an immoderate jest, turned and casually sauntered up the stream. And, utterly ended by that last blow to his hope, he had thrown up his arms. The water choked his nostrils. The swift current tumbled down the stream—

He wakened from the nightmare, coughing and sneezing out the dust of the hay which had entered his nose and mouth. Then he sat up with a sigh of relief. The dawn was just breaking through the night, not with the fullness of morning, but with a dull and uncertain twilight. The great rafters above him were growing visible. The door at the end of the loft was a dim square of hazy light. And near the barn a rooster was crowing energetically. He

ended. A distant rooster answered. Then the silence fell
once more.

The Duke climbed down to the floor of the barn. That
meager portion of sleep had been enough to relax his durable muscles. He was ready for whatever lay ahead of
him now. But, first of all, to shock the last remnants of
drowsiness out of his head, he ran out to the edge of the
lake, stripped off his clothes and plunged in.

The water was newly iced from the snows of the mountains above him, snows which never were quite melted during the whole length of the hot summer. Yet he thrust his
way through the lake with long, powerful strokes and
came back to the gravel of the bank, with the surface of
his body chill as frost, but with the hot blood boiling beneath.

He was dressed before the dawn light had increased to
the true brilliance of morning. And he looked about him
as the east grew rosy behind the summits. From that hill
to the south the valley by moonlight had seemed charm-
ing, but now it was truly beautiful. In the bottom lands
along the river there were cultivated fields where grain and
hay were grown. Over the richly grassed foothills which
spread away from the bottom were hosts of cattle. He saw
them by groups, or singly, spread everywhere. There was
no need of a near view to understand that with such feed
their sides were rolling fat! Yes, wealth must be pouring
out of the ground swiftly in this valley. And he thought
back with a sort of bewilderment to the worn, haggard
face of Guthrie, as the rancher had appeared when he
talked with him.

That thought made him look north and east. There rose
the Black Hills. There could not have been a more proper
name. Masses of green diorite with surfaces weathered to
sooty black had thrust up from the earth, interspersed here
and there with glossy outpourings of iron—iron blossoms
three hundred feet long at the base, and lifting up twice
that distance into the air—huge, top-heavy pyramids
three-quarters rock and one-quarter iron. Even with the
distance softening the rough ridges of the Black Hills,
it seemed impossible that human beings could go there
even to find shelter from pursuit. Actually to live there
was beyond credence! And yet that was what Guthrie had

sworn to the sheriff that the outlaw who molested him was doing.

Yet it was not such a bad idea—to take shelter among the labyrinthine tangles of those rocks, and come down as from a citadel into the lowlands to prey on the workers for all that was needed for the comforts of life. Some commodious cave might shelter the marauder, and he could dwell there at ease save when he chose to step forth and make his levies of money or provisions. The eyes of The Duke shone. If the time came—as he expected it to come—when society resolutely ostracized him and made him an outlaw, he would take a lesson from this fugitive who lurked in the Black Hills.

A clamoring of dogs made him turn around just as the rim of the sun began to push up above the eastern horizon. He found the pack almost at once. They were commodiously kenneled in what had once been the blacksmith shop. But the forge and the tools had been moved out of the old shed. Only the smoke-blackened timbers gave token of the use to which the place originally had been put. This was the shelter for the dogs in case of bad weather or during the cold mountain nights. But now they were out in their yard, tumbling here and there—dogs of all shapes and sizes, except small ones.

One could see at a glance that they were not a congregation of curs, however, no matter how much cur strain there might be among them. They bore the token of many a fight. Here was an ear missing which the sweeping stroke of a puma might have shorn away. There was a great, jagged scar along the shoulder of an old veteran hound, which the stiff claws of a cornered grizzly might have opened. Hardly a member of the pack that had not been injured in the ardors of the trail or in fights with one another. They were clamoring for food now, or falling into brief argument here and there, with a display of teeth and fierce growling.

Another and more mellow calling took The Duke around the corner from this den of tumult to a smaller yard and kennel, where he found half a dozen long, low-bodied dogs with great trailing ears and with pouchy faces and wise-seeming eyes. These were the bloodhounds Guthrie had mentioned. And with these two packs he was to hunt down the murderer. It was work which went against the grain of The Duke. He had rather have met two men face to face and taken his chances with them than to corner a single foe with this pack of brutes and their inescapable powers of scent.

However, that enemy was not yet at his mercy. It would be time enough to think of clemency when he encountered the brigand or had him helpless by means of the dogs. In the meantime, he was suddenly aware of eyes watching him from behind. He turned abruptly and found a big man—with inches fully as many as those of The Duke, and with far greater bulk—standing idly behind him and taking note of him with a sort of quiet amusement which was not at all to the taste of The Duke. He was not accustomed to finding even the shadow of a smile on the faces of those who were about him. However, he took careful note of this stranger. He regarded the powerful body, not too heavily muscled for agility, he took into consideration the narrow waist, the lean hips, the swelling chest and the great spread of shoulders.

And the face of this man was the face of one whose strength had never been equaled by his fellows. He had that dauntless way of looking deep into eyes; he had a proud and determined bearing—all of which spoke eloquent volumes to the keen glance of The Duke.

His face was as interesting as his strong body. It was deeply lined, though the man could not be greatly in excess of twenty-five or twenty-six years of age. But there were seams which would have done credit to fifty. The small gray eyes were sheltered under a great bluff of overhanging brows. There was an aquiline nose, sharply hooked. There was a wide-lipped mouth and a square chin. Altogether, his face reminded The Duke, at the first glance, of one of the warrior dogs he had just been looking upon. At second glance, the face seemed familiar. This was someone he had seen before. But at the third glance he understood. It was not that he had ever seen this same countenance before, but the big man was like a composite photograph of all the fighters whom it had been the lot of The Duke to encounter on his wayward pilgrimage through life.

"You're The Duke, I take it?" said the other.

"That's my name, as they call me."

"I'm Steve Guthrie."

They shook hands slowly, with a lingering pressure, as though they secretly wished to try out the strength of each other with the power of grip as a gauge.

"You've come to get the gent in the Black Hills, then?" said Steve.

"I guess that's to be my main job."

"Well," said Steve. "I wish you all kinds of luck. Uncle Bill is sure worried. But I guess you'll get your man, if all we hear about you is straight."

And just a tinge of mirth curled his lips, as though he had his doubts of the matter.

11

◉

Steve Shows His Caliber

IT WAS NOT a very auspicious opening to his career on the Guthrie place, this meeting with the nephew of the owner. In the old days The Duke would have pushed to the conclusion of an inevitable fight a conversation far less suggestive than this. But in three years at hard labor he had learned a great deal, and, among the other things, he had learned to think twice.

Steve Guthrie took him to the bunkhouse and introduced him to the cowpunchers as the latter came tumbling out in the fresh chill of the sunrise. Their names blurred and passed into a jumbled confusion in the memory of The Duke. What he saw were their faces, the manner in which they walked and stood and the directness with which they met his eye.

And when he had been introduced to each, had shaken hands with each and had taken hold of the whole character of each man, as it were, with the grip of his fingers, he decided that he had never in his life seen a worse lot of cowpunchers. To be sure, they might know their work. They might be expert in riding the range. They might be able to tell a mile away by the actions of a cow what illness or pest was annoying her. They might be geniuses at the roundup. They might be heroes when it came to riding a bucking horse. They might have all these qualities, but The Duke shrewdly doubted it. They were all elderly. They were all half broken in body. They were all hangdog and shiftless in manner and in expression.

There is a singular look which comes into the faces of men who no longer care, who have lost their pride and self-respect. He found that look in the faces of these men, and it affected him like personal uncleanliness. Afterward, he went with Steve Guthrie into the long, low room with a stove in the center and the bunks built along the wall. He chose an empty place at the end of the room, and here he brought his pack, though Steve offered him a room in the ranch house. But The Duke declined with thanks. If he were working on a ranch he preferred to throw in his lot with the other cowpunchers. He was simply one on special duty, so to speak.

"Now come into the house and see Uncle Bill," said Steve. "You'll find him a pile changed, even from what he was yesterday. Every day puts a couple of years on the old man's back, you might say."

The Duke protested that he must take care of his horse, so Steve followed him to the barn. But he had no sooner seen Monday than he became greatly excited. It was easy for The Duke to see that his companion was deeply stirred, but he could never have guessed it from the speech of Steve. In fact, The Duke discovered at once that the only proper manner of getting at the thoughts of Steve was by watching his face. The words he spoke said one thing; the manner of his speech said quite another. Though he simply grunted at the sight of the tall gray, his eyes were on fire.

"Kind of leggy, ain't he?" he asked after a time, watching The Duke working over the stallion.

"Sort of leggy," said The Duke noncommittally.

"Most like he wouldn't do no good under hard work," suggested Steve.

"Most like he wouldn't."

There was a sigh from Steve. Strange was the man who could keep from defending his horse in the face of such accusations as these.

"Might be he could step along pretty well over the flat, though."

"Might be he could go along pretty good," admitted The Duke.

"Hey, Tom!" called Steve to the cowpuncher who at that moment passed the open door of the barn. "Throw your saddle on Sandow, will you?"

He turned to The Duke.

"D'you mind giving your hoss a run before breakfast?"

"Not if it ain't too far."

"Just down the valley a ways."

"Sure!" The Duke nodded cheerfully, but he wondered what could have aroused this profound interest. He tossed his saddle on Monday and led him out into the open just as the cowpuncher whom Steve had hailed came forth leading a long-bodied, bay gelding whose heavily muscled quarters and shoulders gave a sufficient explanation for his name. But his legs, his long neck and the elastic step with which he walked—all promised great speed.

"Give him a whiz, Tom," said Steve.

Tom, in the saddle, winked and grinned at his boss.

"Down to where the old mill used to be on the river," said Steve. "Tom, unless you look out and ride hard, I guess Sandow will get beat. There's a look to this gray hoss—"

"Down there and finish back here?" asked Tom.

"That's right. Are you ready?"

"Ready!" answered Tom and The Duke.

"Let 'er go, boys!"

He had snatched his revolver from its holster at the last moment and fired it into the air, and the explosion started the horses away. Sandow, settling to his work like a dog starting after a jack rabbit, was half a dozen lengths in the lead before Monday seemed to understand what was expected of him. But no horse which has ever run on the open range passes beyond the days of colthood without coming to know what a race is. Sandow headed straight for a fence, sailed over it deftly, with hind feet tucked under him, landed, and was off on the far side like a bird swooping.

And as he looked ahead and watched, The Duke understood why that course had been picked. Sandow was a good fencer, and Monday might never have jumped a fence in his life. However, as he pricked his ears and started in pursuit of the gelding, The Duke put him squarely at the fence, and by the determined manner of Monday's approach he guessed that the big horse was not entirely new to such a business. Now he reared, flung himself into the air, landed lightly on the farther side, and was off again, with Sandow a scant four lengths away.

After that, there was nothing to the race. There was a succession of half a dozen fences, one after the other. By the time Sandow had cleared the last one Monday was sailing over it at his side, and Tom, the rider of the bay, turned his face with a curse and a look of amazement.

He doubled his mount sharply around beside the old mill and scudded back for the finish. But The Duke had no desire to win that race. There was nothing to be gained by revealing all the speed of Monday. It sufficed him to know that over the flat or over the fences the gray horse could run in circles around the bay. And as for Steve Guthrie, what was to be gained by letting him know exactly how fast the gray stallion was?

So The Duke took the gray around in a loose and open circle and brought him slowly back toward the first fence. In the meantime, Sandow had doubled around and, darting away, had regained the half dozen lengths he had lost. Monday snorted with eagerness as he saw the gap which had been opened before him, but on the return to the starting point of the race he received no help from his rider. Tom was like a feather, bobbing in the saddle on Sandow, whipping him on, swinging with the swing of the running horse. But The Duke sat heavily, a leaden figure, on the back of Monday, and they cut down the lead of the bay horse slowly. With only a gesture The Duke knew he could double the speed of the gray. But he sat quietly. He leaned forward to make a hollow pretense of jockeying his horse. And so he cleared the last fence and drew up, loser by a full two lengths.

Tom was jubilant.

"When you come shooting up beside me down at the mill," he said, "I thought you had me. But I jerked Sandow around and gave him the ride of his life coming home. And here we are, Sandy, old kid!" He laughed joyously. "They don't make the kind that can beat you, old hoss," he assured the gelding.

"You sure gave him a good ride," assented Steve Guthrie. But it seemed to The Duke that there was not a great deal of heartiness in the voice of the boss, and the eye of Steve was running back and forth from Sandow's heaving sides and bowed head to the erect crest and easily drawn breath of the gray stallion. There was much to be deduced from that comparison, and The Duke was uncomfortably sure that Steve would make no mistakes. It was rather odd, he decided, as he put up the gray again, that the nephew of the owner should have taken this very keen interest in the new man and his horse.

"It was the fences that beat your hoss Monday," Steve was saying as they went back toward the barn. "If that race had been over smooth ground, poor old Sandow would have taken a trouncing."

But the glimmer in his eyes said quite another thing, and The Duke understood that Steve had easily seen through all of his maneuver to let Monday be taken. But no more was said about it on the way to the ranch house for breakfast. Steve picked up a new topic.

"When you talked to Uncle Bill," he said, "what did you make out of it?"

"What d'you mean?" asked The Duke.

"Did you figure that he talked a little queer?"

"He talked a little scared, seemed to me," said The Duke.

"Well, you got brains of your own, and you know how to use 'em. I just want you to remember that when some folks begin to get suspicious that other folks are trying to kill 'em, it simply means that—"

He paused and tapped his forehead significantly. The Duke regarded him with horror.

"You mean he ain't just right in—" He could not complete the phrasing of that inquiry.

Steve shrugged his shoulders.

"I've said too much," he said. "That's the trouble with me. Always talking too much!"

And he shook his head sadly. If there had been any doubt in the mind of The Duke as to whether or not his companion was a fox, the last doubt was instantly removed by this remark. From that moment he decided that he would not trust Steve out of sight. Yet he entered the dining room of the big house, chatting with the boss in the most friendly fashion.

12

◎

A Man in Terror

HE PUT ONLY one question to Steve as they crossed the threshold: "Does your uncle do all the hiring?"

"Sure. He does the hiring, and I do the firing. So what's the difference?"

There was no doubt that he was right. The man who did the "firing" certainly controlled the policy of the ranch. But The Duke was amazed by what he heard. That an elderly rancher who had been reduced to a semi-hysterical condition by several attempts made on his life should have surrounded himself with obviously harmless cowhands, was one thing; but that a burly young giant like Steve Guthrie should have made such a selection, was almost beyond credence. Steve could have taken them three at a time in his arms and crushed them.

There was a distinct reason behind the fact that he had weeded out all except such fellows as these. What could that reason be?

Indeed, every moment that The Duke stayed on the Guthrie place, he became more and more convinced that there was work to be done here in unraveling a mysterious situation. And he made a resolution, to begin with, to make no man his confidant, but would work entirely through his own strength and his own discretion.

Breakfast is the fastest meal on a farm. In fifteen minutes it was ended, and Steve told The Duke that it was time for him to see William Guthrie himself. The latter, it appeared, slept late in the morning for the reason that he could not sleep much at night.

"He keeps himself walled in like he was in a little fort," said Steve Guthrie. "But you try not to smile when you see the inside of his room!"

He chuckled as he spoke, and it seemed to The Duke that there was a cruel relish in his voice. So The Duke merely nodded with a vague agreement. He had been gravely impressed at the breakfast table by the silence of the cowpunchers and the manner in which, even when they spoke in a monotone, they furtively cast up their eyes to the face of Steve Guthrie as though to ask permission. What was the secret of this power of his? How had he been able to reduce free men—and cowpunchers above all —to this condition? Or, what was more likely, why had he chosen such specimens as these for the work on that big ranch?

These speculations were cut short as they arrived at a door where Steve Guthrie tapped once, made a pause, tapped twice sharply and close together, and then after another long pause, rapped heavily again, a single stroke.

"That's the password." He grinned at The Duke over his shoulder.

"You think there's nothing in this scare he's got?" asked The Duke point-blank.

"Sure I do. That crook that he chased, that bandit from the Black Hills, was sore because Uncle Bill gave him a hard run that day. So he came back and tried to plug him through the window. But since then he ain't showed up, has he? Uncle Bill acts like somebody tried to kill him every day of his life. Matter of fact, there's been only one attempt—"

Here a key turned heavily in the lock. A bolt jarred back, and presently the door was opened, though only a few inches, while the face of the rancher appeared masked in the gloom of the room. As he perceived who stood before him, he flung the door wide and at the same time he stepped back and to the side, as though to avoid encountering even a ghost of danger face to face.

"Here's The Duke," said Steve.

"Come in, John Morrow," said Guthrie.

The Duke stepped in with Steve at his heels.

"I'll stay here alone with him," said the rancher.

"Alone?" echoed Steve with pointed emphasis.

"Yes."

Steve retreated with a grunt of surprise, and Guthrie closed the door behind him. That interim gave The Duke a chance to look about the room, and he used the opportunity as only one with well-trained eyes can do.

The room was furnished as though for the poorest cowhand. Upon the slats of the bed a bedroll had been unfurled. The bed itself was of unpainted wood, darkened by some thirty years of use and exposure. There was one chair drawn up before a little rudely made table littered with a tangle of papers which evidently represented the business of the ranch. The floor was carpetless, without even a rag rug. Spur scars were here and there, and in places the surface wood had been worn away near the bed and in front of the table. The window was blank of curtains. Such was the sleeping chamber and office of a man on whose land ran three thousand head of fine cattle!

The indoor life meant nothing, however. The real roof was the open sky, and the real walls were the mountain-piled horizons. All of which The Duke understood perfectly. To be sure, he was himself a devoted lover of comfort. If he had had the income of that place for a week—but that was another story. He turned to face his employer and found him still engaged in relocking and rebolting the door. Presently Guthrie finished, waved him to the only chair, and himself began to walk hastily up and down the room, his shoulders bowed, his gait shuffling, and pausing many times as sudden thoughts struck home in him.

"You've looked things over?" he said at last.

"I ain't had time to look everything over," replied The Duke, glancing out the window and down at the jumble of buildings. The headquarters of the ranch was like a small town, actually with more timber in it than went to the make-up of many a crossroads village in the mountains.

"You've seen the men at breakfast, anyway?"

"Yep."

"What do you think of 'em?"

"I dunno," said The Duke cautiously, for the first thing a gambler learns is to hide his opinions of other men. "I ain't had the time to make up my mind."

"Say!" exploded Guthrie, though he kept his voice soft. "Man alive, d'you mean to say you ain't seen through the whole lot of 'em at a look?" And he turned his weary and sleepless eyes upon The Duke.

"Well," confessed John Morrow, now that he was pressed to the wall, "they didn't look like much to me."

"They're a pile less than they look. I got eighteen men doing a dozen men's work!"

"Why don't you fire 'em?"

"Steve handles that end. And it's hard to keep real men out here. Steve ain't the easiest man in the world to get along with. He's a downright sort. He talks like he was a captain and they were soldiers. And men that've got any backbone don't stand it very well. How about you? How are you going to stand it?"

"I dunno," said The Duke. "I aim to get along. I owe you three months' pay."

"You mean you'll stay?"

"I sure will."

The rancher sighed.

"That does me a pile of good," he declared. "Have you seen the dogs?"

"Yes."

"They're a good working pack. Not much on looks. But they'll run a man trail as soon as they'll run a bear trail. I got 'em from below the border and"—he paused, and a grim smile twitched at the corners of his mouth—"they ain't unused to the scent of man."

"Has Steve had any luck running 'em?"

"They only been here a few days. And Steve can't run nothing. He's too heavy for the hosses around here. He weighs close onto two hundred and forty pounds. Needs about a dray hoss to carry him, and a dray hoss can't keep up with a pack. That's the reason why I ain't had much help from Steve in catching this hound from the Black Hills. Footwork is where Steve shines. He's gone out on the trail on foot for me, but he ain't happened to have no luck. In them Black Hills among the rocks it's pretty hard to read a sign. A sight trail is about all that a man can follow."

The Duke nodded. He had not realized just how great was the bulk of Steve. His respect for that young giant increased. Two hundred and forty pounds of muscle! That was certainly "considerable man!"

"Has anything happened since you got back?"

Guthrie glared at him. He hesitated as though afraid that he would not be believed.

"Last night—" he muttered and glanced toward the door as he subdued his voice to a whisper.

"Look here," said The Duke suddenly, "are you afraid that someone around here will hear you?"

"And think I'm crazy!"

The Duke shrugged his shoulders. He was beginning to think that Steve Guthrie had diagnosed the situation correctly. Fear would produce insanity, of course. And the fact and actions of Guthrie showed that his nerve was very far gone.

"Last night," said the rancher, "he came here again! He tried to sneak up on me. I heard him walking up the stairs. And then his footsteps come right down the hall and—"

"Easy!" said The Duke, jumping up in alarm. "You'll be getting a stroke or something, Mr. Guthrie!"

For the rancher, as he told the story of that midnight horror, had grown splotched with livid patches over his face.

"But did you actually see anything?" continued The Duke as Guthrie drew in a great, sobbing breath and passed a hand over his face as though to erase the memory.

"I heard the steps come up to the door!" said Guthrie.

"The wind'll make queer sounds like that that seem to walk up and down," commented The Duke.

"I had a lamp turned low," said Guthrie. "I was sitting up in bed with a gun ready, and I seen—I seen the knob of that there door turned!"

He gasped out these words, pointing straight toward the door, so that The Duke turned toward it with a shudder of apprehension. And suddenly the tale of the rancher was lifted from the region of hysterical fancy to the purest fact. He was not a foolish old man letting his nerves get the best of him, but one hounded by a murderer.

"And I don't dare tell Steve. I don't dare tell none of the men. They'd laugh at me!" And Guthrie groaned.

13
◉

Red Mud and Black

THAT WAS A LITTLE twist of tragedy of which The Duke had not thought—to be surrounded by succor in time of danger and not to be able to call out for help without drawing on one's head ridicule which was more to be dreaded than death—that was torture worse than any The Duke had conceived. For his own part, Guthrie's frantic gesture toward the door had convinced The Duke as well as though he had seen the slayer lurking in the hall and then stealing away with a soft stride before the dawn.

"If you'd called for someone—"

"My voice would have scared him away before the boys could of come."

"How did he get to the window of your room the time he fired in at you?"

"Lowered a rope from the roof, took a shot through the window, saw me drop—because I tumbled back out of my chair with the scare of the discharge—and then slid down the rest of the way to the ground."

"And he got started after you with all of this just because you tried to hunt him off'n your ranch?"

"That's it. Look here!"

He hurried to his table. He came back bringing a piece of paper on which was typewritten:

Keep off my trail and I'll leave you alone.

"And you wouldn't do it?"

"I'd see him hanged first! The day after he sent me that warning I was out on his trail again!"

The Duke nodded. There was a fine courage in this time-worn cowman.

"If I could face him—if we could shoot it out!" Guthrie groaned. "But he sneaks around in the middle of the night—"

His words were interrupted by a heavy knocking on the front door of the house and, almost immediately, a loud calling as that door was thrown open.

"Guthrie! Bill Guthrie!"

"It's the sheriff, Tom Onion!" cried the rancher, starting for the door. "Maybe he's learned something—"

He tore the door open and ran into the upper hall, with The Duke at his heels. Down the stairs—steep as a ladder, well-nigh—ran Guthrie, The Duke close behind.

"What's up, Tom?" he shouted as he descended.

"We're looking for a man," said the sheriff. "We're looking for a man and—by heaven!—here he is!"

He thundered out the last as Guthrie reached the level and The Duke stepped down behind him.

"Hands up, Duke. Jerk 'em up lively and keep your elbows stiff!"

He shoved his revolver at the chest of The Duke, and the latter thrust up his arms obediently. Tom Onion meant business of the most deadly seriousness. Behind him a mutter of deep satisfaction rolled from the voices of a score of men and The Duke, looking about him, found that he was surrounded by many faces, every one weary but determined. They edged in toward him. In spite of the fact that the sheriff had his gun under the chin of the helpless man, these others watched him as a hawk watches, and kept their hands near the butts of their revolvers.

The Duke was impressed. And, being impressed, he

smiled upon the sheriff, and smiled still upon the men behind him.

"What's up, Tom?" he asked.

"The last of your ructions," said the sheriff fiercely. He was not in the habit of trying and convicting a prisoner before arrest, but today his mind seemed to be made up before he laid eyes on The Duke. "Get his gun, Toby!"

The revolver was drawn from The Duke's holster. Toby stepped back.

"Why hang it, Toby, don't you know better'n to think that a gent like The Duke carries only one gun?"

Toby hurried back to the job, and presently, after much patting of The Duke's person, he located another weapon beneath the clothes, and drew out a snub-nosed pistol.

"You'll get a killing one of these days to teach you to be thorough," said the sheriff. "Are you sure he ain't got anything else on him?"

"Positive certain," declared Toby, hot-faced because of his first failure.

"Lemme see," said Tom Onion. "If you're wrong, a couple of us that are alive now may be dead before we're a minute older. Get a couple of guns onto The Duke, some of you boys!"

The order was obeyed to the letter. A dozen Colts came flashing forth on the instant, and a dozen hard muzzles were jammed into the ribs of The Duke.

In the meantime the sheriff stepped close and reached for the throat of his prisoner. The Duke wore his shirts of an exceedingly large neck size. Even in that country of loose clothes a number eighteen on a fifteen and three-quarters or a sixteen neck was conspicuous. The sheriff dipped into The Duke's clothes with his forefinger and presently raised his hand with a dark string outlined against it, a mere wrapping string in size, but it was, in fact, a bit of fine horsehair woven and braided together so that it was of the greatest possible strength. And, running this thread over his finger, the sheriff presently drew up through the loose collar of The Duke a dainty little derringer so small that a card expert could well-nigh have palmed it and escaped detection. But it had two short barrels of large caliber.

"Two dead men is what I said," said the sheriff, "and two dead men is what I meant. Maybe one of 'em would of been you, Toby!"

Toby, crimson with shame, stepped back into the crowd and strove to lose himself. But his disgrace was covered by the mutter of wonder which came from all those stern lips.

"You see how he was fixed up," said Tom Onion, stepping back. He talked of The Duke as though the latter were an inanimate creature, or a beast of prey behind bars, at the best. "Suppose there was no gat in his holster? If somebody tried to jump him, he had that other gun tucked away in his clothes where it wouldn't show. Or suppose a gent got the cold drop on him and told him to put up his hands. He puts them up, right enough, but just as he gets his hands above his shoulders, and just when the gent with the drop figures that there's nothing more to worry about, The Duke hooks his thumb under one side of that little lariat he wears around his neck and fishes out his derringer. He takes the other fellow while the other fellow thinks that he's through with his hard work. And The Duke can shoot from the height of his chin as well as he can shoot from his hip or his shoulder. Duke, that's the way you killed Pete Sankey!"

The Duke smiled again, and still he said nothing.

"You don't have to talk," said Tom Onion. "Turn around!"

He was obeyed.

"Keep those guns on him, boys, and if he stirs, let him have it. Now, lower them hands of yours and put 'em behind you."

The Duke obeyed carefully, and as his hands came behind him the handcuffs were snapped into place.

"Now," and the sheriff sighed, "I guess I've finished the job!"

"A mighty good job, too!" exclaimed a chorus.

"Turn around," said the sheriff to The Duke and emphasized the command with a prod of his revolver. The latter turned and faced his enemies.

"Mind telling me what it's all about?"

"Curse your murdering heart!" shouted a tall, wry-faced man who now burst forward through the pack of men. "I'll tell you what you're going to hang for! You—"

Instead of the oath over which he set his teeth, he drove his fist into the face of The Duke.

"Stand back, Martin!" thundered the sheriff. "Ain't his hands tied?"

He thrust Martin away, but the crowd did not seem to share the sheriff's indignation over that coward's blow. There was a wolfish lifting of lips and a deep-throated growling. When anger passes a certain point it brings all the brute to the surface. As for The Duke, a thin trickle of blood was running down from his lips, but he continued to smile. His face was a mortal paleness, but his eyes were gentle, and they were fixed full on Martin.

"But I'll tell you if you ain't guessed. They ain't any way out this time, Duke. You was seen! But there ain't no use dodging. Come out like a man and confess, Duke. You killed 'Dud' Martin on the Gaveney Road last night!"

"No."

"You lie!" came the voice of the crowd.

"Mrs. Martin!" called the sheriff. "Stand back, boys!"

The cowpunchers pushed back and opened a narrow path, and down this came a little, erect, middle-aged woman with a sun-browned face and sun-faded wisps of hair streaking down from beneath her hat. Like the rest of the party, her riding clothes were streaked with red mud. She halted a step away from The Duke, and he would never forget the gleam of her eyes.

"John Morrow," she cried, "you killed Dud Martin!"

It brought a roar of hatred and indignation from the crowd. The men swept a little closer. Thoughts of a lynching were in every mind.

The sheriff threw himself in front of his captive as though he guessed the storm which was brewing.

"Clear away, boys," he said. "Let me get him back to town and—"

"I'll save you a trip," said The Duke.

The sheriff whirled back on him.

"Well?" he barked.

"Lemme ask a few questions."

"Fire away."

"Mrs. Martin, you seen me do the killing?"

"Yes!"

"What time?"

"Eleven fifteen last night on the road where—"

"That was tolerable dark."

"He counts on the darkness saving him!" cried Mrs. Martin. "But it wasn't too dark to see the gray hoss you was riding, John Morrow!"

"Maybe not. You seen a gray hoss, then, but you didn't see my face?"

"Natcherally not, with you wearing a mask! But we all know you were riding a gray hoss. We know you left the dance wanting to do murder for the way they'd treated you, and you took it out on Dud because our girl wouldn't—"

"Will you gents follow me out to the barn?"

His calm was wonderfully convincing. It brought a shadow of doubt over their keen certainty.

"Step out," said the sheriff. "We'll follow you, Duke."

The crowd gave way. Through the front door they went and then down the steps and back to the barn in which The Duke had stabled the gray. Monday was playing in the corral behind the barn by this time, running here and there like a colt, and striking with his forehoofs at whirling bits of straw which the wind bandied here and there. It was a pleasant sight to see. The Duke paused so that the others could enjoy it.

Then he went into the barn.

"Here's my saddle," he said, pausing beneath it. "Will you take it outside for me, Sheriff?"

The sheriff, bewildered, obeyed. Into the sunlight the old saddle was brought, still spotted with mud from the long ride of the night before.

"D'you see any difference between the mud on this here saddle and the mud on the saddles you folks been riding in?" asked The Duke.

They turned to stare.

"You're plastered all over with that red clay that sticks like glue. And here's my saddle with black mud on it. Boys, ain't that a proof that I never rode the Gaveney Road last night?"

They were dumbfounded. Yet it seemed impossible that so small a thing should have undone all of their riding, all of their reasoning.

"Ain't it an easy thing to change saddles?" asked Mrs. Martin, her voice shaking as her certainty left her.

"Where would I of changed it?" asked The Duke. "This is the saddle I bought in Wheeler City yesterday. I can prove that. How did I get it here over the Gaveney Road without splashing it over with red clay?"

The sheriff cursed softly.

"Besides," said The Duke, "the Gaveney Road is a mighty long ways off. If I'd rode Monday all that ways, would he be as frisky as that now?"

And he pointed back to the corral where the tall gray was still gamboling.

There was no doubt about it. It was a convincing stroke. The silence of the crowd attested that the detail had told with them. It was just such a bit of evidence as they were best fitted to appreciate.

"Mrs. Martin," said The Duke, "seen her husband killed in the middle of the night, with the wind roarin' and the rain fallin'. All she knows is that the killer rode a gray hoss. Sheriff, you can't take me on that sort of evidence. I'll thank you to put my saddle back where you found it—and take the irons off my hands! And there's my guns that I'll be troubling you for, too!"

There was nothing for it but surrender. They examined the dried mud on The Duke's saddle. Indeed, where the leather had been soaked through, some of it was still damp. There was no possibility that the red clay could have been removed and such a coating as this put over it. And reluctantly the silent sheriff removed the handcuffs and restored the weapons.

After that they backed away from The Duke and got to their horses, with only the sheriff lingering for a word or two.

"Duke," he said, "I'm sure sorry!"

"Thanks," said The Duke.

"But your record is agin' you."

"Sure," said The Duke, and that was the end of the matter.

They last saw him calmly rolling a cigarette and looking with his mirthless smile after the figure of the dead man's brother. Martin had used his spurs and was now a full mile away and still riding as though the devil were at his horse's tail.

14

◉

Night Signals

WHEN THE NOISE of their hoofbeats died away, the rest of the crowd, consisting of curious cowpunchers of the Guthrie place, still lingered until Steve scattered them with a roar.

"Are you making a living standing around and enjoying the weather?" he thundered. "Git out and stir your stumps!"

They scattered, and The Duke looked after them through a lazy cloud of cigarette smoke. He was not accustomed to hearing men shouted at as though they were dogs. He was still less accustomed to seeing them obey when they were so addressed. But these fellows seemed to have been chosen for their abject docility. He looked back with a curious dislike at Steve Guthrie. The more he saw of the man the more he disliked him.

"Nothing much to that crowd," said Steve. "Not much bulldog about them. They let go their hold about as soon as they got it!"

The Duke smiled at him, his most malevolent smile.

"They didn't have me by the throat," he said. "And they're cussing their luck because they didn't. They ain't sorry that they didn't get the right man; they're only sorry that I didn't turn out to be him. If they could of hung me first and found out they was wrong afterward, they wouldn't of cared at all!"

"There's one main point," said Steve gruffly, "and that is that they didn't stretch your neck. What else matters?"

"Nothing much," said The Duke, and fell into a dreamy silence in which his attention was fixed on a far-off cloud.

"The rest of the hands are starting on their day's job," resumed the boss of the ranch briskly as the rattle and pound of the grist mill began in the distance, taking its power from the eighteen-foot wheel of a great windmill. "I suppose," he went on, "that you'll be aiming to start, Duke?"

"I been thinking," said The Duke, "about—"

"About your job?"

"About a story I heard when I was a kid."

"Yeah?"

"The story was about a growed-up man that wouldn't never work for more'n one boss."

"How come? What're you driving at, Morrow?"

"Bill Guthrie hired me; he'll give me my orders; and he'll do the firing, I figure," said The Duke mildly. "Does that suit you, Guthrie?"

Steve blinked at him. It was a long moment before he seemed to understand the full purport of the words of the new hand. Then he grew purple with rage.

"Why, you—" he began.

"Steve!" cut in his uncle. "There ain't any call for you to start making a speech. It's a pile healthier for a young gent to save his wind for his work."

Steve favored his uncle with a poisonous glance and then turned on his heel. And in The Duke a little tingle of gratification ran up and down his spine. He would have welcomed a battle at that moment. Every fiber in his body was crying out with the desire for action. He had chained down an earlier impulse which had urged him to ride in furious pursuit of Dud Martin's brother. The ache of his injured mouth, where the fist of the dead man's brother had driven home, was a small thing, but the torment in his soul was an exquisite torture. So regretfully he saw Steve take his uncle's order and leave the contest. But old Bill Guthrie was now smiling on him.

"When I was a kid," he said, "I used to be all wrapped up in game chickens. Darned if they don't love fighting jest for the sake of the fight. It's like pie and cake to 'em. Ain't you kind of the same breed, Duke?"

He did not wait for an answer. He came closer and laid a kindly hand on the shoulder of the younger man.

"Don't you be paying no attention to Steve," he said. "It's like Steve not to see that there's things worse than hanging, and one of 'em is to have most of the folks one knows all dead set against one. I know how you feel, son. All I say is: Ride slow. Wait till you get sunlight before you jump any ditches. And if you wait long enough, one of these days you'll have all those folks back on your side just as strong as they're now against you!"

"Them?" said The Duke as he jerked his thumb in the direction of the last of the disappearing posse. "I ain't wasting any time worrying about what they think! When gents hunt in a pack they don't amount to no more'n a pack of coyotes. When one of 'em yelps, the whole crowd starts in hollering, not knowing what it's all about. A crowd don't do no thinking. It can do a hanging or a murder, but it can't do no thinking."

"That's true," said the rancher. "That's true for a young gent to have said!"

His words, his kindly manner, warmed the heart of The Duke. Moreover, having put into words the anger which he would rather by far have expressed with violent action, he felt in a far more kindly mood toward the world in general. He set off immediately to round up his forces for the long trails which he was about to ride.

The dogs were what first mattered. He whiled away the long hours of the morning looking them over. He took them out one by one and in couples. He caught and saddled a tough mustang in the corral. He wore out that durable little brute with two hours of racing back and forth with the dogs. He saddled another and wore it out in the same fashion before noon. But by that time he had been able to give the dogs fine exercise, and he had seen the fashion in which they worked. He already knew the fast ones and the slow ones. He knew the ones which were inclined to snap and snarl and give trouble. He knew the doughty old trailers whose noses were hungry for a good scent, and who would be most apt to cling like death to a trail. They had been well broken, that pack. And once they started after a man, it would go hard if they did not trail him closely.

Such were the thoughts of The Duke when he reached noon of that day. He was already washing when the cowpunchers came in. He was drying his hands on the long, community roller towel while they chattered and cracked jokes and told the tales of the morning's work. But when they went inside to the cheerless dining room the cloud fell over them even as it had fallen over them at breakfast time. Those who spoke, spoke only to ask that dishes be passed to them. And their voices were lowered to a churchly hush. There was only one free and voluble speaker. That, of course, was Steve. He held forth in a loud voice while the others listened. He did not cease his talk until, at the end of the meal, William Guthrie fell asleep in his chair, succumbing to the weariness of many a night of scant sleep, and to the lulling influence of the shaft of sunshine which fell through the tall window and over his gray head.

That was taken as a signal. The cowpunchers rose and tramped out. The Duke followed. But at the door he paused to look back. He saw Steve leaning beside the chair of his uncle.

"Wake up, Uncle Bill," he was saying. "Wake up and go upstairs to bed. You're plumb wore out."

"I'll do fair enough," said Guthrie.

"You won't either. You're tired out. Go upstairs and lie down on your bed, and I'll come along and watch in the room with you."

"Will you do that, Steve?"

"Sure I will!"

"You're a good lad, Steve. A little rough-spoken sometimes, but I always know that your heart is right!"

The Duke pondered over that scene while he was out riding during the afternoon. Guthrie must be right. There was much tenderness and much goodness in the big fellow. The Duke himself decided that he must postpone the judgment which he had been forming.

In the meantime, he covered a large section of the ranch with a twisting course which he rode on Monday. The big gray seemed to have quite recovered from the effects of the long ride of the day before. He had showed it by his frisking in the corral that morning. He showed it again in his eagerness to go that afternoon. But his master kept him at an easy jog mile after mile. He could not tell when that reserve speed might be a priceless asset on the trail. He did not intend to use it up in foolish frolics. For the interest of The Duke in his work had grown immensely since that story of the turning of the doorknob, and since he had stood in that fear-haunted room of William Guthrie.

He skirted around the ranch with his eye sharp for every peculiarity of the land. He studied the contours around the ranch house, as, in the old days, he had studied the face of an opponent in a gambling game. And, finally, the map of all the flats and all the hills and all the draws was printed in his brain. By this time it was late afternoon. By the time he had put up Monday and come to the house, supper was ready.

After it, William Guthrie drew him apart. He pointed out that The Duke could not adequately protect him unless The Duke were near during the night. And for that purpose he suggested a room next to his own. Accordingly, John Morrow brought his bedroll from the bunkhouse into the main dwelling. There he made it down in the designated apartment, smoked a cigarette and turned in for the night.

His sleep was solid. Yet, as he slept, his mind was open and ready to hear so much as a whisper fifty feet away— so prepared, indeed, that when William Guthrie groaned in his sleep in the middle of the night The Duke bounded to his feet with a gun in his hand, ready for instant action. He slipped into Guthrie's room with his feet bare. But he found the old rancher sound asleep, though he was frowning in the middle of another nightmare, with the sweat gleaming on his brow.

The Duke looked down at him for a moment in wonder and pity. Then he returned to his own chamber. He could not sleep, however. Three or four hours of complete rest were enough for him in the day, so now he determined to put on the rest of his clothes and go for a walk around the house and wait for dawn.

Accordingly, he slipped down as softly as he could and stepped out into the night. Outside, he went off at a brisk gait. He walked down by the river. He skirted back to the barn. He went in and found Monday lying asleep. He continued from the barn and the perfume of sweet hay until he was beside the star-scattered surface of Lindsay Lake. There he paused to listen to the soft crisping of the waves along the shore.

While he waited he raised his head by chance and saw what seemed to him a faint glow of light near the top of a tall pine tree which bordered the lake. It appeared and disappeared. It was a ghostly light indeed. The Duke turned in bewilderment toward the house, and instantly he found the explanation. From the back of the house, from a little attic window, a light was being flashed— covered and exposed at unequal intervals. Someone was signaling far off through the night.

To whom was the signal sent? Whom was it meant for? What were the words?

15

◉

"Dogs First"

PLAINLY THAT LIGHT was winking out a regular code. How much of the message had gone before, he could not guess, of course. Moreover, he had no knowledge of a telegraphic code. If only he had taken the time to study that Morse code which was on a page of his little pocket dictionary! He ground his teeth. Here was an almost certain way of looking into the heart of the Guthrie mystery. That signal was flashing away from the direction of the Guthrie house toward the Black Hills.

The Duke took out an old crumpled envelope and the stub of a soft pencil. As fast as he could work he recorded the flashes of the light—a dash for a long exposure and a dot for a short one. No doubt it would be an illegible mass of pencil markings which he accumulated in this fashion, but at least it was worth the attempt.

Frequently the light went out. He waited a moment, but the signal did not flash again. But since the signaler had ceased his work the next important thing was to find out who had been doing the flashing. He ran around to the front of the house. The door which he had closed behind him as he went out was too apt to make a noise if he forced it open suddenly, so he slipped through a window which stood gaping upon the interior blackness.

It brought him into a room from which he hurried into the main hall of the house, and down this he went straight to the rear stairs, which wound up toward the second story and then to the attic above. But, as he was in the act of putting foot on those stairs which wound up steep as the rise of a ladder, well-nigh, he heard a light whisper of fluttering cloth above him, and then the slipping of leather against wood. Someone was coming softly and swiftly down through the darkness, and it could be no other than the midnight telegrapher. The Duke shrank into a corner to wait and watch.

Presently a figure loomed strange and bulky coming down the stairs. It was the unmistakable whisper of silk against silk which The Duke was hearing, and his heart leaped in him. Had a woman come to the ranch house? In another moment the figure was on the first floor, to which the rear stairs descended straight from the attic.

And that preconception that it was a girl filled up the mind of The Duke. It seemed to him that he breathed a slight fragrance newly come into the room where he crouched. It seemed to him that he could almost trace the features of her face. A woman! Lurking in this old house mysteriously, invisible by day and wandering about at night to send strange signals flashing toward the Black Hills—

Here the kitchen door was opened, and against the dull light of the midnight sky The Duke saw the bald sconce and the swinging queue of Bing, the Chinese cook!

The Duke stiffened with rage and disgust. He was on the verge of leaping on the celestial. But he restrained himself. He knew nothing, so far. At least, he knew nothing of importance. Far better to wait and to bide his time. If he tried to spring the trap prematurely, nothing might come of it.

Instead, he trailed Bing like a ghost until the China-man sat down beside the pump in the back of the ranch house and calmly lighted a long-stemmed pipe. There he crouched like a heathen idol, gathering the end of his queue into his lap, and there The Duke left him and stole back to the front of the house.

He entered it again. He went up to his room once more, making no more noise than a drifting shadow. There he lighted his lamp and found that little old dictionary. He opened it at the supplement which was so crammed with facts and data of all sorts, and among the rest, the Morse code. Over this he pored earnestly.

It was after considerable study over these strange characters that he eventually produced the envelope on which he had attempted to register the fraction of the message which he had spied out. He found it a crazy jumble in-deed. Here and there the pencil had slipped away from dot or dash and left a streak as irregular as the queue of Bing in a high wind.

And out of these undivided characters The Duke was to produce letters and then combine the letters into words!

He began, however, to figure out the problem as well as he could. If one dash meant "T" and one dot meant "E," the message might be supposed to begin "Teet." But then followed four dashes.

The result of his first exploration of the code brought him a message which began:"Teetoniu—" But here he decided that no combination of words could be brought out of such a chaos. He went back and began to work in a new fashion. And he struggled over and over again until at last, by fantastic slicing of the dots and dashes into singular groups, the light struck suddenly upon his mind.

"Dogsfisstandmanlater," was the result of his ultimate triumph. And that dissected into "dogs fisst and man later." There was certainly meaning to this. There was very much meaning indeed! Obviously he had made one mis-take in transcribing, and that was in failing to register with his pencil one of the flickers of the light. That "fisst" plainly meant "first." The message informed him that the dogs were to be "gotten" first and the man later.

The hounds were to be destroyed, it seemed, and after they were disposed of there would be time to pay attention to "the man." Who was "the man"? Was it William or Steve Guthrie? Was it himself? An instinct told him that he was the goal of this hidden threat.

By the time he unknotted his brows and looked up from the deciphering of this message the dawn was beginning, had passed the stage of cold grayness, and was spreading rosy light across the eastern horizon. Here an outcry of snarling and growling among the pack of hounds in their pen straightened him suddenly to his feet. He was down the stairs instantly and started for their yard, and he found them still busy at work, both the bloodhounds and the other pack. Their muzzles were red, and yonder were two of them fighting over a bone. They had been fed raw meat not five minutes before.

The Duke regarded them with dismay and then started for the barn. He was on the back of Monday in a few seconds and cutting across through the morning light, to come on the trail of the night visitor who had thrown that meat to the dogs. But there was neither sight nor sound. He had cut swiftly away where his horse would leave no trail, using the packed gravel along the edge of the river where the trail of this morning could not be distinguished from the trail of yesterday.

That is to say, such must have been the line of the flight of the stranger if it were indeed someone outside of the household of the Guthries who had fed the dogs.

As for the significance of that feeding, The Duke had not the slightest doubt, and before he returned from his ride he had confirmation of his fears. From afar, as he came back, he heard the howling of the dogs, and then a coughing and snarling. And as he drew nearer he saw men gathered around the fence which shut in the poor brutes.

One glimpse of the pitifully convulsed animals told The Duke all he wanted to know. It was arsenic. And enough of that poison must have been put on the meat to have slain an entire battalion of men. Otherwise, it could not have acted so swiftly.

He rode away from watching their wild efforts to get at water. The entire pack was gone—the big hunting and fighting dogs, and the bloodhounds themselves. The Duke was stopped by William Guthrie.

"Just when I was beginning to hope that with them dogs and with you to hunt them there'd be a chance of cornering that rat! Duke, it's too much for me! I'm going to give up and leave the ranch. I'll leave Steve here. He ain't afraid of the devil if the devil comes up with fire and brimstone and all. But I'm through. A gent that'll poison dogs will poison men. And I ain't going to be killed by the food I eat—not if a thousand miles between the Black Hills and me will do any good!"

"But if you go I'll have to stay on here alone—"

"What good am I to you, lad?"

"When you're gone there'll be nothing between me and Steve."

"I'll cancel that three months' work you owe me. You can ride back to town with me. I'll give you that three months for making another start."

The Duke shook his head.

"I've got to take one try," he said. "I've got to have one look at them Black Hills!"

"Good old Leaper!" called one of the cowpunchers. "He was the brains of the pack, anyway, and he ain't touched the stuff."

The Duke hurried back to the inclosure. And there he saw, in the smoke-blackened entrance to the old blacksmith shop, a black-and-tan hound of great size, looking woefully around on the death agonies of his companions, but apparently untouched by the poison himself.

It seemed like the interposition of fate to The Duke. There was one hound left to aid him in the unriddling of the trail of this murderer of beasts and men.

16

Trailing

THERE WAS NO doubt now about the meaning of that message which he deciphered. If the soft-footed Chinaman, Bing, had sent out the call, he had signaled a far-off confederate that the first step must be the slaughter of the hounds. And that confederate had prepared the meat, poisoned it and straightway had ridden in to do the murder. It might be wise to accuse Bing simply in order to keep him under surveillance so that he could do no further damage.

A moment of reflection showed John Morrow that such an accusation could not be made to hold water. He had seen a message flashed from the garret of the ranch house. And then, a little later, after the signaling stopped, he had seen Bing come down from upstairs. But the Chinaman's room was in the second story of the house. Could he not easily say that he had simply been having a sleepless night and had come downstairs to gain the open air in the hope that it might prepare him for a real rest?

Such would, of course, be the answer of Bing, and The Duke, remembering that masklike, ivory-colored face, decided that an inquisition would bring him no results. It was far better, he decided, to take his fling at the Black Hills and discover what he could of the trail of the fugitive and marauder. It was difficult to persuade the panic-stricken rancher to wait one more day before he started for town. But when that had been accomplished he took Leaper and started on the trail.

But before any trail could be run it had to be located. He rode first to the bridge. There was a patch of soft ground on the farther side of the bridge, as he had noticed the afternoon before, and if a horse had approached it during the night there might be distinguishable sign. He hunted accordingly on the farther side of the bridge across the Lindsay. But he found nothing. Marks of a drove of cattle covered the approaches to the bridge on both sides. They had gone out that morning and would have obliterated any hoofprints of a horse.

There were other possibilities which must be exhausted before he began to pronounce the case hopeless. He went back down on the bank of the river, still keeping on the side farthest from the ranch buildings, for he began to see that the marauder would not have crossed the bridge in his stealthy approach. No matter how soundly the ranch buildings seemed to be sleeping in the blackness of the night, a solitary horseman would not be apt to venture the loud and hollow sound of his horse on the boards of the bridge. There was a scant possibility that he might have come across on foot, but this possibility was actually small indeed. The stranger would be daring indeed if he trusted to mere speed of foot to get him away from danger should he be surprised in the midst of his work. No, he must have ridden close to the dog pen and then thrown in his meat and departed with his horse, though the hard gravel round the kennel failed to show the prints of his hoofs.

How and where, then, would he have crossed the river? If he really came from the direction of the Black Hills he must have crossed the river unless he undertook a long and painful detour around the headwaters of the stream. That was most unlikely. But farther up the valley, beyond the big forking, where two creeks, swollen and noisy with snow water, joined the Lindsay River, the Lindsay itself dwindled to a rather insignificant stream. It might be possible to ford it there without a considerable distance to be swum. And where the drenched horse came out of the water the bank must show one place which was spattered with water, and which would be not yet dried by the chill morning sun of the mountains.

That thought came like a glorious inspiration to The Duke. He turned Monday around and cantered him across the bridge. On the farther side he saw Steve Guthrie leaning against the corner of the noisy grist mill, smoking a pipe and grinning in mockery after him. It took some of the high heart out of The Duke to see that he was being laughed at, but nevertheless he kept on. He whistled to Leaper. The good hound sprang into the lead and ran wavering back and forth with his nose close to the ground, hunting for what scent he knew not, but eager to be of service. Now and again he ran back to the horseman and trotted nearby with his head canted to the side, looking up into the face of this new master with anxious eyes.

And the sight of the wise-headed dog was infinitely comforting to The Duke. Better to hunt quietly, the two of them, than to start out with a thundering pack in full cry, a noise which would warn the hunted many a precious mile ahead of the actual danger.

In the meantime, they skirted along the southern or ranch house side of the Lindsay, proceeding at a smooth canter, until they were three miles to the east, where the two creeks joined the main river. From this point The Duke jogged ahead at a moderate trot, scanning the bank of the stream anxiously. And not half a mile farther up he came to the thing he had expected and prayed for. At a point where the river bed widened and became proportionately shallow, the gravel along the bank was dark where water had been washed upon it from the main body of the stream. The stain of the water diminished at once and disappeared at a point where a trail of a horse began. To the intense disappointment of The Duke, however, that trail led inland! For a moment he was too disgruntled to do anything but swear, but eventually he forced himself down the trail, riding mechanically, with no heart in his work. Leaper, however, could no longer doubt that this was the day's work now really beginning, and with a glad whine he darted ahead down the line of hoofmarks. A quarter of a mile away he bent sharply to the west and continued running rapidly, his head high, which was sure proof that he did not need the scent to run by. The moment The Duke saw that change of direction, his heart jumped.

It had been simply a clever little maneuver to becloud the pursuit, if pursuit there were. And indeed, except for him, the cowpunchers and Steve Guthrie seemed to take it for granted that nothing should be done to come to close quarters with this scoundrel. They would have allowed him to go without striking a blow. If he had worn a hood of darkness he could not have been more impregnable.

The moment he saw that the trail ran west toward the ranch house again, The Duke called in Leaper with a shrill whistle. And then he led the way to the bank of the Lindsay again. It was perfectly easy to cross. Monday picked an adroit way across from stone to stone and gravel bank to gravel bank. Only in the center he dropped into the water up to his withers, well-nigh. And so they came out dripping on the farther bank.

Here they found the trail at once. It was the trail of a shod horse with a bar shoe on the off forefoot. That horse was a powerful traveler. When he walked his step was long and even. When he trotted he went with a swinging and large-stepping gait as though he had true trotting blood in him. And when he galloped the stretch of the brute was amazing. The Duke noted these things as he cantered down the trail, letting Leaper run ahead to read the sign with his accurate nose. The Duke followed, making out what he could with his inexpert eye.

He would have given much now to have been thoroughly schooled in the intricacies of cutting for sign and all the other mysteries which go toward making a good man on a trail. There are lessons which cannot be learned out of books. Men are born to that work or not born to it. But, as for The Duke, the trails he had most closely observed had been simply the lines on the faces of his opponents in a game of cards. And such skill as he had gained could not help him here!

He made out, however, that a large, heavy and fast horse had made that trail. The presumption was that the rider was of the same type as his horse, although, as a matter of fact, it might well be a little fellow with a mere passion for a lofty mount.

And so they kept on. For the first mile or two he could not be sure just which direction the marauder had taken, for his course wound in and out among the riding foothills. But at the end of that time it was plainly to be seen that he had pointed his course out of the Black Hills, and The Duke rode on with a shout of triumph. In the meantime, wise-headed Leaper roamed in the lead, sometimes raising his head to look back at the rider, and sometimes whining. But on the whole he was a silent hunter, and no quality could have delighted The Duke more than this. Had he been backed by a score of hard riders and hard fighters, he would not have cared so greatly. But, now that he rode alone, a noisy dog would have meant the quiet laying of an ambush, and then a bullet through the head of John Morrow.

In the meantime, they were climbing rapidly out of the lowlands. They left behind them the deep grass of the hills. They left behind them the last group of sleek-sided, red Herefords, staring after the horseman and the dog with looks of mild unconcern on their white-striped faces. They pressed now into a barren and stern region of stone. They entered the district of the Black Hills proper. Now that he was so close to them, The Duke could see that it was distance which gave the Hills their really sooty character. But near at hand, though they were made up of dark stone, it was not nearly so funereal an effect. But the great iron blossoms, as they were popularly called, were even more gloomily impressive near at hand than when they pricked the distant horizon.

And through that wilderness of stone he would have been helpless had it not been for Leaper. Only here and there he saw where the shoes of the horse had scarred the glossy surface of the rock, but Leaper found even on that stone scent enough to carry him along.

It was a slow, slow trail, to be sure. And as the sun rose higher and rolled toward noon, Leaper was more and more often baffled. Yet he kept on, one faint thread of the scent remaining true with him. He kept on until they came to the roaring of a stream which bubbled out from the foot of a great iron cliff. The trail went straight to the water on one side, but it did not come out on the other, for when The Duke sent Leaper across, the hound scurried around in vain.

Here the trail, it seemed, pinched out.

17

◉

The Bandit's Cave

BUT, GREEN AS WAS The Duke in the working of a trail, he was by no means foolish enough to give up the task at the first check. He tried the stream. It was not eight feet wide, but he could not reach to the bottom, and it was too swift to swim. So he took Monday back, gave him the advantage of a short run, and then jumped the water. The good horse slipped on the treacherous surface of the rock beyond. But, though he staggered, he did not fall. From this position the hunter began his work again. To be sure, the surface of the rock showed nothing to his eye. But that rock was almost as hard as steel and might well fail to reveal a trail which existed on it. And that surface, now being backed by the heat of the sun, was sure to let the scent melt away rapidly as water through a sieve. Still he sent good Leaper here and there to try to pick up a new lead. It was quite in vain. The honest hound worked like a Trojan. He cast far and wide. He probed here and there as though he might find the scent tucked away in a corner. But at last The Duke was forced to admit that the trail had evaporated. He had done exactly what the other men had done when they chased this marauder. He had followed straight on into the Black Hills, only to have the trail pinch out to nothing. Perhaps this was the very point where the others had been baffled likewise!

The Duke dismounted, rubbed the nose of Monday, and stared mournfully. And Monday rubbed back and sniffed at the back of his master's hand and then bit at the fingers mischievously. But there was no solution of the mystery to be come at in this fashion. He rolled a cigarette, and, as the smoke drifted fragrant into his nostrils, he regarded the black flow of the water as it poured out beneath the lower lip of the rock.

It did not bubble and boil forth like water imprisoned underground and springing to the surface and to freedom. Instead, it glided forth as though proceeding at the mildest inclination downward. The lip of the rock merely skimmed and flattened the surface.

It was, of course, the wildest waste of time. But The Duke was not one who regarded carefully the spending of every moment. He stripped off his clothes and was straightway in the water. It was difficult to swim across the stream, so violent was the current. And therefore, of course, it was entirely impossible to swim against the force of that rushing water. But The Duke climbed along the edge of the rock until he was directly by the orifice from which the stream flowed. Here he lowered himself carefully. He reached under. It was as he had suspected. The rock projected only a few inches under the surface of the stream. It might, of course, continue to curve downward.

But The Duke was bent on exploration. He plunged beneath the surface, a mournful wail from Leaper sounding in his ear as he disappeared. Then, by the ragged projections of the rocks, he drew himself forward, feeling for the top of the rock and struggling ahead into the current.

In this fashion he had progressed perhaps five or six feet, and his lungs were beginning to ache and burn with the strain of holding his breath. But here his head popped above the surface of the water, and he found himself breathing perfectly fresh air.

He had pushed through under the ledge to absolute darkness. But now he was at least out of the water. If he himself were an outlaw fleeing for his life, what could be more opportune than such a hiding place? He put his hand to the side and discovered that the bank of the stream now sloped away. He worked a little to the side and then, thrusting down his feet, he found that he encountered rock beneath him. A moment later he was sitting at the side of the stream on the stones, regaining his breath.

It was slimy and slippery rock on which he was sitting. And in the darkness an instinctive horror of all that he could not see set him shuddering. It was very cold here, also. The snow water made the rock chamber as chill as a refrigerator car.

Apparently this pocket in the rock, then, could be used as a refuge by men. But what of the horses? How could a horse be brought into this dismal vault? It was barely conceivable that an animal could be taught to submerge its head and, with a strong pull on a rope, could be brought under the shelf of the rock and into this open space. But it would be odd quarters. And if the horse began to plunge it would be consummately dangerous for the rider.

Indeed, if a horse were brought here, it must be taken still farther on to a more ample shelter. So, feeling his way with his hands and his bare feet, The Duke pushed ahead through the darkness until the wall gave way on his left hand and he found himself looking toward a tiny eye of light at a great distance before him. Another step, and there was the crunching of gravel under his feet—sharply pointed gravel which cut his flesh and bruised his feet. But he kept on. Curiosity made him immune to the pain. He remembered that he had foolishly come with empty hands on this exploring expedition. He hesitated, half determined to go back for a weapon, and then decided that it would be as well to continue straight before him until he at least had sight of whatever dangers there were—if indeed this were a resort of that shifty marauder who had terrorized the Guthrie place.

His going now became easier every moment. The eye-hole of light widened, grew brighter. Presently he found himself walking in a very faint twilight. He pressed on with a greater caution. One of the rocks he stumbled over he now picked up as a weapon of a sort if he should blunder into an enemy, either beast or man. For in the recesses of this cave he was most apt to come upon either a lurking human or a sleeping wildcat.

As far as he could see in that strange light, he was advancing up a long cave, the roof of which was lost in the gloom, or with only now and then a faint glistening of a downward projecting rock. The width of the cave increased just as its height increased. It might be twenty feet broad in this section. The black water of the stream darted through the middle of the cavern and filled it with a continual loud roaring and boiling noise. That confusion of sound and the many hollow echoes which were rolling around him could make him reckless of any noise on his own part. But it would also as effectually mask the coming of danger.

In this uneasy mood he now found himself drawing near to a three-foot rift in the rock, through which the mild daylight poured into the cave. And from the opened space in the rock wall he saw more than he could have dreamed of seeing!

What he beheld was a veritable home under a mountain—a commodious home, at that! Water, he believed, could not have hollowed such a place. Rather, it was a rent and breaking away of the rock. He could make sure that it was not the work of water by a glance to the side, where he saw the jagged walls of the room. Perhaps a great fold of rocks had here, too cold for the immense pressure which was bending them, split apart in the heart of the mountain. And through the crack this stream of water had poured.

This was understandable enough. He had heard one of the cowpunchers speaking of the place where this stream rushed down into the heart of the rock, a vertical plunge, well-nigh. It could not be from such a source, however, that the cave was lighted. There must be another aperture through which the sun was streaming. It lighted an immense room, the floor of which was covered with clean sand, though of dark color. A color of blackened rock fragments in the center of the floor showed where the cookery was performed, and where the fire burned for heat in the winter. The space was partitioned into smaller sections by bits of canvas. And all these sections looked toward the central fire for warmth. It was a very convenient and simple arrangement which assured comfort, together with some degree of privacy.

There was only one person in the cave as The Duke looked into it, and that was an old man with a long white beard—a very old man in whom the years had so sapped the strength that his head was permitted to fall forward on his chest. His withered hands were folded in his lap. He sat in the center of the shaft of sunlight which streamed down into the cave. But in spite of that warmth, smoke embers were smoking in the fireplace, and his feet were close to their warmth. Moreover, his old, thin body was wrapped in a thick Indian blanket. Upon this patriarch The Duke gazed with awe and admiration. The hair of the old man streamed down over his shoulders. And his beard, thin and glistening like silk, was spread with apparent care all across his chest and washed down to his elbows.

If this were the only garrison in the secret place, all was well. The Duke stepped farther into the crevice to make sure. From this better point of vantage he could see more details—the complete circle of weapons of all sorts which hung on the walls, and the chambers which had been hewn into the rock here and there, as closets are built into a house. Moreover, he regarded the cleft in the roof through which the sunlight poured. And he saw at once that this was not a way which could be used for entering the cave. It was a wide and raw-edged hole, but it was fully sixty or seventy feet above the floor of the cave. At such a height the smoke from the fire would rise gradually and be dissolved in the upper air as the thinnest mist—that is, unless a veritable bonfire was built. There needed only care in the size of the fire they made, to keep from being betrayed by the rising column of the smoke.

But where was the entrance to this singular home? Certainly they could not habitually use the dangerous and difficult entrance upon which he had stumbled by chance. Neither could they use that rent in the rock roof. It must be that the common door lay alongside the stream of water which poured in out of darkness at the upper end of the cavern.

It was beyond doubt that he had come to the habitation of the marauder—that cold-hearted murderer who had destroyed the dog pack on the Guthrie place, and who had been attempting the life of William Guthrie himself!

18

◉

Bluff

"WELL," SAID A mellow bass voice, perfectly smooth, but very faint. "I guess you might as well step in and tell me who you are, stranger!"

It was a moment before The Duke could realize that the voice had actually come from the old man in the chair. How he could have been seen, he could not tell, unless the patriarch possessed an eye as keen as, and with the field of vision of, a hawk's eye.

However, he decided to accept that invitation. There was an Indian blanket similar to that which covered the old man, thrown over a camp stool near the cleft where he stood. He threw this around his wet, chilled body and stepped into the open space. From a peg on the wall—or, rather, a little projecting rock—hung a cartridge belt and a Colt revolver. He buckled that belt around his waist. He snapped open the gun and saw that it was loaded, that the action was free and easy. After that he was more steady of nerve. No matter who besides the old man might be lurking unseen and unheard in a far corner of the cave, he was confident of upholding his end in a possible battle.

He came squarely before the octogenarian—for his years seemed at least as much as that. And when he was in front of the old man he was confronted, to his astonishment, by a smiling pair of eyes as bright and blue as could have gleamed in the head of any youth. It became impossible to watch all the corners of the cave at once. It was impossible to note its rough comforts in detail. All he could do was regard the old man.

"Who might you be?" went on he of the white hair.

"My name is John Morrow, that some call The Duke."

The other blinked and nodded. Whether or not the name had meant something to him, John Morrow could not decide. And there was a suggestion of such strength in the calm of the ancient man that The Duke made up his mind on the spot: this was the crippled leader, the passive brains, of a whole gang of robbers and outlaws.

"And what brought you here?" went on that involuntary host.

"I been trailing a gent that come down to Guthrie's Ranch and poisoned the pack of dogs. And that trail brung me here. Where is he?"

He had raised his voice at the conclusion of his speech in the vain hope that he might frighten a confession out of the other. But it was like threatening a face of stone. Those cold blue eyes looked through and through him without faltering. And The Duke, shuddering, wondered what manner of man this fellow must have been when he was younger. Certainly he would have been at all ages a good fellow to avoid in a fight. Even at this moment, sitting helpless in the chair, he seemed more formidable than many a young hero who had clashed with The Duke in his rides to glory.

"I ain't got no idea what you mean," said the other at last. "You mean that you run your man into this place?"

"He came in here," said The Duke with less conviction.

"I ain't been sleeping, but I ain't seen him come."

"He came in under the water just the way I came. And he brought his horse in with him."

"Tut, tut, young man," said the white-haired cave dweller, "you ain't aiming to tell me that and hope I'll believe it?"

He laughed softly. If his voice had been raised The Duke knew that it would have trembled into quavering weakness. But it was kept low, and it sounded like the deep laugh of a middle-aged, a strong man.

"I'm aiming to say," said The Duke, "that you know a pile of things other folks are beginning to know."

He had been baffled and cornered, so to speak, and

he struck out blindly in the dark. The ancient raised his head a little. It was plain that he had been struck hard by that random remark.

"I know what?" he asked sharply. "What do I know that the rest of you got any right to listen to?"

"A pile of things," said The Duke, and he smiled.

"Bah!" snorted the other. "You ain't doing nothing but trying to draw me out!"

"Draw you out? I don't have to. I know enough."

"Eh?"

"I know enough," said The Duke.

"About what?"

The old man was growing excited, and the more he leaned anxiously forward, the more The Duke fell deeply into a noncommittal attitude.

"D'you figure that I'll tell you what I'm driving to learn?"

"Why not? What's there agin' me? I live here in a cave. Is there anything wrong in that? Other folks don't want to live this way. Does that make it a crime for me? Can you answer me that?"

"It ain't your living in a cave—"

"Well?"

"Things you done a long time ago," said The Duke, "are what's—what's making me—"

There was a murmured oath from the man of the cave. His eyes grew brighter and wider. Plainly he was very much frightened. And The Duke was delighted. He had struck at random repeatedly, and each blow seemed to be going home. What was the guilt which weighed so heavily on the conscience of this old man? What had he done in the dim past which made him now stare in terror at his visitor?

"There ain't a thing against me," said the man of the cave. "Nobody can make a thing against me."

"Oh," said The Duke, "I ain't denying that you were a fox about it. I know you were that! But even the trail of a fox can be followed, stranger!"

It was very odd. To fumble in the dark and find the handle of a door which opens upon dazzling brightness, is wonderful enough. But to feel that one is knocking at the very conscience of another man—that, indeed, was a strange sensation. The Duke saw his victim change color and stir in his chair.

"What trail?"

"An old trail—a mighty old trail," said The Duke.

"It's a lie! There ain't a suspicion of anything agin' me!"

"Well, you can think that."

"If there really was, would you come here to tell me about it? No, sure you wouldn't!"

"Why not tell you? You won't run away. Oh, no, you won't run away while we're keeping such a guard over you!"

"Who's watching me?"

"Why, that would be telling something worth knowing."

"Curse you!" said the other with heartfelt emotion. "It's all a lie, and I'll make you sweat for it! Now get out of my sight. If I was five years younger I'd take you and throw you out."

The Duke smiled upon him in that cold way for which he was famous.

"I ain't going to bother you much longer," he said. "I just want to look around."

And he began to saunter carelessly around the cave. It might be dangerous to stay here. He saw equipment enough to have furnished forth half a dozen men. And any one or all of the half dozen might return at any moment and take him unawares.

In the meantime, however, he was finding enough to make sure that this was indeed the seat of the outlaw who had been preying upon the Guthrie Ranch for so many years. There could be no doubt of that. The bridles and the saddles which he found bore the "G" which was the stamp of the Guthrie properties. The entire furnishings of the cave had been stolen and taken one by one from the ranch to the cave. It was incredible that a single horseman could have taken away so much. And had it not been for the general laxness with which a ranch is often run, surely those thefts would have become an intolerable annoyance long before. But The Duke had no doubt that for every known stealing there had been half a dozen to which no regard had been paid—which would never be made known except by a close accounting of the properties.

He was pondering what he should do. To take the old man back with him through the water was, of course, impossible. To force him to show any other exit would probably call for methods more brutal than The Duke was willing to employ. But to leave the old fellow behind him would be to undo all the good work which he had done.

He had come to this point in his reflections when, lifting the lid of a rudely homemade box, he found himself staring down upon a mass of women's clothes. The Duke could hardly believe his eyes. This must be actually plunder which the outlaws had carried away from one of the adjoining ranches. He plunged his hand into it and lifted up a shower of silken stuffs. And below this, neatly folded, he saw a rose-colored dress with a pair of rose-colored satin slippers at his feet.

The Duke gasped. He raised the gown and shook out its folds. He could have sworn to it in any court of law. It was the same color, the same fabric, the same high, closely fitted bodice which Sally Smith had worn when she danced with him!

Slowly he refolded the garments and put them back. His mind was racing from one conjecture to another. Here was the place where she lived—among outlaws. Here she lived under the domination, no doubt, of that gray head in the corner of the cave. Beyond a doubt he was her father. Driven out from society somewhere, he had brutally chosen to make his daughter share his exile. He had brought her here in her infancy. And now he supported her and himself through the operations of a gang which he controlled through the superior force of a high intellect.

It was a gloomy-minded John Morrow who finally closed the lid on the box and turned away. Here, within the grip of his hand, were the means of accomplishing all that was nearest and dearest to his heart. He could solve the problem of Guthrie by arresting this old man and taking him away. While the leader was imprisoned, certainly none of the gang would dare to disturb either Guthrie or Guthrie's ranch.

It would mean more than that. To repay the faith which Guthrie had lodged in him was only one thing. But it would mean the crushing of a formidable band. It would scatter the marauders and, among others, that daring, dark-faced youth who had attempted the rancher's life by shooting through the window and then staying to laugh at his pursuers before he fled into the night. It would dislodge that other man who had ridden a gray horse and murdered Dud Martin. And in so doing The Duke would restore himself to good standing once and forever with the citizens of Wheeler City. And that was the most crying need of all. He saw it more clearly the more he pondered upon it. Better to die at once than be thrust aside as an outcast. He would be instantly known as the one who had changed parties and had become an ally of law and order against crime.

Once let them recognize the change in him, and he would show the doubters what he could do. He would burn across the mountains like a sword of fire. He would stamp out crime. The eyes of The Duke filled with tears of joy as he thought of fighting his way back to the hearts of his people just as he had fought his way out of their hearts long before.

But if he seized the old man he was taking the girl's father. If the cave were sealed, her only place of refuge would be taken from her. And with her father gone she would be forced to wander through the world with a band of rough-handed men—

The Duke rested a hand against the wall of the cave and bowed his head in thought. When at length he stood straight again, he had made up his mind. Great as the price was, it was not enough. The memory of that waltz music still swung in his ear, and the smile of the girl was dawning and dying beneath his eyes.

He looked at the ancient. That worthy was watching him with eyes of fire. And The Duke, with a groan, turned and strode straight for the cleft in the wall through which he had entered the main enclosure. He had not taken a step beyond it when he heard a sharp whistle shrilling through the main body of the cave. The Duke waited neither to see nor hear, but in a blind panic he fled.

19

The Taste of Defeat

THE DUKE DID NOT recover from the dread which filled him in that shameful route until he was around at the dark end of the passage. He threw off the blanket, dived deep into the black heart of the water, and swam to keep down until light poured through the water and all around him. Then he rose to the surface and found himself at his starting point.

Leaper sprang upon him joyously as he climbed out upon the hot rock. And Monday came up snorting and sniffing. By the time he was dressed again and in the saddle, the adventure in the cave already seemed strange and far off—a thing no more real than any dream.

He leaped Monday across the stream of water, and they went slowly back among the hills, with the heat growing rapidly less as they passed from the valleys of rock onto the rolling ground. The Duke strove to whistle to raise his spirits. It would have been as wise to whistle to an eagle in the skies and expect an answer. The sound of the music made him all the more dreary.

Indeed, he was in a hopeless position. If he did not strike at the nest of outlaws, he was failing to fulfill his contract with Guthrie. Furthermore, he was failing to re-deem himself in the eyes of the men of Wheeler City, and every random crime which was committed would be laid at his door. But if he struck, he was striking at Sally. And his heart failed him with this thought.

He came out of his brown study as he heard the ring-ing and clattering of the hoofs of a galloping horse approaching rapidly around the shoulder of a hill. He looked up and saw a rider swing into view, a dashing rider on a beautiful pinto. It was a slender fellow who sat in the saddle, and with his sombrero pulled low across his forehead and a black mask obscuring the upper part of his face, he was well enough disguised. Yet The Duke thought that he certainly recognized in the approaching rider that killer and youthful daredevil who had fired at Guthrie through his window. There was no doubt that he was coming now to head off The Duke and keep him from escaping. He jockeyed his pinto into a lightning burst of speed and rushed the brilliant little horse to the throat of the canyon down which The Duke was riding.

As if the latter would dream of retreat! He pulled Monday back to a walk at the mere thought and touched his Colt automatically to make sure that it was loose and ready for the battle. The pinto, in the meantime, had been shot into the mouth of the gorge and the rider now twisted him around and charged down at The Duke, a quarter of a mile away.

And what a charge! It was like something out of a book. Such madcap carelessness of life and limb The Duke had never seen! He had only to draw his long rifle from its case and send a bullet through the body of the masked man. He even touched the butt of that weapon as the thought occurred to him. He could strike down his enemy while the latter was still far out of effective revolver range.

But it should not be said of him that he had ever taken an advantage in weapons. He whipped out his Colt instead, and, bringing Monday to a halt, he waited.

It was a strange excitement, this waiting for an attack. It was a new role for him. As a rule it was he who went like a tiger at the enemy, but now he was to receive the brunt instead of dealing it. And, in the meanwhile, his swiftly moving mind had time for many things. He had time to admire that feeble old man who, with a single command, had been able to launch forth this fiery horseman to strike down the enemy. He had time to admire, too, the consummate horsemanship of the approaching rider, weaving deftly among the boulders without ever abating the speed of his closing rush, and all the time keeping the revolver poised before him.

The Duke, with a shout and a touch of spurs, sent Monday into a plunging gallop. Instantly they were under way at full speed—a racing start. Like lightning now the gap between the two antagonists decreased. The joy of battle rose in The Duke, but never such a joy as he could see in the whole body of the man who came toward him with raised gun. Every sway of that young, slender body spoke of fierce happiness. He came carelessly, confidently, as a young lover coming to meet his love.

He jerked down the gun. He fired. The bullet snipped a nick in the edge of The Duke's sombrero. What was John Morrow thinking of to let another get in the first fire? He wondered at himself as he raised his gun. What madness had come over him, that even as this young murderer spurred upon him he was filled rather with admiration for the grace and gallantry of the stranger than with a desire to crush and to kill? He did not aim. His return fire missed that incoming foeman by a dozen yards, and the lead splurted into water on the face of a great black rock nearby.

He saw the fire jump from the other revolver. A thunderbolt struck him into darkness. He was plunged into a bottomless wave of black.

Then he felt that he was struggling up toward the surface of the darkness. He was coming into a dim bordering of light. And dimly he became aware of a thousand small aches and pains and then of a sword of fire which was pressed against the top of his head. Someone had poured water over his face and chest. The coolness of it suddenly revived him. He pushed himself into a sitting posture. And far off, wavering among the rocks, he saw that brilliant and gallant young horseman riding, and then disappear over the edge of a hilltop.

It was after he had seen all this and noted it automatically that the bitter truth thrust itself through and through the soul of The Duke. He had been met in open fight and he had been beaten! The wonder of it crushed him. Then he was torn with iron shame. He had been struck to the ground. He had been actually despised by the conqueror.

Yes, so easy had been that victory for the rider of the pinto that he had even descended from the saddle, not to finish the task, but to bind up the wound of the clumsy blunderer whom he had just shot from the saddle. For a moment, so great was his anguish, The Duke wished that the bullet which had furrowed its way through his scalp had been an inch lower!

Then he flung himself into the saddle and rode wildly in pursuit. His fury communicated itself to the horse. Monday stretched out at a racing clip and tore among the boulders. They whipped over a hill. On the next rise The Duke saw the other, the victor, galloping at ease. He shouted his challenge. But the masked man, turning his head, instead of waiting for the attack of the foe he had already beaten once, simply leaned over the pommel of the saddle of his horse and jockeyed the pinto into full speed.

The Duke ground his teeth in an agony of mortification. He understood. This gallant warrior of the plains had no desire to butcher a clumsy fool. He was fleeing rather than risk another meeting in which he might be forced to kill the stupid rider of the great gray horse!

Ah, what a tale there would be told to the old man of the cave if this fugitive got there alive! But he should not reach the wily old fox who ran the gang. No, he should die here among these same hills which had witnessed the overthrow of John Morrow. Groaning with rage, The Duke lifted himself stiffly in the saddle. As they shot over that next rounded summit he would start shooting just over the head of the fugitive to show him that he must turn and give battle. And when he turned—The Duke ground his teeth in exultation!

But as he topped that next hill he saw beneath him only stupid Herefords raising their lazy heads to watch! It seemed that the other horseman had vanished from sight, and John Morrow drew up his charger in wonder.

There was no one to be seen in all that hollow. And yet men cannot vanish completely out of view. They cannot melt into rock and sand! He started slowly ahead again. And before he had gone a hundred feet he saw the explanation. There was the bed of a dry stream in the middle of the little ravine—one of those stream beds which are filled with water only at the very prime of the season when snows are melting. This narrow trench, a dozen feet across and hardly deeper than that, cut the length of the ravine. Into it the rider of the pinto had jumped his horse. Down its length he had raced. He was already out of view and out of hearing. It was folly to continue the pursuit.

The Duke could not even tell what direction he had fled unless he took time to read the trail, and that time he could not spare if he hoped to run down his enemy.

There was nothing for it but to pocket the defeat, swallow the disgrace and turn back to the ranch. But, oh, how his gorge rose as he turned the head of Monday and rode slowly, sadly, away from his first great failure.

20

◉

Murder

SOME MEN ARE chastened by defeat and humiliation, but the proud heart of The Duke was merely roused to a frenzy by it. He reached the ranch in a humor which made him fit to do murder. Even poor Leaper lagged behind Monday instead of running ahead, and dared not even sprint after a baby cottontail which jumped across their path.

All in dead silence they reached the Guthrie place, and Monday was put up without the saddle being taken from his back. Into the house tramped The Duke, banged on the front door, and sent his voice thundering through the chambers. William Guthrie came down at once in answer to the call. He cried out in excitement at the sight of the red-stained bandage which surrounded the head of his new hand.

"I ain't got time for a lot of talk," said The Duke. "I got just this to say: If you want to go into town and have a bodyguard along with you, I'm ready to go this afternoon. But after today I'm going to be a pile too busy to waste time hanging around this here ranch. There's something out yonder in them hills that needs to be got, and I'm going to do the getting!"

He turned on his heel and stamped out of the house.

In turning the corner he almost ran into Steve Guthrie. And Steve started back with a grunt of astonishment, as he saw the bandaged head of The Duke. His astonishment, however, changed by degrees to a satisfied grin.

"Looks kind of like you been out fishing for trouble, Duke," he suggested. "And it kind of looks like you found some!"

The Duke hesitated. There was a wild tingling up and down the length of his right arm, a jerking and twitching of the long striking muscles. His eyes rested on a spot just a little to the side of the point of Steve's chin. But he did not strike the blow. Instead, he smiled and went on. The voice of Steve pursued and halted him.

"What's the main idea now?" he asked.

"I'm taking your Uncle Bill into town," said The Duke. "I ain't going to have time for the next few days to play bodyguard for him out here. I'm going to be busy. Out yonder!"

He waved toward the Black Hills.

It seemed to him that Steve became strangely thoughtful. The bantering smile died from his face. And without another word he turned on his heel and walked off.

Then minutes later The Duke was in the saddle, with William Guthrie on a horse beside him, and they were jogging on the trail toward Wheeler City. The rancher had asked no questions. He had accepted the decision of his bodyguard as though it were immutable. And on the way he talked of other things—of all the stories with which the country was rich. As for leaving the ranch, it was plain that he was glad to go to town, as he had himself suggested that morning.

"And yet," he said suddenly to The Duke, "if he can sneak down here to the ranch in spite of all my men and take pot shots at me, why can't he sneak into Wheeler City and finish me up?"

"Because these men that you got on your ranch ain't worth a hang," commented The Duke. "You got fifteen of them outside of Steve. And outside of Steve there ain't the makings of one good fight in the whole lot. What I'd like to know, Mr. Guthrie, is why Steve hires hands like that at a time when you need real men out here working for you?"

The rancher shook his head and shrugged his shoulders.

"I've finished my worrying and my thinking," he said. "Steve had been running the ranch pretty well lately. Him and me don't agree on all the details, but still he does pretty well. And I'm going to let him go on now and do all the thinking for himself. I've made my pile. I've got enough to rest on as long as I last!"

He chuckled softly as he drew out his wallet.

"When I come out to make my start, Duke," he went on, "I didn't have much. I've got eight hundred in this here wallet. I had seven hundred when I started working for myself. That was a pile before you was born. Well, three years ago I was able to buy that ranch. And now I've got enough to stop work. I ain't going to stay out there and ask questions while that skunk from the Black Hills is sneaking around, aiming to get my scalp. Ain't that logic?"

The Duke admitted that it was.

"And you, too, Duke," went on the rancher kindly. "There ain't any good reason why you should go out there into the hills and throw yourself away. You—you've had one piece of bad luck. Maybe you'd have another, and maybe you wouldn't have luck enough to come in to tell about it afterwards. Now, son, I've taken an interest in you. All you need is a chance to work on something worth while."

"I'll get no chance to do that," said The Duke, "until I've proved to folks that I'm on the side of the law."

"And you aim to prove that by fighting some more? Nope, Duke, there's only one way to prove it, and that's by hard work!"

"I'll do my share of that later on."

"Will you tell me what's started you in thinking so strenuous about work and a quiet life, Duke?"

"Can you make a guess?"

"What mostly does it is when a youngster finds a girl that looks like home to him."

"Guthrie," said the fighter, "I'm in the soup with the rest of 'em, then."

"It's the same thing?" The rancher raised his head and

laughed happily. "I'm mighty glad to hear that," he said. "Here's shaking hands and wishing you luck, Duke."

Their hands had barely closed when a heavy blow struck William Guthrie. He reeled in the saddle and pitched forward, and a crimson spurt from his chest flooded over the hand of The Duke. Then he rolled heavily to the ground as the laggard sound of the rifle report came clanging among the hills.

As for John Morrow, he raised his head and looked about him in bewilderment. Then with a shout of fury he started at full gallop in the direction from which the gun had been fired. He stormed up the hillside through a scattering of dwarf mahogany, behind any of whose trunks the murderer might have sheltered himself.

But over the brow of the hill The Duke found himself confronting a young forest of shrubbery as tall as a man's shoulder. Behind this there arose a thicket of trees sweeping along a narrow valley. He cut for sign along the brow of the hill, but his inexpert eye failed to find the print of either horse or man. Neither was there a sound of a retreating man through the brush. And suddenly he was wheeled around by the thought that, after all, the bullet which struck down the rancher might not have passed through a vital place. Perhaps Guthrie still lived.

Back he went at a mad gallop, flung himself from the saddle and knelt beside the victim. But it was plain that the slug had torn out the life as it passed through poor Guthrie's body. He had not stirred from the position in which he lay when he first slumped off the horse.

The Duke stood up again, sick at heart. Far away, a lessening speck down the valley, galloped the horse which had borne Guthrie. It would return to the ranch, and its empty saddle would bring the cowpunchers on the run to find out what had happened. They would follow the trail to Wheeler City, find the body and care for it and take it back to the ranch itself. But, in the meantime, the wheels of justice must begin to grind. And The Duke must set them in motion at the earliest possible moment. Poor and green trailer that he was, he knew that he was incompetent to attempt to track the slayer on the spot. There were scores of keen-eyed men in Wheeler City, however, who could start on fast horses and comb the country. So he started on for the town, swinging along with the loose, easy stride of Monday.

It had been a strange day! There was a faint ache from his wound, and a slight fever in his veins. But his physical injury was small enough. It was the wound to his spirit which cut the deepest. And pity for honest William Guthrie ached in his heart.

This was a trenchant comment on all of his old doctrines. Perhaps the man who fired that cowardly shot had begun somewhat as he began—a happy, carefree youth who fought for the joy of fighting. Perhaps those youthful battles had been prolonged into manhood. Quarrels with a revolver leave traces which never rub out, enmities as deep as the bone. And in the end this man had been outlawed as perhaps The Duke might well have been. But in the end he had degenerated to this—a veritable wolf, killing unscrupulously, recognizing no tie which bound him to honor.

It was a full burden for the head of a youngster of twenty-one. And The Duke was a sober youth before he saw Wheeler City spring up in a hollow among the hills. Into it he rode, and straight to the house of the sheriff. He drew his revolver and banged against the post on the veranda with the butt of it. The sheriff made his appearance with instant speed and then shouted and drew back at the sight of the naked gun in the hand of The Duke.

In spite of himself, Morrow smiled as he dropped the Colt into the holster.

"Sheriff," he said, "there's been a bit of the devil raised today. Bill Guthrie was killed riding in with me to Wheeler City!"

"Riding in with you?" cried the sheriff with a plain note of accusation in his voice.

"Riding in with me," said The Duke steadily. "He was dropped with a long-distance rifle shot. I'll take you out to the place, and I'll ride in the posse that starts for the skunk!"

The sheriff looked anxiously at him, as if he were striving to push away a veil and look at the truth.

"Go to Doc Morgan and get your head fixed up first,"

he said. "There ain't any hurry. It'll be half an hour before I get a gang together. A slow start makes a quick finish. But—Duke, I'm going to be glad to have you with us on this ride!"

21

◉

Steve Guthrie's Charge

THAT LAST REMARK made but small impression on John Morrow. He knew that even now the good sheriff was only waiting to seize upon the first small evidence to turn against this ex-convict. He knew that if suspicion ever were turned strongly against him, the entire town would rise to get rid of him once and for all. And with this thought making his face black, he returned to the hotel.

He did not, however, immediately go to the doctor as Tom Onion had advised. Instead, he went first with Monday to the stable behind the hotel. There he saw that the honest gray was well cared for and fed. He saw that his lodging was the only box stall in the barn. Then he went back to look for Doctor Morgan.

He found that gentleman in the hotel itself. He had been riding all the night before, had brought a new life into the world far away in the mountains, had plunged back to Wheeler City, and now he was barely rousing from his sleep. But the sight of The Duke effectually opened his eyes. In ten seconds he was rattling away with a rapid fire of questions, uninterrupted by the process of changing the bandage on The Duke's head. To his questions, however, he received only brief monosyllables as answers. And, finally, since talk he must to keep his weary eyes open, he took up what was happening in the street beneath his window as a topic.

"They've had a bomb thrown into the town, it seems,"

said the doctor. "And I've an idea that you brought it. But you're as uncommunicative as a mute. In fact, you won't even talk by signs. Down yonder in the street comes the sheriff. Old Tom Onion is on his war hoss, the old brown."

"That's the Grafton hoss?"

"That's the one. There isn't a thing around here that can beat that hoss."

"Except one," said The Duke, thinking of his own rangy gray.

"Eh? But there's Tom Onion stopping Jerry Mafferty and the Newton boys. They're as excited as hens over a grain of corn. What's it all about, Duke?"

"Bill Guthrie was murdered while I was riding into town with him."

"While you were—" gasped the doctor.

"D'you think that I might of done it?" growled The Duke. "It was a gent with a rifle. I tried to get at him, but I couldn't locate the trail of him. So I come in to get the sheriff on the job and to ride along with him."

"There's Steve Guthrie himself come in in a cloud of dust!" exclaimed the doctor. "He looks like he's traveled quite a distance and at top speed. He's sure been wearing out hossflesh!"

"Steve in town?"

"And full of news!"

"Sure. The hoss with the empty saddle must of come back to the ranch. And he come rattling along to—to—town—"

"There's a crowd gathering," said the doctor, putting the finishing touches to the bandage around The Duke's head. "And the sheriff and young Guthrie are the center of it!"

Over the clamor of many voices which had grown up in the street rose the clarion call of the sheriff.

"Hey, Doc Morgan, is Morrow up there in your room?"

"He's here!" sang out the doctor. He added, turning to his patient: "Is that comfortable, son?"

"Fine," said The Duke, and he rose leisurely from the chair and stretched himself. But as he did so he heard a thundering of many footfalls on the stairs, and, looking through the open door, he saw the sheriff appear, climbing in haste, with a grim expression. Ordinarily he would have thought nothing, done nothing, but this day his mind was equipped with a lightning of sharp suspicions. He sprang from his chair as he saw half a dozen other men following up hastily at the heels of the sheriff. And he reached the door of the doctor's room in time to confront Tom Onion.

The instant he saw that working face and the hard, glittering eyes, he knew that danger lay ahead—serious danger.

"Duke," said Tom Onion, "you got to come with me. Put up—"

As he spoke his hand flashed back to his revolver and twitched out the weapon, but The Duke did not wait to take a gun in his hand. Instead, he lashed straight out. His right fist drove into the face of Tom Onion, and the sheriff staggered back, struck the railing which ran down the hall beside the stairway, and fell with balustrade and all crashing down the steps—a mighty ruin which involved many others who were hurrying up to pretend to be helpful in the matter of this arrest, and who were at least eager to be witnesses of all that happened.

That blow had removed Tom Onion. But from either side three men sprang in, tugging out their guns. The Duke smashed the door shut, turned the lock just as their shoulders thudded home, and then drove a bullet through the upper part of the door. It would prevent them from trying to smash it open and rush him. In fact, the explosion of his gun was answered by a chorus of groans in the hall, and shouts of fury.

The Duke disregarded them. He turned in time to see the good doctor reaching his revolver from beneath the pillow of his bed.

"Drop that!" cried The Duke.

The doctor dropped the gun and turned a convulsed face toward his visitor.

"You murdering young rat!" he said.

And The Duke watched him curiously. This, then, was the true exposition of how the good men of Wheeler City felt toward him! They were ready to sink their teeth in him at the slightest provocation. Here was the doctor turned into a very picture of indignant scorn and rage, almost ready to run in on the leveled Colt in the hand of The Duke. And John Morrow wondered at him!

"Stand still and don't try nothing," cautioned The Duke. "I'm going to listen to what they got agin' me."

"Duke!" the voice of the sheriff was shouting from the outer hall. "We got you, and you might as well walk out and give yourself up."

"I'm going to hear the charge agin' me," said The Duke. "What's wrong with me this time, sheriff?"

"You killed Bill Guthrie and robbed him!" shouted the sheriff.

"That's a lie, and a loud one!"

"Here's Steve come in to tell us what he seen. He found his uncle with his wallet gone, dead on the trail to town. Duke, you can't get away with a cock-and-bull store like you tried to tell me. Open the door, Duke, and give yourself up. Or are you going to make us starve you out like a rat?"

"I've got a fat man in here to keep me company while I'm starving," said The Duke. "You can do what you please, but that door stays shut!"

There was a snarl from a dozen throats.

"Don't hold back on my account, boys!" roared the angry doctor. "I'm willing to die ten times to see this rabid cur brought to justice."

There was a cheer of applause from the men outside.

"Good old doc!" called the sheriff. "If anything happens to you, we'll burn this fellow by inches, and he can lay to that!"

A thunder of agreement came from the other men.

"Wait a minute!" called The Duke. "What is there agin' me except what Steve Guthrie has got to say? All he's got to say is just what he thinks might have happened!"

"You wouldn't stand for arrest," called the voice of Steve Guthrie himself. "That's proof enough!"

"Mighty good proof enough!" broke in the chorus. "Give yourself up, Duke. You're in a losing game."

"There's time for that later on," said The Duke slowly. "I need a while to think things over. And mind you, I'm watching that door."

He gestured to the doctor with his gun.

"Is that your case of instruments over there?"

"Yep. What of that? Need a surgeon's knife to cut my throat, you blackguard?"

"Take up that case. You might be needing it. Climb out the window yonder. You can get down onto the roof of the veranda. And from there down to the street will be easy."

"You mean that? You're letting me out, Duke?" echoed the doctor.

"I seem to be meaning that. Start moving. I need to be alone."

The doctor, with a puzzled face, got together the essentials of his profession and approached the window. Beside it he paused and turned back to The Duke.

"Maybe I've been wrong about you, son," he said. "I've certainly believed that you would keep me here just for the sake of having a partner in misery. But it seems— Duke, for heaven's sake, tell me the truth! Did you commit that dastardly murder, or are you innocent?"

"Innocent," said The Duke.

"By the Lord, I almost believe it! Then give yourself up, lad. The law never makes mistakes! If you're innocent it will be found out. I have money to hire a good lawyer for you, and you shall have one! I begin to think—"

"There may be justice in the law for some folks," said The Duke, "but there ain't none for me in Wheeler City. They tried to hang the Martin murder on me. Now they accuse me of killing a helpless old man that had hired me to guard him! Doc, ain't that unreasonable? Have I ever had a fight with a gent that didn't have a fair and square show of beating me? Have I ever jumped an old man in my life? Have I ever even taken a man so much by surprise that he didn't have a chance to get his gun out of the leather?"

The doctor, assailed by this storm of protest, nodded his head slowly in agreement.

"That sure sounds straight," he muttered. "Come out and let the rest of the boys hear you say the same thing. They'll believe you. They got to!"

"They'd hang me," said The Duke. "They'd hang me without waiting to hear me talk. Move along, Doc."

"John," said the doctor, "I've used some harsh talk to you—"

"I've forgotten it already. It's all right, Doc."

They shook hands. The doctor was immensely moved.

"I'll have this thing straightened out in an hour," he said. "I'm going to tell them about a side of The Duke which they've never seen!"

"Thanks, but before that hour's up you'll have heard so many bad things about me that you won't know where you're standing. Good-by, Doc!"

22

◉

Escape and Pursuit

THERE WAS A GREAT uproar of applause when the doctor reached the street. The Duke saw people at windows across the street, shouting and clapping their hands. There followed a little silence. Crouched close to his window, The Duke heard the doctor give a most flattering account of the crowd's prisoner in the room upstairs.

But, as he ended with a plea that The Duke be assured fair treatment, he was drowned by a roar of dissent.

"He just acted a part with you, Doc," they assured the latter. "He wanted you to come down here and talk for him. And so he turned you loose after he'd filled you full of talk that don't mean nothing—"

The doctor's voice was raised to shrillness as he protested, but the wave of dissent drowned him out, and The Duke, kneeling and listening, nodded his head until a rifle bullet clipped through the wall and whirred past an inch from his face. One of those watchers from the windows across the street had spotted him.

He withdrew to the center of the room and sat down cross-legged. It was a long afternoon and evening and

night which stretched before him. He could hear them
mustering in increasing numbers. The exciting report had
gone out from the little town. Men had poured in from
the nearest ranches. They filled Wheeler City. They were
on watch everywhere. A thousand rifles were ready to
claim the credit of having dropped John Morrow.

The Duke dragged the mattress from the bed and placed
it in the center of the floor. On it he stretched himself. It
would be odd indeed if they had the courage to attempt
to rush him at this early stage of the siege. And, closing
his eyes, he was instantly sound asleep. It was not the
first time that he had gone to sleep in a time of peril, and
he knew well enough that should an attack be made to
break down the door, or should anyone attempt to climb
up to the window of his room, his watchful subconscious
senses would note it and alarm him.

It was pitch-dark in the room when he wakened. He
had slept through the fag end of the afternoon and the
twilight. He had slept through the early evening. When he
pulled out his watch and shoved it into the shaft of moonshine which had crawled across the floor, he saw that it
was after one o'clock in the morning. It was rather wonderful that he should have been able to slumber through
all this space of time. But here he was, alert, perfectly
rested, ready to make the battle of his life. The effects of
the wound which had stunned him the day before in the
Black Hills were now hardly noticeable.

The Duke stole across the floor, silent as a passing
shadow, and peered out. There was no doubt that the
citizens meant business. Under the veranda he could hear
a subdued murmur of voices. On the roof of an opposite
house, beside the black shadow of the chimney, fell the
shade of a man crouched behind the chimney, rifle in
hand. There were others, no doubt, tucked away in nooks
and crannies and corners which he could not see. And his
first hope of escape vanished like an exploding bubble.
He had dreamed that when the night came and the small
hours of the morning were there he could break through
from the window and make his escape with a sudden
plunge for liberty.

There was no suddenness, however, which could take
a dozen well-practiced riflemen by surprise. A skill which

could drop a tree squirrel as it scurried through the loftiest branches would certainly think nothing of riddling a grown man with lead in this bright moonshine. The window, then, as an avenue of escape was absolutely closed.

Yet something must be done on this first night. Already thirst was tormenting him. His wound began to burn again. If he waited here for another twenty-four hours he would be in a serious state, weakened and far less capable of making a resolute drive toward freedom.

There were other possibilities, however. He might work a way through either of the two walls which did not open on the outdoors. Or he might try the ceiling or the floor. The door through which he had first retreated it would of course be foolish to even consider, for in the hall he could hear the guard walking slowly and steadily up and down, up and down.

He contemplated the walls, the ceiling. But he saw that the chances were so small as to be negligible. Other watchers must be in those two rooms. Others would be beneath him and above him, for there was no lack of men to undertake the work in Wheeler City. Only too many were willing to volunteer, hungry for a chance to get in a shot in the name of law and order.

With a sudden thought he slipped to the door. It was the last means of exit of which he had thought, simply because it was the normal means. And it was quite probable that the watchers would think the same thing. While they might have their guard there, ready for an emergency, no doubt the guards in the hall took their work simply as a dull matter of course, without the slightest hope that they might be called upon to use their guns to ward off an attack.

The Duke tried the key. It was either a new lock or newly oiled or both. The bolt slid without friction and without noise. And he left the door unlocked. He stood up, tightened his belt, considered removing his boots; and then he decided that this would be a useless precaution. If he should actually succeed in breaking away from the house he would need protection for his feet outdoors.

Next he drew the revolver from the holster and laid his hand on the knob. He turned it slowly—very, very slowly. For all he knew, there might be a dozen pairs of eyes fixed even now upon that knob and waiting with wolfish eagerness to get at him the instant the door should be opened. The pacing of the guard had ceased.

He waited until it began again. He heard the steps approach the door, heard the man yawning—and then he opened the door—not with a jerk, but as slowly as though a gust of wind had blown it wide. With a startled exclamation the guard turned, snatching up his revolver. And at that instant The Duke struck with his long arm. The heavy barrel of the Colt landed squarely alongside the head of the other. Down he went with a crash along the floor. And The Duke was out.

Along the head of the stairs he saw a tumult of confused figures starting up. He saw the gleam of a dozen guns. Yes, even outside the door they had posted a guard as heavy as this, and not one of them had fallen asleep in spite of the lateness of the hour.

He saw that in one flash. Then he was down the hall like a scared rabbit whose first leap is its longest one. A dozen guns boomed. He felt the twitch of a slug as it cut through his blowing hair. Another jerked at the bandage around his head. But he reached the turn of the hall unhurt. Around it he went, sloping at a sharp angle as racing cyclists do at a curve. Then he straightened for the end of the hall at full speed.

He had the start, both in space and in the fact of running, over those others who had to rise, climb a few steps of the stairs on which they had been sitting, and then break into motion. But they had only to reach the turn of the hall to open fire, while he had to continue to the farther end to an open window which terminated the hall.

Moreover, their shouts had filled the house, had overflowed it, and now other voices were answering from every quarter. The Duke knew that his chances were just one in twenty. He reached the window at the end of the hall. No, his chances were not one in five hundred!

It was a long drop below him. And at the alarm from the hotel the yard behind it had suddenly swarmed with figures climbing on horses or already in the saddle. Suppose he survived the drop without a broken limb or without being stunned. Even then how could he hope to get away from that tangle of mounted men?

He wedged his way into the window. There was a shout directly behind him as the first of his immediate pursuers rounded the corner of the hall. The gun exploded. A slug crashed into the wall beside him. And then The Duke dropped. He had not hung there in the window idly. He had waited, indeed, until the tumult had caused heads to be raised, so that eyes saw him and guns were being drawn below. But he also waited until a horseman passed directly below him. Then he let go with his hands, thrust himself clear of the wall, and dropped.

His knees struck the shoulders of the equestrian. The fellow was flung, stunned and sprawling, to the ground, as though a thunderbolt had struck him. The Duke tumbled beside him, but was instantly up. The horse from which he had knocked its rider was starting away at a gallop. That was all the better for the needs of The Duke. He required a running start if he hoped to get clear of these swirling antagonists.

He leaped at the horse and clung to the side of it even as a cat might have clung with four sets of claws. One hand had found the flying mane. One gripped the saddle horn. One leg was thrown over the back of the horse and behind the saddle.

They shot away. Fear thrust into the flanks of his horse. The little mustang went wildly through the crowd, dodging here and there. As for the men who were following with guns poised, yelling to one another, they would have had a far better chance to hit a snipe in its dodging flight than to land this elusive target with a pistol shot aimed in the moonlight and blurred by the shadows of the houses.

From behind the hotel they curved, reached the main street of the town. Looking to the side, The Duke saw that two score men had swung into the saddle in front of the hotel. The street was a seething mass of horsemen. And now they were getting into their stride with a rush. They could have riddled him with a score of bullets, but they dared not shoot, for down the street and facing them came another charge of fifty horses, making the ground quiver, and filling the air with the thunder of their coming. Valiants enough were there, with sufficient lead under trigger to have blown a dozen Dukes into nothingness. But if they fired it would be into one another's faces.

The Duke saw, understood, and, half laughing, caught for the reins. He jerked himself into the saddle, he swung the mustang to the side and cut in between two houses. He doubled around one house, and, while the main stream of the pursuit went rushing out and off into the outer night, The Duke cut straight back across the main street, across the town, and then slipped away toward the hills.

He had been seen, and he was followed by literally scores of hard riders. But for the moment at least he had thrown off many a man—yes, perhaps he had thrown off the cream of the posse!

23

◉

Outlaw Aid

HIS CHANCES WERE now what? John Morrow wondered as he sent his horse shooting off into the night. They had been five hundred to one against him not many minutes past. And now they were what? If gray Monday had been beneath him—ah, then indeed he could have laughed at them. In a minute he would be out of revolver range— effective range by moonlight, at least.

But gray Monday was back in the stable, no doubt, crunching hay or sleeping a sound sleep. No, worse than that, perhaps he was being ridden here to capture his master. The Duke groaned at the thought and turned his head. There was no gray in sight, however, among the pursuers. Only to the far right of the scurrying horsemen he saw one which, when it came out of the shadows, might prove to be gray. But it had not the size. Even in the distance The Duke knew that that was not the stride of Monday!

But they were gaining! That was the meaning of the silence of their guns. They found themselves overhauling the prey, and who would fire prematurely in such a case? Why might they not even take their man a prisoner alive? That would be glory indeed!

They were gaining! The Duke swung his weight forward so that it would fall more over the withers of his mount. With the spurs he strove to drive the little brute ahead. He held up the lumpish head with a stiff pull on the reins. He drove the horse ahead by his own will power. He jockeyed the animal as he had never jockeyed another. Yet it was not the first time he had ridden for his life. For all of that, the posse still gained on him. They widened their front. A dozen men were riding in a line, and those on the farther flanks were pushing their horses furiously in the hope that they might cut in and eventually surround the fugitive.

In fact, there was no doubt that he was simply mounted upon a horse which was slower than the average of cow ponies, even, and behind him were the picked horses of the range! No doubt they could swallow him up with their first rush. But they held back. Perhaps they were not yet any too eager to push their horses within close range of that famous and terrible fighter.

They struck an upslope. And the roan on which The Duke was mounted ran well indeed. Short-legged and thick-bodied so that he was useless as a sprinter, he yet relished hard work. He had plenty of bottom. And if they delayed their final rush long enough the roan would begin to wear them down.

Perhaps there was one chance in ten of that—one chance in ten, then, that The Duke would not hang from the limb of a tree before the morning dawned! He topped the hill and found that he had actually gained. He went down the hillside beyond. It was cut to pieces with boulders and jagged rocks. He threw the roan at that hard going, and the gallant little beast responded with his best. Bravely, they went down among those ruins of big rocks. A slip would have meant a ghastly fall, with rock teeth to tear them to pieces as they slid. Behind them the pack of the pursuit held up a little and picked its way more daintily down to the bottom, and more daintily, again, across the ravine and to the lip of the farther side.

He had increased his lead to a position of momentary safety as he drew away into the night again, spurring his horse at every jump; but in five minutes of desperate running he saw that he was lost indeed. Before him stretched a limitless, rolling plain. He could not dodge into difficult going again. Not until the far-off, shadowy hills were reached would he be in a place where the posse might be embarrassed by the brave riding of the fugitive, and long before The Duke reached that far-off land he would be run to death.

Again he looked back. It was very pretty—if one could adopt an impersonal attitude. The horsemen to the rear were opened out like a great fan. They were sure of themselves by this time. They saw that the game was in their hands. The pace which was so desperate for The Duke's horse was so easy for these well-bred ponies that practically the entire mass of horsemen from Wheeler City had caught up with the chase. The slowest horses were kept well bunched in the center of the pursuit. The faster ones sifted out onto the flanks, and these gradually, very gradually, began to gain. They were in no hurry. He who outdistanced his fellows was sure to get a bullet through his brain as he pressed in upon the pursued. So they kept together, a spreading, almost fluid, mass of riders.

A mist which had blown across the moon was now cleared away again by the same restless wind. All became clear on the plain, and The Duke saw it with a groan. It had become clear in order that his death might be the more clearly seen, run down by numbers.

Here a great shout from the crowd behind made him jerk back his gloomy head. And far before him to the side a rider on a gray horse was cutting across the line of his flight. There was still a considerable distance between them, but it could not be doubted that at their rate of going the gray horse would cross them.

And The Duke, looking back to the men behind, hesitated. Suppose he should wheel his horse, draw two guns, and fly at them, dealing out death from either hand. Since they would have him a murderer whether it were true or not, he would show them a death scene in which as many fell as in the whole life career of any two ordinary desperadoes.

His mustang had slackened its pace somewhat as though in sympathy with the thought of its rider. But The Duke changed his mind. It was better to let them go. They were cowards, and they admitted their cowardice because they dared not spur to the full of their speed and challenge him, one by one. They were cowards, but this fellow who was cutting in ahead was a brave man—a hero willing to take a chance. And The Duke, gravely acknowledging that fact, drove home the spurs again and changed his course so that he was driving squarely into the way of the newcomer.

Nearer they came now, with great speed. And behind John Morrow the posse had gone mad with excitement. Those men on the flanks were spurring to get up with the kill. Thundering shouts were striving to warn that solitary horseman in the lead not to be too rash—not to throw himself away in attempting a task singlehanded which would probably prove too much for him. But he still kept on.

And now, as he came closer out of the moon mists, The Duke saw a singular thing. The rider disappeared from the back of the gray horse. Instead, he was seen to be mounted on another horse. Indeed, all the time it had been simply a gray horse led beside another.

The Duke, breathless with wonder, stared and stared again. And now—he could not be mistaken, for the moonshine was glimmering along its flanks—he saw that the horseman who approached with such speed was sitting the saddle on a fleet-footed pinto. It was a young-looking rider even by that light and at that distance. Yes, and the body was poised and slender in the saddle.

What could it mean? What under heaven was in the mind of the stranger? An odd explanation came to The Duke. This crafty murderer had killed Bill Guthrie with a long-distance shot. But when he heard that the killing had been attributed to an innocent man he determined to save the latter from the workings of the law. He had saddled the gray horse. Yes, it was indubitably Monday himself, swinging with matchless stride across the plain!

Whatever the explanation, The Duke raised both his hands with a sudden Indian whoop of joy that threw his mustang ahead with redoubled speed. The posse, too, had seen that he who approached had probably not come to intercept but to save. And they were riding madly. Five hundred men, perhaps, with a roar of fury were closing on the prey which they might have ridden down three miles back had they not foolishly delayed! There would be an unpleasant session for Sheriff Tom Onion if he allowed this chance to slip through his fingers.

Now The Duke swept closer to the stranger who rode ahead of him. There was no question at the last, for he could see the mask over the upper part of the face of the stranger. And he could see his right hand raised in sign that he came on a friendly errand.

A moment more and the other ranged alongside. The pinto was turned so that the gray horse came close to the mustang. The Duke rode, and with a great neigh Monday greeted his true master. In two seconds The Duke sat in the saddle on his own horse.

And now what a difference! It was a mere loosing of the reins, and away shot Monday. Now let those proud riders of high-stocked horses attempt to close in on him! Now let them drive with all their might and main to close the gap! But Monday was playing with them, drawing ahead with every leap. And a yell of frantic hatred and disappointment went up from the five hundred.

Yes, there were fully that many. The spurt of the last mile had spread them out. They extended behind over a wide sweep of ground, trailing away to a few stragglers whose horses were obviously incapable of maintaining the pace, and who had drawn back their mounts to an easy canter.

Only the cream of the pursuers could live with such a pace as now developed for even an instant. And even these could not keep it up long. There was only one drawback. That was the pinto. And The Duke discovered with a single glance at the smaller horse that all was not as well as it might have been.

Monday had come out from Wheeler City without the weight of a rider in his saddle. But the slender-limbed pinto had been asked to carry a burden over a greater

distance than any of the men in the posse, and at a greater
rate of speed. And it had told on him. He came on gallantly now, to be sure. He ran with his head still up, un-
flagging. But it was plain that he could not increase his
gait. Monday alone could have walked away to safety.
But The Duke found himself now chained by his rescuer.

The outlaw was riding with consummate skill, crouched
low over the withers of his horse, and pushing the pinto
along over ground rough and smooth. But in spite of his
best efforts he could not gain. Here was Monday rocking
along with perfect ease. Truly he was a marvel! At any
moment he could step out and leave the crowd behind.
But what was to be done to save the outlaw who had
saved him?

24

◉

Miscalculation

HE DREW THE LONG rifle from its case beneath his right
leg. With it he tried a snap shot, not at the body of horse
or man, but pitching his bullets cunningly, just before the
reaching hoofs of the horses. Again, again, and again he
fired. It amounted to genius, this ability to turn in the
saddle and handle the heavy Winchester as though it were
a light revolver. It amounted to great genius indeed for
him to be able to shoot accurately without bringing the
long gun to the shoulder, and twisted as he was in the
saddle. But he chipped the rocks just in front of the riders.

Had there been two or three or even half a dozen, that
display of uncanny skill in marksmanship would have
made them draw rein rather than rush ahead into the
jaws of certain death. But here was no small group. Each
man felt that he enjoyed a strange immunity because there

were so many of his fellows who could take his place. Each man realized that if he himself did not set an example of drawing rein to discourage the others no one would draw back. They would all push straight ahead. Perhaps some fell back for a time, but only because their horses needed a slower gait. When they breathed a moment or two, they would come up into the press again.

Now they paid no attention to the rifle of The Duke. They knew that he had not enough bullets to kill them all. They were poured full of mob courage which, as well as mob fear, is a terrible and hysterical thing. And as they swept across the plain there was not a man in the lot who did not feel that he was making history. He would be able to tell his grandchildren he had been among that famous band which rode The Duke to death on the night he escaped from Wheeler City. An exultation filled them. They were capable of dying a dozen deaths for the sake of their great idea. And so they pushed on. It would have been as well for The Duke to pour his slugs at the face of a granite wall.

He realized his failure and shoved the gun back into the holster. And there was a shout of triumph from the crowd. They could understand this maneuver only in one way, which was that The Duke was confident he could not escape; and since he faced certain capture he wished to have the case against him as easy as possible, with no new killings to madden the crowd.

It was impossible, then, to frighten back these men. And, in the meantime, they were using their numbers adroitly. The great body of their horses pounded along at a regular pace. But from time to time a few spurred out before the rest and sprinted at the fugitives. This pushed The Duke and his companion away from the main pack of the pursuers. But when the handful which had rushed to the lead had exhausted their horses, they would fall back and let their horses trail the mob until they recovered and could join again. But there was no chance for such trailing with The Duke or the outlaw who rode beside him. No sooner had they finished one sprint and were letting their weary horses flag again than another group of sprinters rushed out from the pack.

Monday could keep them well in hand. He seemed

full of untouched reserves of strength. The few days of good care and good feeding had rounded his barrel and sleeked his hide. He had increased five-fold in beauty. And he had increased five-fold in strength, also. Oh, to pour some of that unneeded power into the failing legs of the pinto!

That graceful little horse, not more than fourteen-three in height at the utmost, delicately shaped and slender in modeling, had strength enough and to spare as compared with most horses. Or at least, carrying the slight bulk of its rider, the pinto could hold off most of the horses of the posse. There were only a few here and there which could have outrun it, even with the handicap of weight against them. That handicap was severe. Indeed, The Duke was amazed as he turned his head and studied the lines of his companion. That frail boy could not weigh, he thought, more than a hundred and thirty pounds. It was hardly more than the body of a child. Yet he remembered how the wild young fellow had come charging at him among the Black Hills, as confident as though he were a giant on a giant horse. But here in the moonshine, as they rode together, both horse and man seemed small indeed!

It was the last mile of the pinto's strength, The Duke saw at last. The brave little horse strove hard and heavily. His speed had not diminished. It would not fail him until he fell dead under his rider, but he was weak and weary with the strain of the long going. There was no bound to his stride, no elasticity in his supple body. His head was straight ahead of him to begin with, but now it was perking up—sure sign that he was badly spent.

The Duke looked wildly around him. If it came to the worst he must give his saddle on Monday to the outlaw and let the posse sweep around him. There was no succor before him. Far off to the right and well ahead was the Cumnor Mesa—a great black-shadowed wall in the moonlight. It swung in a broad curve across the plain, a hundred feet high and many a mile in length. And then a big idea came to The Duke.

There were two alternatives left to him if he wished to preserve his honor. He could either give his horse to the outlaw, or else he must draw the entire force of the pursuit away from the rider of the pinto and take the full danger upon his own shoulders. The latter, of course, was much to be preferred. The first way was certain destruction for himself. The second way was at least a fighting chance. And in the Cumnor Mesa he saw the trap into which he might be able to draw the posse after him as one man. It was his death they wanted. It was that sight which spurred them so hotly across the plain. No matter how close they were to the capture of the rider of the pinto, they would turn from him to a man to get at The Duke on tall Monday.

What The Duke planned was simply this: Cumnor Mesa with its lofty face described a sweeping arc so sharpened in the center that it was really a V-shape. Suppose he were to turn to the side and ride straight for the center of that V. The posse would instantly turn to pursue. They would sweep ahead and at once so narrow the gap that he could never hope to swing to the left again and break away into the open. His only hope would be that he could swerve to the right when he was near to the face of the mesa, and, riding at the full of Monday's great speed, plunge back between the cliff and the posse and so squeeze out to liberty. It would be tight work. At the very best he would be under close-range fire for a time. But he had better take that chance than keep desperately straight ahead with the pinto weakening more and more every moment.

He drew Monday closer to his running mate.

"Partner," said The Duke, "your hoss is plumb tired out. But keep on going. Feed that pinto the spur and raise him out of his skin. Give him the quirt. He's a game little beggar. Squeeze him out and make him work. Get another fast mile out of him and you're safe. Lord bless you, pal. You sure gave me a lift tonight. I dunno your name, but I know you're as game as they make 'em. So long!"

He waved his hand. The other, sitting straight in the saddle for an instant, waved back. The pinto staggered. But in an instant the rider was hard at work jockeying his mount along, holding him up, running him straight and true in spite of exhaustion. The wavering of that moment was a sufficient proof to The Duke of the wonderful horsemanship of his companion.

In the meantime, he turned to make his dash for the open. One word in the ear of Monday, a slight leaning forward in the saddle, and then he was off. There was no need of whip or spur to tell the eager gray what was wanted of him. The little-bodied runner plunged into full speed in a twinkling of an eye and darted off to the right. He had gained a dozen lengths in the new direction before the posse seemed to realize what was taking place.

Then, with an uproar of bewilderment, they surged about in the new direction. The right flank became the leaders. The left flank became the trailers. All was confusion. For so many hundreds of fast riders could not change direction smoothly. Yelling to one another, cursing, they poured about in the new course.

And The Duke, peering anxiously behind him, saw around the edge of the sweeping mass how his late companion was flying away toward safety, unpursued by a single one of the men from Wheeler City. The latter saw the main object of their interest turning into the mouth of a perfect trap, so it seemed, and every man crowded his horse so that he might at least see the finish. The weary pinto, after his gallant run, was allowed to continue peaceably.

As for The Duke, he rejoiced from the bottom of his heart that the outlaw had escaped. No matter if this were the very man who had twice attempted to murder William Guthrie and on the second effort succeeded. No matter if he were, in fact, that rider on a gray horse who had murdered the other rancher, Martin. Both of these crimes might be laid to the account of that fellow who was now drifting away into the moon haze on the pinto.

What The Duke really knew of him was that in fair battle that stranger had shot him down and crushed him with his first defeat. And again this queer man of the Black Hills had saved him from among his enemies and done so at the imminent risk of his own life. There was such reckless bonhomie in this behavior that the heart of The Duke leaped and warmed. If he ever lived through this night he would find out that man, forget the trouble which had been between them, and buckle him to his heart as a friend.

All of this went through his mind as he glanced back

to the form of the solitary rider which was melting into the distant night. But the next instant he was looking forward into the face of his danger. It was worse than he had expected. The deceptive light had made the mesa seem farther away than it actually was. Now, rough of face, it grew swiftly upon his eye, black and huge. There was not time enough to draw away from the posse, it seemed.

He called on Monday. Oh, gallant stallion! His body quivered with his effort. He sank lower as his stride increased. The ground poured like water beneath him, and the posse dropped swiftly behind him.

Now to break through. Now to edge to the right and skim between the hard riders and the front of the rock. He called again on Monday, and there was ever in the gray horse a reservoir of power which could be tapped and drawn for a little more and still a little more in the crisis. The wind in the face of The Duke was a veritable gale as he swung the stallion to the right. But with the first stride and his own first glance in that direction he saw that he was blocked, that his scheme had failed, that he had ridden into a trap as perfectly sealed as a cork seals a bottle.

25

◉

Safe Through

WHEN THE DUKE planned his maneuver it had been on the assumption that all of the scores and scores of horsemen behind him would be close up and would turn in one jumbled mass to pursue him. He had fogotten that many of the posse had fallen back a considerable distance. And these—no sooner did they perceive the new direction of The Duke's flight than they simply turned to

their right and in so doing formed a long, loose line across
the whole front of the V-shape which the mesa made. And
now for the first time the pursuers understood what had
been the plan of the fugitive, and their yell of exultation
thundered into the ears of John Morrow and made Monday shudder with fear.

And truly it was a terrible spectacle—that long line of
riders, here rank behind rank, and there a thin scattering—with the revolvers now held ready for the final rush
and the final burst of shooting. Mist of the moonshine
wrapped around and over this wild cavalry charge. Men
were black silhouettes. The horses were like monstrous
dragon forms. Behind him to the left looked The Duke,
but there was no chance of dodging back by the same path
in which he had come. The whole wide mouth of the V
was choked with enemies.

He could gain the wall of the mesa and climb to the
top of the rock, perhaps. But that was merely to postpone his fate. He knew the top of that tableland. It was
bare as the palm of the hand. It was chiefly a straight
stretch of wind-scoured rock with an occasional drift of
sand across it. But there was not even a respectable
bunch of grass to break the monotonous level, the deadly
lifelessness. If he strove to take refuge on the top of that
fortress, they needed only to send a detachment to the
top, then to surround the mesa with watch fires; and,
when the day dawned, they could bag him at will.

It was not a pleasant prospect, but this was the only
means of avoiding sudden death. An hour gained was—
an hour gained. But to give up his horse, to die on foot
—surely it was most unknightly!

That thought made him tighten the reins. He was on
the very verge of swinging the stallion around for the
death-charge when his eye was caught by a dark streak
down the face of the mesa, a place where a slide of rocks
had recently crushed away part of the old wall.

He rode closer, rising in his stirrups. He was eager as
a rabbit that leaps high over the stubble to take view of
the hounds and the distant covert. He saw that at the foot
of the cliff there was a rubble of huge boulders where they
had bounded into the plain or else lay split and smashed

by the force with which they had dashed upon one another.

It might have happened a year before, but still the scar of the rock slide was dark on the pale face of the cliff. And The Duke resolved to try to ride up this gash across the brow of rock as though up the gentlest incline. What chance he had of succeeding he dared not estimate. And as Monday brought him flying closer and closer he hardly dared look at the peril before him.

Yet he cast back a glance at the hurrying multitude and decided that it was far better to be brought down by bullets while making that effort than to charge hopelessly against the hundreds. He hoped that Monday would die with him, horse and man toppling from the cliff—

That wild picture had hardly formed in his mind when he rushed the gray at the ascent. Well for him then that the stallion had been pastured among rough rocks and sharp-sided hills! Well for him that the colthood of Monday had been a long school of mountain climbing! He took the first boulders with agile bounds. He based his feet upon the slippery rocks as confidently as any mountain sheep. And there seemed to be in his legs the same iron muscles which drive the sheep up and upward to the top of a cliff, moving from footholds which seem no more than wrinkles on the face of the stone.

The Duke, amazed by that exhibition, merely crouched low in the saddle and shouted encouragement. Up they went with dizzy swiftness. There was altogether a rise of some hundred and fifty feet to accomplish. And they went up it on a stairway which would have broken the heart of a hero. Sometimes, as the stallion sprang forward, the boulder from which he had leaped lost balance and plunged over the side of the rock. Sometimes, as he rushed on, he was basing his feet on a ridge scarcely six inches in breadth.

There was a crash of guns from beneath. A score of bullets splashed on the rocks near The Duke. He looked down. Horses were whirling and dancing. The scores of horsemen, lunging together at the apex of the V, had jammed one another into inextricable confusion. Moreover, they had ridden in too close. They should have stayed out if they wished to fire effectually.

Now some of the rearmost rode out for that purpose. But all was wildest confusion and thunder of guns and voices of men and squealing of terrified horses as they kicked and bit in the jam. And one or two even attempted to follow the fugitive on that wild way to the top of the cliff, only to halt their horses before they had gone a dozen yards, where the leading horse and rider toppled and rolled headlong to the bottom of the rocks. Others threw themselves from their horses and began to labor up the face of the cliff on foot. But more than all that wild tumult The Duke would have dreaded a single good shot kneeling quietly in the plain and drawing a perfect bead. One man would have meant certain death. But five hundred meant five hundred ways of distracting one another.

He felt bullets clip through his shirt. His sombrero was knocked from his head, and he caught it in midair with a hole punched through the top of it. And still Monday rushed on up the slope. It was not an incline. It was a terribly precipitous ladder. Even a man would have shrunk from attempting it. Perhaps even Monday, in broad daylight which showed the distance of the fall, would have been unnerved. But in the moonlight, with the excitement of the chase to drive him, he was unconscious of fear.

They were near the upper verge now. Another leap, and they were at it. A yell of disappointment, shame, rage, incredulity, from the mass of the pursuers—for certainly when this thing was told it would not be believed by those who had not seen the hunt—and with a last glance down toward them The Duke saw them wheeling their horses and riding like mad to cut around to the other side of the mesa and intercept the fugitive before he could come down.

But at that hope he merely smiled. All the advantage was now on his side. He pitched forward in the saddle as Monday stretched into his long, striding gallop across the top of the plateau. He patted that sleek, wet neck. He called affectionate and foolish words into the ear of the stallion. And Monday ran on with his head high, one ear pricked and one ear flattened as though to drink in every word with understanding.

They reached the farther wall of the mesa. This was

quite another affair. The descent here was comparatively easy. To be sure, Monday had to sit down on his heels and coast half the way to the bottom, but that was a small thing to a mountain horse. They struck the level of the plain among a cloud of rattling pebbles and rocked away again with that effortless and machine-made perfection of stride. Far off around the curve of the northern end of the mesa poured the first of the posse, but they were out of it now beyond hope. There had not been one of the entire posse capable of living with the gray stallion for ten minutes of hard running, and now that they had taken the last edge from their strength by their sprint around the end of the mesa, they faded away to nothing when they attempted to stretch out after The Duke across the plain. Not more than twenty, indeed, had made the last forlorn attempt and ridden around the rock wall. These kept doggedly to the chase for a mile or perhaps two. Then they drew rein of one accord and rode sullenly, silently, back toward their companions. Ahead of them they had seen the Black Hills looming, and they knew that it would be vain to attempt to trail the fugitive among those mountains of glossy stone.

They went back to Wheeler City. With what comments would they be greeted, who had allowed a single man to slip through their midst in the hotel where they had him blockaded, to ride cleanly out of their midst, to gain his confederate and the led horse, and, finally, to rescue his tiring companion by an exploit which showed his sublime contempt for his enemies? So they went back groaning. But every man was vowing that the troubles of John Morrow had not ended if there still was any manhood in the men of Wheeler City!

As for The Duke, he thought not of them. No sooner had the pursuers faded into the night behind him than he also drew rein. It was on a small plateau where he was out of danger of being stalked close. And here he dropped from the saddle, loosened the cinches and looked carefully over Monday.

There was not a scratch from the bullets which had flown. The tall stallion was as sound as the moment he started. The Duke walked him the next mile. Not that the horse was dangerously hot, but because his rider was for the first time in his life actually glad to walk! The grit and grating of the pebbles and the sand under his feet; the thick silence of the mountain night; the immense sweep of the sky; the steady glittering of the stars—it seemed to The Duke that he was seeing and hearing and feeling to the full extent for the first time in his life.

And all around him were things wonderfully good! Simply to breathe was a delight. And now and then, pausing, he listened until it seemed to him that the rolling thunder of many hard galloping horses rose out of the desert behind him. That fancy died away to the perfect silence again. The mystery and the hush pressed against his upturned face. And here was John Morrow left alive in the world!

He had been through a thousand perils before that day. But everything which had gone before was dim—was nothing! He could live through the horrors one by one from the time he had first seen the face of the sheriff appear above the head of the stairs and he had slammed the door and locked it in the nick of time—from that moment his memory traced the stages one by one, and every stage was hopeless until, by a miracle, Monday had brought him to the top of the mesa wall. He was not proud of what had happened. On other occasions he had saved himself out of his own strength. But here he had been rescued by fate itself. The Duke grew humble and as simple as a child.

26

Sally Delivers a Message

HE FOUND a little fertile valley among the Black Hills, and there, just before dawn, he paused. He took off the saddle. He rubbed down the stallion, and since the night was chill, the wind rising and the gray horse hot with the run, he covered Monday with his own tarpaulin.

For his own part, he needed only a moment of warmth and relaxation. He had had his sleep in the early part of the night in his besieged room at the hotel. So he took a blanket from his pack, wrapped himself in it, lighted a cigarette, and, sitting with his back against a rock, he waited for the morning.

The dawn came and found him still blowing smoke toward the east. The rose of the morning spread. The sun was not yet up. It was the most thrilling and beautiful moment of the day. Monday was cropping the grass at a little distance. And now it was that the peace and the calm mind of The Duke was shattered by the sound of an approaching step. It froze him with horror. There was no time to rise, throw off that entangling blanket and get out a gun. Far less was there time to saddle the stallion and attempt flight.

But who could have dreamed that there would have been one in the posse clever enough to trail him by night, and tireless enough to follow that trail to this conclusion? He turned his head, with his teeth set, prepared to find the sour face of Tom Onion, and instead he found himself staring straight into the eyes of Sally! He blinked at her like an owl.

She was dressed in a khaki skirt and a loose brown shirt, with a red necktie knotted under the broad collar.

Her bare elbows rested on a rock. Her fists were under her chin. And she smiled down at The Duke.

"Sally!" he cried. "Sally!"

He started to his feet and cast the blanket away.

"If I'd been one of Tom Onion's men, this would of been pretty easy for me," she responded gravely to his greeting.

"It would," said The Duke with equal gravity. "I sure sat down here and went to sleep with my eyes open. But it's a good thing that a friend found me."

"H'm! I dunno about that."

"Anything made you hostile?" asked The Duke.

"You mussed up my clothes when you were in the cave the other day," she remarked.

He flushed.

"Which I sure was surprised," said The Duke faintly.

"How come," asked the girl with sudden directness, pointing a straight, brown finger at him, "that you didn't sick the sheriff onto this here cave we been living in, to get at the gent that's been bothering William Guthrie?"

"I was aiming to have a talk with you and find out about things first," said The Duke. He studied her face with mortal earnestness.

"About what?"

"Who is he?" he asked.

"Who is who?"

"The gent that brought me Monday last night?"

"That's Sam."

"Who's he?"

"He's my brother."

The Duke exclaimed under his breath— "Asking your pardon, Sally, but I sort of half guessed it. There was something about him that started me thinking. When I first seen him come tearing along through the hills I didn't have the heart to take a square shot at him——"

"That's what they all say that fight Sam." Sally sneered.

"I ain't dodging the fact that he beat me," said The Duke, flushing. "Only"—he swallowed his sullen anger and made himself smile upon her—"I don't suppose you could understand, Sally. Anyway, it's over with. He dropped me with a slug of lead one time. The next time he comes along and risks his neck to save me! I'll bet you, Sally, that you were the one that talked him into doing that!"

"Doing what?" asked Sally coldly, and stared at him with lack of emotion.

The Duke sighed.

"Maybe I'm wrong again," he said. "Leastwise, I'm sure glad that Sam is your brother. Is he around?"

"He ain't," said Sally.

"He's out again, after all that he done last night?"

She shrugged her shoulders.

"That ain't nothing for him," she said.

She wandered to Monday. She began to pat and rub the velvet muzzle which Monday raised as she drew near.

"Now look here, Monday hoss," she said, "I've heard a whole lot about you, and how you climb up cliffs and suchlike. But you sure got good manners."

She kissed Monday between the eyes.

"I sure wish that you could stay, Monday!" she said.

"He ain't in any hurry to go," said The Duke.

"You're plumb wrong," declared Sally. "Him and his master are about ready to start."

"How come, Sally?"

"My brother Sam told me to bring you out that message."

"Well?"

"Can't you take a hint? He says for you to start on traveling. He says that you've made the Black Hills a pile too popular as it is. You'll have sheriffs and posses camping all over the hills. And Sam says that the best thing for you to do is to drift away any place you please so long as it's far!"

"D'you hitch up with Sam's idea?" said The Duke.

"I sure do!" said the girl.

It was so carelessly cold, so perfectly indifferent, this manner of Sally's, that he shook his head in amazement. She was as stony of nature as the rocks of the Black Hills.

"How come?" he asked.

"Sam ain't got much use for a gent that does a murder on an old man," said the girl, and her black eyes were on fire with scorn.

"You mean Bill Guthrie?"

"I mean just him!"

"Sally, I swear by everything that's over me, I didn't kill Guthrie."

Some of the fire went out of her eyes. But there was still a wealth of scorn and disgust.

"Who did kill him, then?"

"I thought—" He stopped, bringing his teeth shut with a click.

"You thought what?"

"I knew that your brother hated Guthrie."

"Sam hated him? Sam!"

"I don't know nothing," said The Duke, scowling. "I just figured that maybe he—"

"Sam do a murder like that?"

She laughed at him, but the laughter was full of angry abruptness.

"Anyway, he took a pot shot at Guthrie through the window of his house. A gent that would do that would shoot him from a covert—"

"A pot shot through his window—what are you talking about?" cried Sally. "Try to murder an old man like —Bah!"

She stamped in her rage.

"Why not him as well as me?" suggested The Duke. "You got no proofs, but you're sure anxious to say I done the killing."

"I respect a murderer more'n I do a gent that goes around spreading scandal!" said this fierce girl of the hills.

The Duke lighted his cigarette and then let it fume and go out. He would have given a great deal to find a loophole through which he could escape.

"Well," said the girl, "I ain't going to tell Sam what you think. If I did he'd come out here raging. He'd clean you up in about a minute."

The Duke was angered past endurance. Courtesy to a girl he felt to be a main essential, of course. But the best of men cannot bear more than his strength, and The Duke had passed the margin.

"Ma'am," he said to Sally, "I aim to say that your brother Sam would be tolerable welcome."

"If he was here," she answered more hotly than ever, "you'd be talking different."

"Look here," protested The Duke. "He sure played

white when he helped me out last night. And he appears to be a handy gent with a gun. But if it comes to a pinch—say, keep him clear of me, Sally! How come he dropped me, I dunno. But something tied up my arm. I couldn't work my trigger finger. If we was to have a run-in again—"

"Ain't you ashamed!" she cried. "Ain't you ashamed to talk about what you'd do to a man when there's only a girl to hear you!"

If there was one sin in all the catalogue from which The Duke was free, it was the sin of vanity. Or if he were a trifle vain he was certainly never vainglorious and boastful. And he could only regard the girl with an anguish of rage. He managed to beat down the first wave of fury.

"If your brother is dead set agin' me," he said, "why did he work so hard to save me tonight?"

"Because he was a fool," said the girl, "that thought you might be grateful. He didn't know—"

She could not complete the sentence, and The Duke stared blankly at her. It was impossible to say anything. He was mute in the presence of this terrible storm of words. And the wild desire grew in him to do something, since he could not speak.

"Tell your brother," he said, "that I'll sure be waiting around in case he wants to talk to me."

He took from a pocket a case full of playing cards. He removed one. He spun it into the air until it whirled away, presenting to him only a glimmering razor edge. Then he jerked out his revolver and fired. The card fluttered down in two pieces. He picked them up and gave them to Sally.

"When you see your brother Sam," he said, "give him these from me and tell him that they're my calling cards."

27

Flight

HE THREW the saddle on the back of Monday, flung himself into the stirrups, raised his hat on high to Sally and disappeared among the rocks. For a quarter of a mile he rode furiously fast. But at the end of that spurt he swung his horse around, made a detour to the rear, dismounted and ran cautiously back until he heard, before him, a sound which was curious in that wilderness of mountains of stone. He stopped and listened, and now he made sure what he had at first suspected—the laughter of a woman!

A moment later, stealing to the right and into a clump of boulders, he came on the view of Sally proceeding at a most leisurely walk and, from time to time, breaking into fits of immoderate laughter. At another time he might have feared for her sanity. But now he realized that she was roused to mirth by the thought of him!

The Duke could hardly believe that which he saw. He was quite accustomed to inspiring fear and hatred, but he had never before made any person break into hearty laughter such as this! Gradually she gained command of herself, but she was still chuckling as he trailed her—when his foot struck a small stone and he stumbled heavily to his knees.

Luckily that fall threw him headlong behind a jutting stone. Around the edge of it he peered as he fell, and he saw the girl suddenly sobered by the noise behind her.

She whirled as a wolf whirls when it hears the snap of the dog's teeth. In her hand was a long Colt revolver dexterously balanced, and she was crouched low, as though to present a smaller target to an enemy. The Duke marveled at her. Now she ran a few steps forward with strange swiftness, weaving from side to side so as to disconcert the aim of a hidden foe. Behind a big stone she dropped out of view and remained there for some minutes.

At length she seemed to feel assured that the noise she had heard must be, since it was so single and isolated, merely a natural fall of a stone. Suddenly she stood up and went on in her original course while The Duke stole behind her more cautiously than ever. And there was doubled need of caution, for now, though she felt there was nothing behind her, she kept the sharpest lookout. A dozen times she turned her head sharply, wheeling around to search the ground behind her in the dread of finding a foe.

And The Duke wondered. There had been times in his life when he had had to go on guard against many foes. And now was beginning a period when he must exercise the most constant precautions. But how could he ever hope to achieve the vigilance of this girl of the mountains? She was as swift-moving as a wildcat, and as full of alarms. There was not a moment, as she walked along, that she was not scanning rocks and sky and ground in the deepest anxiety. What a life she must have lived to have acquired such habits!

Suddenly he was able to forgive that passion with which she had just denounced him. To attack a friend of hers, to say nothing of a brother, was to put a greater tax upon her undisciplined spirit than she could endure.

Now he came to that part of the trail for which he had waited. She came to a place where the rushing sound of water rolled loudly around her. And here, where that overmastering sound drowned such lesser noises as fugitive footfalls behind her, she broke into a run. And The Duke marveled again! He remembered the running even of boyish cowgirls, raised on horses as much as their brothers, and accustomed to all manner of hardships and exercise. But none of them possessed a tithe of the ability of this girl to cover the ground. She ran with the free leg action of a boy athlete. She swung around among the rocks. She darted out of view down a hollow. She came into his sight again farther away, while The Duke hastened to follow her.

He could see where the river now dropped underground, diving headlong into the mountain, just as it issued on the farther side. It was into this foamy vortex that he half expected the girl to plunge. Instead, she swerved to the left, bounded up among the boulders and disappeared.

The Duke now stood up and gave vent to his amazement in a series of drawling, soft-voiced oaths. It had been more than he could have believed. This could not be the gentle-voiced girl who had danced with him that night at Warner's Springs! But at least this last burst of running explained one thing—it explained the reason she had been able to dart away from him and gain covert around the dance hall so swiftly that when he pursued he had been unable to find a trace of her. No wonder— for, fast as he had run, he could hardly have distanced her in a short spurt.

At length he followed onto those boulders among which she had disappeared. But there was nothing to be seen. It appeared that the girl had dived into the blank stones of the mountainside. But The Duke knew that miracles are story stuff and not fact, and that a hundred and thirty pounds of girlhood does not melt into thinnest air. Among those rocks he worked here and there.

He was fastening his eyes upon the ground and working with a feverish earnestness to find the trail. For trail there surely must be if this were the most-used entrance to the cave where several persons lived and kept their horses. But the hard, glossy surface of the rock showed him nothing. Not until he had crouched over and begun to search the surface on his hands and knees did he arrive on the first sign. And this was not at all what he had expected. It did not come in the form of a chipped bit of rock such as the shod hoof of a horse will strike away. Instead, there was a fluttering and gauzy bit of fuzz which clung to a rough bit of the rock face. He worked some of it loose, thinking it merely an odd growth. But when he twisted it in his fingers it did not rub away as vegetable matter should do. It merely rolled into a hard thread. With a sudden thought urging him, he lighted a match and touched it to the thread. And at once his nostrils sniffed the familiar tang of singed wool.

The Duke jumped to his feet with a cry of relief. This was the explanation why the surface of the rock left no trail. Those who dwelt in the cave issued forth upon shod horses, but over the shoes there were wrappings of cloth so that the iron might not scar the rock and wear out a trail. He followed that trail straight up to the surface of a great boulder. And there it stopped.

He was in the midst of this quandary when a faint noise warned him to take cover. He shrank down among the rocks barely in time. A section of that massive boulder, to the face of which he had followed the trail, now yawned open, swung wide like a door, and in the throat of the pass The Duke saw the brother of Sally on the pinto.

There could be no doubt that he was the same man. He rode the identical horse, as fresh and wiry as ever after a few hours of rest and a feed. He wore the same short, black mask. Yes, this was certainly he who so gallantly had brought to The Duke the tall gray stallion. The recollection of the peril which this fellow had undergone for his sake moved The Duke immensely. No matter what the treacherous girl had told her brother, no matter how vindictively she had poisoned his mind against The Duke, the latter remembered how this slender youth had swept across in front of the hundreds of savage riders from Wheeler City and brought safety to The Duke—yes, had thrown away his own chances to save another!

It was a very fine thing! It sent a little chill of appreciation through The Duke. And, let come what might, he vowed that he would never lift hand against this wild adventurer.

In the meantime, the subterranean horseman advanced out of the shadow. And The Duke saw, as he had apprehended, that the hoofs of the beautiful and fleet pinto were heavily swathed in cloths. One glance at the horse sufficed. It was a fine little animal, but not worthy of being named in the same breath with tall Monday.

As for the rider, now seen at close range in the sun for the first time by The Duke, he was even smaller than he had formerly surmised. The daring and brilliant carriage of Sally's brother, indeed, made up for his lack of size, so that at a distance he became an imposing figure. But here, viewed close by, it was plain that he could not have lasted a moment in a grapple with The Duke. His sole force was in his ability to shoot quickly and straight.

All of these things The Duke took note of with the greatest care. Who could tell how vitally his estimates might affect him before many days?

The rider looked about him hastily for a moment, then sent his mount down the hill. The pinto trotted quickly along the slope. He continued for a quarter of a mile until he was by the bank of the stream just before it dived underground. There the rider dismounted, removed the bandages from the feet of the pinto, and then, remounted, spurred away in the direction of the place where Sally had left John Morrow.

The Duke watched with a falling heart. It had not seemed possible to him that the girl could actually be so fierce as to send her brother out to do a murder. But this seemed to be the truth of the matter. There went the sprightly young brother to hunt down the man who had spoken against his reputation. And in the subterranean chamber the girl waited with her hands clasped and her eyes on fire, eager for the return of Sam and the details of the death of the interloper among the Black Hills.

It was a gruesome picture. It half obscured that lovely memory of Sally as she had been in the dance hall when she had brought him triumph in the very hour of defeat. Now that he thought upon it, there had been two great crises since his return from prison. In the one he had been buried under the heaped-up scorn of his old companions. In that case Sally herself had most conclusively, most brilliantly, saved him. In the other case he had been in danger of his life, and here it was Sally's brother who brought him safely through.

Though it was now a great temptation to go out to face the youthful rider, The Duke refrained. Better even to be known as a skulker and suspected for cowardice than to shoot down this wild young hero.

He went thoughtfully back through the hills to the point where he had left Monday. There seemed little likelihood that he would encounter the outlaw of the Black Hills on the way. Indeed, he was lifting his left foot to the stirrup when he heard the rattle of iron hoofs on iron-hard stone, and, glancing over his shoulder, he saw the pinto and its rider shooting down the slope toward him with gun drawn. When he found that he was sighted, the young warrior shouted—a shrill, small cry of triumph—and swung the revolver before him.

The Duke did not wait. Another moment, and the outlaw would be in point-blank range. In another moment it meant either killing or being killed. And John Morrow could not shoot at his late savior.

He twitched Monday around as he threw himself into the saddle and lifted the gray at once into full gallop. An instant of that and then, glancing behind him, he saw that the pinto was already dropping behind, though the rider was spurring furiously in an effort to get closer.

Then a gun spoke. A bullet smashed against the rocks near The Duke. Another explosion, and the slug whistled through the air over the head of John Morrow. But that was all. He shot the gray around the corner of a hill. Before the pinto and its rider came into view of the fugitive again, he was far, far away.

And still The Duke forced his horse on at a terrific pace. For the first time in his life he was fleeing from less than threefold odds. What if the world should see him now? And what, worst of all, would be the words of Sally when her brother returned triumphant with this tale of cowardice and flight? The Duke groaned, but though he looked eagerly back at the pursuer he did not slacken his pace. Another five minutes, and he had broken out of the heart of the Black Hills and into the lower and more rolling ground. The rider of the pinto was safely distanced, and now The Duke drew up the gray stallion for the first time and went on at a pace slow enough to admit of thinking.

28

A Community Aroused

WHAT IS ONE FRIEND to a man whose days are filled with good-fellowship? But to The Duke the loss of the girl's good will was a more crushing blow than his exile from Wheeler City. She meant more to him than the esteem of a thousand. But now her brother would carry back to her a story of his cowardly flight and— He could not think of it. He was choked with shame and confusion.

He left the Black Hills and climbed among some low hills to the east. There the day was spent on a knoll where the grass was rich and thick for Monday, and from which there was a wide view spread before The Duke himself. And with his glass he pored solemnly over the landscape through the late morning and the afternoon. A rabbit roasted impromptu was his own meal. Monday had sumptuous fare.

With the glass he could see enough to convince him that the good people of Wheeler City were by no means minded to let the matter of the escape of The Duke die. This time they were thoroughly roused. Not since the day of the Parker Boys had the entire community turned out in this fashion. In groups of not less than half a dozen— as though this were taken to be the smallest unit which could handle The Duke even if it succeeded in finding him—scores and scores of men were riding up and down through the plains around the Black Hills and into the Black Hills themselves. The marvelously clear and pure mountain air enabled The Duke to watch everything that was even distantly in range. Many a long mile away he made them out against the plain or, more distinctly, as they climbed into the hills.

Why did they not search these hills where he now found covert? Or why did they not pass on into the great, rough-sided mountains which spread to the north of the Black Hills? There could be only one explanation of the persistence with which they focused their attention around the Black Hills themselves, with their masses of weathered rock and towering iron blossoms. They had seen the other outlaw of the Black Hills save him. And they had taken it for granted that The Duke would be admitted into the strongholds and the concealed places of the other bandit.

It was quite a stirring sight, in the meantime, to see the manner in which they mustered and poured forth to hunt the desperadoes to the ground in this great effort. But the more The Duke saw, the more he was convinced that he would never again be able to sit among law-abiding men. His exile was complete. There was never a jury in the mountains that would fail to convict him without a shred of testimony against him. They would require no more than a few character witnesses. On the strength of their testimony he would be a dead man.

Such was the conclusion of The Duke. And now the sorrow began to leave him, and the dark anger began to rise. There was a hardening of the heart, a grim carelessness such as he had never felt before. He began to understand what was really meant by the word "desperado." He himself had been called by that name, but it had never been one tithe deserved. As a matter of fact, he had been simply a wild-headed youth out for a good time, one who chose to find his fun in battle with other men. He could see that now. But a desperado, properly so called, was a man who had lost the fear of death because he had nothing left to live for. He was a man who could not miss in his gun plays because a single miss meant that he himself was killed. He was a man who had only one thing left him with which he could gamble, and that last stake was his own existence. He juggled it in an open hand. He lasted perhaps a week and perhaps a month, and perhaps, if he were very great, half a dozen years. But in the end he was killed like a cornered rat.

Such was the desperado, justly so called. And The Duke could understand, because in him there began to appear some of the same elements. Since there was no longer any hope that he could go back to men in peace, he would go back to them in war. The wise resolves which three years of torture in the prison had built up in his mind melted away. After all, there was such a thing as fate, he decided, and fate had certainly taken a hand against him. So, now that the struggle was definitely turning against him, he would resign the battle to be law-abiding. If he were foredoomed to be a destroyer of life and property, then he would show them how truly terrible such a destroyer could be. He raised his head, his eye gleamed with a melancholy happiness, and the resolve hardened in him to a fixed purpose.

He determined to wait, however, until the next day before he sallied forth. It would be mere suicide to venture out into this maze of armed men unless there was absolute need. But when another twenty-four hours had dulled the edge of their watchfulness, when they began to weary of their work, then he would try to slip away. He would aim to strike his first blow—but where? Perhaps in Wheeler City itself, while the majority of the fighting men were away in the Black Hills searching for him; would it not be a beautiful victory to signalize the beginning of his outlawry by riding back to the town and harrying it as it had never before been harried by a single man?

His heart grew warm at the thought. And then he ground his teeth in mortification and sorrow. How completely he had failed! But when the wise old warden had warned him that he would need above all else in his work of self-reclamation endless patience, he could not have had in mind such a situation as this one.

He drew back into a naturally made camp toward the evening. Within a circle of shrubbery he prepared to spend the night. There, when the light was still so strong that the gleam of his fire would not be noticed, and while the shades of the evening were sufficiently thick to shroud the smoke which he sent up by mingling with it, he cooked his supper. He went out again, while the stallion was peacefully cropping the grass in the inclosure, and looked down to the plain.

It had greatly changed in the last few minutes. The yellow haze of light which had poured across the landscape was now quite gone, and the blue and the faint purples of the twilight were pooled in the hollows and flowed up the canyons into the mountains. And here, there and in a score of places he saw campfires beginning to throw out their long rays of light.

The Duke was amazed. And, likewise, he was over-awed. He had not dreamed what the power of an angered countryside could be. Neither had he dreamed that public wrath was ever more than a momentary flash which either struck down its prey at the moment or else forgot! But it seemed that the Black Hills were girt with campfires, yellow gleam on gleam, lying in a long, loose circle. He could hardly give credence to the eyes which saw it! For the Black Hills must be a good four miles across, and the circle of fires, if it were complete, covered a dozen miles. He could count less than half of that circle, and yet he made out, as the evening thickened, no less than seventy-five fires!

A hundred yards apart or a trifle more, and there must be half a dozen men to each fire. But could it be that a thousand men had joined to draw that cordon around the Black Hills? The more he stared, the more bewildered he grew. Then he traced back through the last stages of the story as he knew it. There had been the depredations of the outlaw of the Black Hills—the raids on many ranches—the attempt to kill Bill Guthrie at length. Then John Morrow returned to his old town. And, in a short space, Martin was killed on the high road by a man riding on a gray horse, and Guthrie was killed while under the escort of The Duke, and, finally, the entire town of Wheeler City had been disgraced by allowing the captive to slip through its hands!

That was enough, surely, to madden the entire community. They had two murders which they felt they could directly attribute to The Duke. There were others, perhaps, which they now began to rake up out of his past. Every bad story that had ever been told about him was doubtless magnified tenfold in this time of his downfall. And so recruits had poured in. Every ranch made sure that it was represented by a man or two. Every village sent representatives. Every idle man and boy capable of riding and shooting was on hand. And, in addition, practically the entire force of the men of Wheeler City were here on the ground! To have seen them marshaled in the full brightness of midday could never have been so impressive as to see them here represented only by scattering rays of lights through the gathering blues of the evening.

Still The Duke could hardly believe, any more than the man who drops a match in stubble can believe that that small spark started the wall of fire which, in a few seconds, gallops across the acres, tossing up great red arms of flame.

Though they had gone to catch him, though they made sure that he had taken to the ground somewhere in the hills, their net would not close on him. He laughed and shook his fist in the air. They would not get him. Their net would close on quite other victims!

At the thought his exultation left him. Sally was yonder, despising and hating him, no doubt, for what she would be sure was his cowardice. And the net of the men of the law would close over Sally's brother, who had saved The Duke's life.

He groaned at the thought. But he decided, after a moment, that this could never be. So wild a man, so adroit a hunter as Sam, could never be lured into blundering abroad at night. And if he did go abroad, the lights which these men kindled, if sufficient to show anyone who attempted to ride through the lines, were also sufficient to warn back anyone save a rash-headed fool. There was only one real danger, The Duke decided, and this was that the risk of running that gauntlet would prove too strong a temptation, and the boy might run into the peril for the sheer peril's sake.

However, he could not be so wild-headed as this! Or if he were— What of the old man sitting in the cave? What of the girl? It was too horrible!

It preyed on the mind of The Duke so long that he decided he could not endure the silence of the camp there on the hilltop. He saddled Monday again, and he jogged the horse down into the nearest canyon. From this he went out into the plain, and instinctively he headed toward the lights.

Once he drew rein suddenly and asked himself, with a start, if he were about to do the thing which he dreaded lest the brother of Sally might attempt. Was he about to be drawn like a moth by a fire?

One thing at least he knew as he sat motionless in the saddle with the gleaming arc of the fires far before him and the stars shining overhead: He loved Sally with all his heart!

29

◉

The Root of Information

THERE WERE several clumps of dwarfed trees between him and the line of the fires. Toward one of these he headed, and, riding into it, he made his survey more closely.

From this nearer point of vantage he could see that his estimate of the number at each fire was about right. At one fire there were five, as his glass told him, and at another there were six. And this could be used as an estimate for the number in the entire line. A thousand men, then, were encamped around the Black Hills to destroy one man or two at the most!

It was as though the full power of the law were displayed to him at the very moment when he had decided to live with the aid of the law. But he was not disheartened. The greater the odds, the greater the glory.

Here his thoughts halted in midstride, so to speak, for from a clump of trees just before him there withdrew a man riding on a tall gray horse—either gray or white, for no other color would have showed through the gathering night—and the rider turned south and jogged slowly away.

The Duke watched him, fascinated. There could be only one reason that kept a man peering at the campfires from a distance. It must be that, like The Duke himself, he dreaded the force of the law which he was now beholding.

Another surmise came close on the heels of this. There had been a rider on a tall gray horse, like Monday, who had held up Martin and murdered him for the sake of the money which the unfortunate rancher had been carrying with him. Might it not be that the man he saw fading into the night was the same?

The Duke reined Monday back and rode in pursuit.

It was not easy work. He had to keep Monday so far back that the form of the other was a mere glimmering shadow, guessed at rather than seen in the distance. If he pressed closer, Monday himself would be seen by the other. Indeed, at any moment the other might spot the pursuer, and that would probably mean that the hunted would become the hunter.

South and south at a steady canter the stranger passed over three miles or more of ground and then veered suddenly to the right. The Duke followed, intensely curious and wild with eagerness. They rounded the foothills. They put the Black Hills to their right and north. Still the stranger rode on, until he struck the bank of the winding river which flowed through the Guthrie ranch itself.

Down the south bank of the Lindsay he rode at a more rapid pace, and The Duke felt his heart come into his mouth. His mind went back to another night when a signal had flashed from the attic window of the Guthrie ranch house and had spelled out a strange message to someone east and north—someone hidden in those same Black Hills, perhaps.

He had surmised before that it was the brother of Sally, that strange young rider. But might it not be this same wanderer? Might not this be the marauder who had pillaged the Guthrie ranch of old?

At least there was the possibility. He pressed a little closer. It was the thick of the night now. His eyes ached from straining toward that impalpable shadow which drifted before him.

A quarter of a mile from the ranch the shadow suddenly began to draw nearer. The Duke stopped. The man before him had halted. Had he seen, perhaps, that he was being followed, and was he now laying an ambush for his pursuer?

John Morrow jumped Monday into the shelter of a

high-standing boulder and dismounted. Then he dropped flat on the sand, when he found that he could not make out the form of him who had been in the saddle of the other gray horse.

Now he caught the sound—a faint, faint grinding of feet in sand. It was not the horse. The single stepping of a man alone could make that sound. And the noise was diminishing gradually. Yes, the stranger had here dismounted and was going on toward the ranch on foot, no doubt for fear lest his horse might betray him by neighing when near the other animals on the ranch.

It was enough for The Duke. He threw down the reins of Monday and hurried on in pursuit. He passed close by the other gray and paused for a single instant to peer at the animal through the starlight. Yes, it was a horse full as tall as Monday, but heavier and grosser of bone and muscle. They were not more comparable than draft horse and thoroughbred, so far as the fine modeling of the head was concerned. And plainly, if it came to a pinch, this animal could never hold its own in a race with Monday.

The Duke put that comfortable assurance behind him and continued, turning to the left, where there was more grass to mask the sound which he made in running. Bu there was no occasion to continue with such haste for any length of time. Almost immediately he made out the form of the walker ahead of him. The man went on steadily Certainly he was not approaching the ranch for the firs time. He went with the steadiness of assurance. Entering the tall pines near the lake, he paused here a little time with John Morrow lurking behind him. Then he went on dipped to the left so that some shrubs lay between hin and the lighted bunkhouse, and continued straight to th Guthrie house itself.

By this time The Duke was walking with his hand o the butt of his Colt. He had little liking for Steve Guthrie, but if this gray horseman was about to attack the rancher as he had attacked poor Martin, he would interfere with a forty-five caliber bullet.

Yet there was no stealth in the manner of the other. He now went straight up to the front door of the house. From his pocket he produced a key. He opened the door, to the utter astonishment of The Duke, and disappeared into the interior of the house.

And The Duke followed still! There might be a thousand perils in entering this house, but he slipped up to the front door, found, as he suspected, that the stranger had not paused to lock the door behind him, and entered the dark hall.

Here he saw a glimmer of light from the stairway beyond. And he heard steps going up.

"Hello, Charlie!" called the voice of Steve Guthrie. "Is that you?"

"It's me, all right. How's things?"

"All right."

"Is this safe?"

"There ain't a soul in the house except old Bing. And he's coming out now to watch the foot of the stairs for us."

"The yaller old coyote! But he'll keep a sharp eye. How are you, partner?"

"Finer'n silk!"

The footfalls of he who had climbed the stairs halted in the upper hall, and then they passed into a room. At the same instant the door to the dining room opened, and the whisper and rustling of soft-padded slippers sounded over the splinters of the floor. The Duke stepped to the side, then crouched close against the wall.

Presently Bing stepped into the doorway. He held in his hands a lamp which threw a fiercely concentrated radiance over his face, with the yellow-stained pupils rolling in alarm. Now he put down the lamp on the little center table of the parlor, and as he straightened up he whirled with a frightened little intake of breath. He had sensed danger without either sound or sight of it. And as he wheeled he had brought out his knife.

But The Duke had flung himself high into the air, and as he descended on his victim the stroke of one hand knocked the knife spinning out of the fingers of Bing, and the next instant he crashed against the luckless Chinaman. Bing sank to the floor with a powerful arm crooked around his throat to choke away outcries and with no chance to so much as struggle. The first blow had stunned him. He lay limp and helpless while the other, with Bing's own knife, cut Bing's silk coat into strips and, with that costly stuff as ropes, tied him hand and foot, not as a calf is hog-tied, but so that he could not stir. And last he was gagged so that he could not utter a sound.

That done, The Duke went on. He stole up the stairs to the hall above. And there he found himself at the very root and base of information. There was not even a pretense of guarding themselves, so secure were they that Bing would head off any spy. Their door was ajar, and through it The Duke looked in upon them, through it he saw their faces, heard their voices, was to all intents and purposes in the room itself. He had not missed any great section of their conversation.

"Nigh onto a thousand!" said the stranger, completing a sentence the first part of which The Duke had not heard.

He was a very pale-eyed, pale-haired man. He had hardly any expression at all in the upper part of his face, but the lower part was grim and deeply lined. He was tall —neither so tall nor heavy as Steve Guthrie, but, nevertheless, a big man.

"A thousand?" said Guthrie. "They's more than that."

"You been over to see?"

"Sure I have. I went over and I took the boys with me. Out of the fifteen of 'em, I left ten. Everybody allowed that I was mighty generous!"

He laughed softly, and the stranger laughed with him.

"They don't know," he commented, "that ten of your men are about equal to one real man."

"Less'n that," declared the rancher. "Ten of 'em wouldn't stand up to a scared dog if it come to a pinch."

"You sure picked out a yaller-hearted crew."

"And wasn't it a good thing that I did?"

"Tolerable good, I'd tell a man!"

"If they'd been real men they'd of made life hard for you, Charlie!"

"Yep! They'd of caught me quick enough. It ain't in the books for one gent to keep escaping from fifteen every time he climbs onto his hoss and feels like riding. But they acted like they didn't want to catch me!"

"No more they did. They figured they would of broken some teeth before they finished you. But I had to keep getting them out to chase every time you come near the place and missed. It sure took you a long time to—"

"Talk about that some other place, will you?" growled Charlie.

"Just as you say! But there ain't anybody to hear!"

"How can you tell?"

Charlie rose and walked straight to the door!

30

◉

To Ride for Money

THE DUKE GRIPPED the butt of his gun hard. He would rather have lost an arm than kill these two before he learned their guilty secret, whatever it might be. But if Charlie saw him, kill them he must, or else die himself. So, crouched almost to the floor, hardly daring to look up, he waited.

There was only an instant of suspense. Charlie turned away. He had come to the door not to see into the hall, but simply because he became restless. He stood at the door, but he turned back at once into the room. He slumped heavily into his chair and remained motionless, staring at the floor.

"What's wrong, man?" asked Steve heartily.

"What's right?" asked Charlie with a sudden fierceness.

"Everything!"

"Everything with you. But what about me?"

"So long as I'm fixed, you're fixed. You ought to know that!"

"Thanks," growled Charlie. "I don't think you'd go back on me, Steve," he chuckled. "We got too much on each other, eh?"

Here he looked down, lighting a cigarette, and as his

eyes were averted Steve Guthrie allowed an expression of malignant darkness to cross his face. It was only a momentary shadow. When Charlie looked up again the face of Steve was as calm as ever. But The Duke had seen and understood.

"When I got that word from you about Morrow," went on Charlie, "I sure got worried. But he didn't turn out to be hard to handle, eh?"

"Not so easy as maybe you think," said Steve. "He come here like a wolf, walking around and smelling out trouble. Besides, he begun to get pretty thick with Uncle Bill, and if I'd let 'em stay together much longer there'd of been the devil to pay. That's why I told you to get to work."

"I didn't waste no time," Charlie nodded.

"You sure didn't."

"I got the dogs one day and Uncle Bill the next."

"Pretty neat work, Charlie."

The Duke listened breathlessly. It was more than he could have dared to hope to hear. But what difference did it make, after all, that he was hearing these things? If he were to repeat them to others, would he be believed? And how could an outlaw even gain a hearing with the powers of the law?

"Pretty neat work it may be," said Charlie, "but what I'd like to know right here, son, is when I get the coin?"

"As soon as I get my hands on it."

Charlie swore. "Ain't you rolling in money out here all the time?"

"Nobody but a fool carries five thousand around with him! And—by the way—Uncle Bill had more'n a thousand with him. But call it a thousand even. Take that from five thousand, and it leaves four thousand that I owe you, Charlie."

"Is that your game?" Charlie's pale eyes flashed. "Is that the way you figure it out?"

"Ain't it a square way?" asked Steve heavily.

"Not the way I have of thinking!"

"Let's hear you talk."

"I dropped Bill Guthrie, didn't I?"

"Sure. I ain't denying that."

"I took a chance doing it, maybe?"

"You took a chance."

"There was this fellow Morrow that you think is such a hard one. He was riding right alongside of Guthrie, wasn't he?"

"That's what you said."

"Well, I laid up there in the brush and seen Morrow come up within six yards of me. I had my hoss lying down—a handy trick to have a hoss know! I had my rifle drilled on Morrow. If he'd come an inch closer, one time, I would have let him have it."

"Why didn't you?"

"Because I wanted the murder to be charged to him, didn't I? Oh, you'd be mighty glad if I'd bumped him off, too! But I ain't a plumb fool, Steve!"

"Maybe the day'll come," said Steve, "when you'll be wishing with all your might that you'd taken that first chance and finished with The Duke."

"Huh?"

"I mean it! He's a plain bad one, Charlie. I seen enough of him around here to know. Cool as ice when it comes to a pinch. When they come here to get him for the Martin killing, it would of done you good to see how easy he took it."

"Standing up to talk is one thing. Standing up to guns is another."

"He'll stand up to guns, too. Maybe we'll find out how he can stand up to'em!"

"Let's get back to the money. I ain't found that Morrow had much sense. He never bothered me none, even when he got out after me with that Leaper dog."

"How'd you dodge him?"

"Got up into the Black Hills. I looked back and seen that this Morrow gent was following me, so I just went on until I come to that place where the creek runs out of the side of the mountain—"

"A queer place. I know it."

"I rode the old hoss into the water and let the stream take me down about a quarter of a mile. Then I rode out and went on. And he never followed me farther than the place where I went into the water."

The Duke gritted his teeth. After all, he had been a consummate fool not to have guessed what had been done.

"If he had follered on I'd of picked him off dead easy. He was riding along the trail blind as a bat."

He added: "But this ain't getting down to the money. I say that by bumping off Uncle Bill I had a right to what money there was on him, same's I had a right to the money that was on Martin. Ain't that clear?"

"I dunno—"

"Well, it's got to be clear!"

For a moment the eyes of Steve burned at the other. Then he sank back into his chair and made himself smile.

"I ain't going to fight about a measly thousand dollars," he said. "I ain't that kind."

"Well," said the other, relieved, "I'm glad that's settled. I get the whole five thousand, then. And when do I get it?"

"Soon as I can get my hands on it."

"How long will that be?"

"Are you rushed for money?"

"I'll take what's coming to me!"

The Duke could follow the rise and fall of hard feeling between the two. Plainly these confederates, having accomplished the objects of their union, were ready to lunge at each other's throats.

"There's no hurry, Charlie."

"Where is the money?"

"In Wheeler City."

"In a bank?"

"No."

"Look here, I ain't asking you to tell me where you've stowed away your stuff, but I want that five thousand. Suppose we ride into Wheeler City and I meet you somewhere near the edge of town?"

"Tonight?" exclaimed Steve.

"Why not tonight? Are you afraid of riding in the dark?"

The sneer with which this was spoken brought a dark flush to the cheek of Steve.

"If you insist," he said with some dignity. "I suppose I got to go. You got the money coming to you."

"Then let's start now."

"Charlie, you act like you thought I'd try to beat you out of that coin!"

"Oh, no!" The other chuckled. "I ain't afraid of that. I figure that you'll pay, Steve. Something tells me that you ain't going to try to back down."

There was no mistaking the threat which was in his tone and behind the words. And there was no mistaking the smile with which Steve met the words. He knew that his confederate, or hired tool, was like the poison of the snake—as fatal to him who used it as to him who was struck by the fangs.

Suddenly Steve rose.

"We'll start now," he said. "Go ahead, Charlie."

"That sounds like the right sort of talk to me," remarked the other with a grunt.

He stepped forward, and as he went past Steve Guthrie the lips of the latter parted to a malignant sneer, his brow contracted, and his hand tightened over the butt of his revolver. But he seemed to think better of that murderous impulse. He glanced sharply overhead. No doubt he was considering that a murder committed here would be one from the results of which he could not escape. There were too many people near him—and murder will out!

So much The Duke waited to see, then he shrank to one side of the hall door and kneeled again, now with the long gun gripped in his hand and ready for instant action. If only they had not been here in the stronghold of the Guthries, he would have made his savage attack at once. But, since they were here, it was suicide to attack two such men as these. Either one of them would be a handful.

They strode out into the dimness of the hall. And what a giant Steve was, as the eye looked up to him from beneath.

"The thing to do," said Charlie, "is for us to ride till we're close to Wheeler City. Then you go on in. I'll wait out by the Fryer place, out by the pump behind the old house. How does that suit you? You can come out and talk business to me there!"

"That sounds fine as silk to me," said Steve Guthrie.

Their heavy footfalls went down the stairs. Would they go straight on to the front door, or would they turn through the parlor toward the side door?

Into that parlor they turned. They would be sure, then,

to find the prostrate body of Bing, the Chinaman. But no, they walked straight on, and presently the door slammed behind them. Their heels struck loudly once or twice on the outer steps, and then landed into the muffling dirt outside.

The Duke, stealing swiftly down the stair prepared for action, heard those things with a great feeling of thanksgiving, a joy which was abruptly terminated by a shrill scream from the parlor itself.

31

◉

A Lost Cause

THE DUKE WAS inside the parlor in two leaps, one of which carried him to the bottom of the stairs, to the door of the parlor, and the next planted him in the gloom of the parlor beside Bing. The Oriental's yell had hardly ended; another was beginning, but was choked away to a bubbling sound as The Duke dropped to his knees beside him. His hands and his feet were still fast bound, but he had worked the gag from his mouth by inconceivable effort.

"Hello!" called the voice of Steve outside the house. "What the devil's this? That's Bing!"

His footfalls hurried back. A few deft touches of his big jackknife freed Bing, and The Duke caught him by the nape of the neck and yanked him to his feet. He dragged him to the door and opened it. Then, standing back in the shadow, he ground the muzzle of his revolver into the small of the wretched Oriental's back.

The Duke could see Steve outside, running back.

"Tell him you'd fallen asleep in the chair and had a bad dream—tell him anything," said The Duke, "but keep him out of this here room. If you don't—"

There was no time for another word. Steve was before them in the darkness. A final prod of the revolver supplied the place of speech, however.

"What the devil'd you yell about?" exclaimed the master of the ranch as he reached the door.

"I sat down to wait, Mister Guthrie," whined Bing. "And somehow I fall asleep. Just now I catch a bad dream. I holler. I wake up. Very sorry, Mister Guthrie!"

"You yaller-hided old liar!" growled Steve. "What you mean by shouting like that! I sure thought that there was a knife striking into your gizzard! But—you go to bed, Bing. I ain't coming back much before morning."

He was gone again, and The Duke heard his voice as he rejoined Charlie.

"Close the door!" he ordered.

Bing obeyed. In another moment his hands and feet were again tied with a quick turn of the silken strands. The gag was jammed back down his throat.

"I'm going to be busy around here for a while," said The Duke. "You stay here and don't move. If I hear any noise I'm coming back to crack your head open for you. Savvy?"

With that savage warning he stepped back into the hall, closed the door behind him, then slipped noiselessly out the side door of the house.

If he could keep Bing quiet for a few seconds until Steve and Charlie were out of earshot, all would be well. In the meantime, he must cut around the two at full speed and get to Monday before Charlie reached his horse.

It was not so difficult to do. As he turned the corner of the house, running fast, he saw Steve mounting his horse, which had been left under the cover of a big pine before the building. The two went on slowly, with Charlie walking beside the mounted man.

It needed only a broad detour to the right, and then a cut to the left again. He gained Monday, swung into the saddle, panting, and reined back into a circle of shrubbery.

He was only just in time. Monday was barely behind the shelter when the two horsemen came up the trail. He peered through the branches and made them out so distinctly that it seemed impossible they could go by without seeing him.

"The Chink is getting queer," said the voice of Charlie.

"He sure is," answered Steve.

"Besides he knows a lot."

"He knows too much."

"Sometime he'll have to be fixed so he ain't likely to ever do no talking. He could hang you, Steve."

"Sure he could. But he ain't going to. I know too much about him."

"About the way he used to run other Chinks in over the border? He could turn state's evidence on you, and they'd never touch him."

"I never thought of that!"

"You better start thinking now, then!"

"I sure will. I'll get you to tap him on the head one of these days, Charlie."

"Always me when it comes to the dirty work, eh?"

"There's money in it, Charlie."

"That's different, then!"

Their voices died out, and when the silence surrounded him The Duke found that he was shuddering.

He had known many a stern man and many a cruelly wicked man in his life, but he had never known one to mate with these. There was a profundity of villainy about them; there was a perfect coldness of which he had never been able to conceive. He could not imagine remorse giving them a single evil hour. They were complete in themselves.

There could be no doubt about it. He had heard enough to complete the picture of the crime. Steve, weary of a life of submission to the will of his Uncle Bill, had determined that the ranch should be his. He had become aware that the outlaw who was harassing the ranch to get necessaries from it, was no other than some friend of his, perhaps. He had finally made a bargain with the fellow to get rid of William Guthrie. Hence, the bullet was fired through the window.

How Sally's brother came to be seen on the place after that shot was fired, The Duke could not conceive, but he was perfectly convinced that no kin of Sally could have fired such a cowardly shot. That wild young horseman who had come to meet him and fight him hand to hand, could never have connived at an assassination by night.

No, it was the work of Steve—Steve who had failed in the first attempt, but who had succeeded in tying the hands of the rancher by poisoning the dog pack, and who had then finally won his fight by having his confederate kill the rancher with a long-range shot.

Having made all of these discoveries, John Morrow swung Monday out from the thicket and let him run across the open land at full speed. The rush of the wind into his face seemed to cleanse his mind from the unclean knowledge which had been poured into it.

There was time enough to follow on the trail of Steve and Charlie. Indeed, there was no need at all of riding directly behind them, for he knew where they had planned their rendezvous. He would reach that place before them. And on the old Fryer place he would be far differently situated than in the house of Guthrie himself. He could attack as he pleased. If he could not take the powers of the law to help him apprehend these scoundrels, he could at least use surprise as an ally.

In the meantime, he let the gray stallion run gradually to the left toward the Black Hills, and as he rode he wondered. The campfires had burned low. It could not be for lack of fuel with all the shrubbery of the foothills about them. There must be some contributing cause. Indeed, yonder was a gap where no flame showed at all, and where the fire must have burned down to a bed of coals covered and veiled with a sheeting of ashes.

That conclusion made The Duke ride on faster and with a higher head, filled with presumptions. What could have happened? In another two miles he found the explanation clearly enough. Before him, over the plain, streamed a huge troop of riders—hundreds and hundreds in a long procession. And their songs and shouts echoed dimly to him across the plain.

There could only be singing like this in honor of the end of their labors. Did it mean that they had discovered the cave, or that they had laid hands on Sally's brother? The thought brought the sweat onto his forehead. He pushed to the left and skirted along the lower edge of the Black Hills, then cut up boldly into them through the line of the dying fires. He reached, at last, the place where the entrance to the cave had been. And now the opening in the boulder stood wide ajar for any to enter who so chose. But the interior was jammed and piled with new-splintered rocks!

There had been calamity indeed in that cave since he had last seen it! He reined Monday about and went back to the place where the stream had plunged into the mountainside. But it ran in no longer! And a little lake had been formed, with rapidly growing circumference. It was filling the hollow around the stream. Before long it would overflow, and the water must find a way back into the plain.

"Hello!" called a sudden voice behind him. "Who's this?"

He reined Monday back with a start. But there was no chance for escape. While he sat the saddle there, deep in his thought and with the spreading rush and rippling of the waters in his ears, a dozen horsemen had stolen up on him. And, with a stifled groan, he saw that he had thrust his head into the fire of his own free will.

There was no chance either to break away by the speed of Monday or to shoot a path through these enemies. Every man was covering him with rifle or revolver.

"Who's this?" asked the man who had spoken before, and who now pushed in front of his companions a short distance.

"I'm Jim Calkins of Hallowell's Crossing," said The Duke.

"Keep back, boys," said the interrogator. "Keep back and watch him. If he tries to make a quick break, let him have it! You're from Hallowell's Crossing?"

"That's me."

"Say, Jerry!"

"Well?" said Jerry from the crowd.

"Know anybody up to Hallowell's Crossing by the name of Jim Calkins?"

The heart of The Duke sank.

"Ain't never heard tell of nobody by no such name," drawled the answer.

"You ain't. Boys, it looks like maybe we've run acrost something. Come in, a couple of you. Jim Calkins, stick up your hands and keep 'em high! I got to have some talk with you!"

And The Duke, grinding his teeth, but realizing that a lost cause is, after all, a lost cause, pushed his hands reluctantly above his head.

32

◉

The Duke Registers a Vow

"AND A GRAY HOSS, too," someone was saying.

The Duke, in desperation, decided to strike in the dark and see if he could not at least gain a respite.

"Let's have a light here to look at him," suggested someone.

"A good idea," said the leader, and reached for matches.

Now The Duke struck his random blow. He must stand or fall by it.

"Lemme see the gent that says he don't know of a Jim Calkins in Hallowell's Crossing."

"Step out, Jerry."

Jerry pressed closer to The Duke, drawling:

"I'm sure sorry, stranger, but I ain't never heard of no such name."

"How many years has it been since you lived in the Crossing?"

The Duke held his breath. This was his one hope.

"Ain't more'n a year and a half," said Jerry.

The Duke drew a free breath at last.

"Well," he said, "I knowed that must be it. I been over a year at the Crossing, as anybody could tell that sups there now. Ain't any of you boys from around the Crossing?"

The leader, taken aback, dropped the match which he had just scratched. It is one thing to hold a match in the face of a guilty man; it is quite another thing to take the lead in insulting a man who may be innocent and live to show his irritation. Besides, the wild hope which had jumped into his mind a moment before was probably too much to be true.

"Ain't nobody from the Crossing," they answered. "That's a pretty long step, from there clear down here!"

"Don't I know it?" said The Duke. "But when we got the news on the telephone I heard the other boys figuring that it was too far away for them to go down, but I ups and says to myself that if that gent that rides the gray hoss has got a hoss as fast as they say it is, it may be the one that was stole from me six months back—"

"You got a gray hoss stole?"

"I been raising gray hosses ever since pop died."

"That's how come he's riding a gray, chief," said one of the men.

He who was addressed as "chief," and who had taken the lead from the first, hesitated a moment; and then, through the darkness, The Duke saw him nod.

"I got to say that we're still watching you, partner," he declared in a much milder voice, "but—you can put your hands down again if you feel like it."

It was like coming out of the darkness into light for The Duke.

"How come you to be here?" was the next question.

"I come up with the boys that are riding back to Wheeler City. I heard tell that the job was finished, and there was something said about a cave-in in—"

"You didn't hear what happened?"

"Nope. I thought I'd come and take a look."

"Come along with us, Calkins," said he who had been chief, and from whose mind all doubt had apparently vanished. "While we catch up with the rest, I'll tell you about it. My hoss throwed pretty near a fit, a while back, with a stone in his foot. Went plumb lame and I thought he'd broke down. We started fussing over him, and it was ten minutes before we found that it was only a stone. How's that for doggone plain ignorance, eh?" he laughed. "And then when we was about to start on we seen you come up on a gray horse, and I got to thinking—well, you see, we knowed that The Duke was riding a gray hoss—"

"I see," said The Duke heartily. "You ain't hurt my feelings none by stopping me. Only I'm glad that you stopped me with questions instead of turning loose with a few slugs of lead and no talk."

They started on after the main body of horses, which was now far out of sight in the direction of Wheeler City. And as they went on The Duke heard the story.

As the men watched from the campfires that evening, not very long after the falling of the dark, someone had seen a swiftly moving streak coming out of the hills, a streak which developed into a rapid rider. And the firelight flashed on the sides of a pinto with the rider bent far over the pommel of the saddle. Straight between two fires darted the fugitive. The shout of the man who had first taken note of the rider started a dozen guns firing. But such was the speed of the approaching man that he had actually slipped through between the fires and was heading off toward the outer darkness at a rapid clip when a lucky shot struck the pinto and brought it to the ground, flinging the rider afar.

When the men ran up they found the horse dead and the rider, staggering and stunned, was just rising to his feet.

The Duke listened with a heart thundering in his throat, but he made his voice as calm as possible.

"I guess they dropped the skunk without asking no questions," he said.

"Baldy Monfort took a shot at him as he come up running," said the narrator, "but somebody knocked the gun down. They wanted to get the gent alive—and they done it!"

The Duke breathed a sigh of relief.

"They got half a dozen guns jammed under his nose and then took his Colt from him and tied his hands together."

"What sort of a looking gent?" asked The Duke, still hoping against hope that it might not, after all, be Sally's brother, though the detail of the pinto horse seemed to be conclusive evidence.

"Not more'n a kid to look at," said the other. "Just a good-looking kid. Maybe nineteen years old, maybe not quite so much. Mighty fine-looking, with black eyes—"

The brain of The Duke became a blank. Poor Sally! If her brother were taken, what would she do? What would become of her and the old man in the cave—but what of the cave itself? And what of Sally herself?

"We hadn't no sooner got him and sent word around to the rest of the fires for the boys to come in—we hadn't no sooner done that than there was an explosion in the hills, like a real lifter going off in a shaft. We run up to the sound. We found that there was a sort of door opened in the face of a big boulder, and the water that had been running into the mountain was blocked up and making a lake. Didn't need no brain work to tell what had happened, but the kid talked up and admitted what it was."

"Ah?" said The Duke.

"He said that The Duke was in there in the cave—seems that that was where they'd been hiding out. No wonder we wasn't able to find 'em when we hunted through the Black Hills. They'd found this here cave with a big boulder balanced so's they could use it like a door to shut off the entrance to the cave. And right in there they'd been living mighty snug. But when the boys made that line of lights and fires all around the hills, seems like The Duke decided that there was no chance of getting through, and that he finally made up his mind that, rather than give folks the pleasure of saying he'd been caught, he decided to blow up the cave and bury himself in it. But this kid—he won't give himself no name —didn't want to die that way. He come out and run his hoss at the line of the fires. And—you know how we caught him."

There was a little silence. The Duke was thinking fast and hard. What had the tale meant? He could gather but one possible significance. That strange old man of the cave, perhaps with the guilt of many forgotten crimes bowing his ancient head, had decided that, though they were all cornered, he would die by no hand save his own. But first the others left him. And this was the meaning of Sam's mad ride through the fires. He had attracted all suspicion on his own head. He had described falsely the destruction of the other outlaw for whom the posses were hunting, and so he had brought about a focusing of the men at one place, and the line of the watch fires was stripped of guards through the rest of its circumference.

And what was this for? The gallant fellow had sacrificed himself and thrown himself into the arms of the law so that his sister could escape unobserved. She had gone out through the water trap on the farther side of the mountains. Yes, and was it not possible that the old man had been taken out with her, and that the blasting in of the cave had been simply a trick of the tongue to make the watchers believe that The Duke himself was dead?

What motive could have led them, so generously, to shield him?

This bewildered The Duke. He began to listen again to the narrative of the chief, who had been running along steadily with his account all this time.

"When the boys seen that the kid was all that they was going to capture after their trouble, they begun to talk pretty hard to him. He didn't answer nothing. He just stood up as cool as you please and looks them in the face and sneers at them. Jud Tomkins, who'd got good reasons for being out for a killing—he gets so mad because the kid won't talk, that he steps up and cracks him alongside the jaw and knocks him down. And when the kid gets up, what d'you think he does? He just wipes his mouth and says nothing at all! But he looks around at the boys and at Jud like he didn't see them there!"

The heart of The Duke rose in him. He could see the picture of that slender young hero oblivious to his danger.

"Then somebody begun to talk about the story that Guthrie had told, of how the hound had taken a shot at him through the window. When the boys heard that yarn again, they got pretty hot. There was talk about stringing him up. They even throwed a rope around his neck. And still he wasn't saying a word until along comes the sheriff."

"Good for old Tom Onion!" gasped The Duke. "He saved the kid, I guess?"

"He done that same thing, and it wasn't none too easy."

The Duke registered a vow that Tom Onion should not go unrewarded for such an act.

"I guess Tom wanted to have the credit of taking the kid into town and having him tried all right and proper," was the cold comment of the chief. "Well, Calkins, that's the story. And there's the gang!"

He pointed ahead as they topped a rise of the ground, and The Duke saw again the widespread, shadowy mass of the great posse. Even at this distance the air was still filled with thin wisps of the dust which they had raised.

33

To Return a Service

FIRST OF ALL, he must see the prisoner, if that were possible. And a wild hope formed in his mind. Suppose he were to be able to take the immediate guard of Sam by surprise? Suppose he were to be able to dash in, snatch the lead-rope from the hand of him who carried it, and so plunge away into the night, bringing Sam's horse with him?

Of course, there was only one chance in a million, but—

He made good use of the size of the crowd to shake himself clear from the "chief" and his companions. In the mass of the posse he worked his way to the front. And that was easily done, for the riders formed a great, milling mass in which there was a continual shift. The object of it, The Duke presently discovered, was to see the prisoner.

And now The Duke saw in turn. Sam rode between the sheriff on the one side, and a man who was strange to The Duke on the other. He rode with his hands tied behind his back, sitting straight as an arrow in the saddle, with his long, black hair flowing wildly down his shoulders, curling and blowing in the wind. There was no doubt that it was Sam.

For the first time The Duke was seeing that face unmasked. It was like another incarnation of Sally herself. So startling was the resemblance that The Duke gasped at it. There was the same delicately drawn profile, the same half proud and half sneering smile lurking about the corners of the mouth. There seemed to be somewhat more sternness about the set of that mouth, however, and there was a savage determination in the outthrust of the jaw. Plainly the fellow was a tiger and full of tigerish instincts, even though his hands were tied. Now and again he looked from side to side, and there was a fire in his eyes.

The Duke fell back into the procession which followed. What could be done? What should be done? Had he better turn back and ride along the western side of the Black Hills in the hope of finding Sally, perhaps with the old man at her side?

No, if he wished to serve Sally it would be far better to do his utmost for this brother of whom she was so wildly proud, so inordinately vain! It mattered not that the girl had sent out this wild rider to destroy him, simply because she had fallen in a pit. What really mattered was that the girl was in danger and suffering. What really mattered was that this very same fellow had once snatched the life of The Duke away from the danger of this same huge posse.

The Duke came to his conclusion.

Straightway he worked his way to the outer edge of the crowd and then began to fall back until he was at the very rear. Next he dismounted as though to tighten a cinch. When he climbed into the saddle the posse was streaming far ahead, and John Morrow turned to the side.

The lights of Wheeler City were beginning to twinkle before him, and it was time to beware lest his face should be seen. Indeed, already he had dared a thousand perils in coming so close to the riders. And, as he well knew, only the fact that they were not expecting him had prevented them from recognizing this rider of a gray horse.

What he did next was to make a detour which carried him at a round gallop to the farther side of Wheeler City.

Here he drew rein, and, behind the deserted and broken-down barn which had once belonged to the Perkins family, he dropped to the ground. In the interior—noisy with rats and with the stars looking through the broken roof—he placed the stallion. There was no food for Monday, and no drink, but the leisurely ride from the Guthrie Ranch and past the Black Hills had not scratched the surface of the stallion's strength. He was fit for another great run before the night was ended.

The Duke's next preparation was to go to the barn of Jess Wilcox. For two generations the Wilcox people had been fanciers of fine horses. They made money enough from their ranch to enable them to gratify their whims in the matter of purchases, and there was never a time the stable behind their town house was not filled with blooded stock. If they could not quite afford the luxury of thoroughbreds, at least they were able to buy three-quarterbreds and well-chosen ones.

In the meadow behind the barn The Duke found what he wanted. There was a cluster of half a dozen fine animals. He had only starlight to judge them by. But for a man who knows horses and loves them there is a guiding instinct which tells him of the quality the moment he glimpses it. The Duke wanted the finest horse in the meadow, and he got it. He did not examine their bodies. The light was far too dim for that. He contented himself with looking at their heads, which could be seen in profile well enough. And, finally, he chose a sleek-coated bay, glimmering in the starlight—not a large horse, but one which The Duke could have sworn would run like the wind.

It was not hard to capture his choice. The Wilcox horses were as pampered as spoiled children and as well-mannered as pet dogs. He walked to the colt of his choice, took it by the mane, and led it toward the barn with the rest of the group following. That would not do. He threw up his hand and hissed. The noise and the gesture made the others toss their heads and halt. And so he went on with his capture.

In the barn it was simple enough to fumble his way to a saddle and a bridle, and five minutes later he had lodged his captive at the side of Monday in the deserted barn.

He had secured the means of a swift retreat which would tax the powers of the tired horses in Wheeler City to the utmost. But he who was to fill the saddle on the back of the newly stolen horse was not yet at liberty. No doubt he was still in the jail, and the irons were being fitted on his wrists. They would need small handcuffs to put over those slender wrists, The Duke decided.

And he began to walk slowly back toward the town. He had become a horse thief. It was a depth to which he could not have imagined that he would ever fall. And he thought again of the sad-faced, quiet-eyed warden, and of their long talk before he stepped into liberty. There would at least be one man in the entire world who would grieve when the news of this falling off came to him. But at least The Duke would never have to face him again. There would be no capture this time. Rather than that, a gun turned against his own body—

As he came closer to the town itself—the long, black row of houses with lights spotting it here and there—he dismissed these melancholy thoughts. He needed all of his energies of body and mind for the work which now lay immediately before him.

He recalled the situation of the jail. It lay almost in the center of the town, run by the Swiney brothers. He recalled the jail itself. It was of the most singular construction. It had been pressed into service many years before when Wheeler City was not a tithe as large as it had now grown. The Slawson boys and their famous gang had descended on the town. They had been routed after a pitched battle, and five wounded prisoners were taken by the officers of the law.

There was no jail to place them in, so they had been removed to this building, and by popular subscription it had been voted a jail and bought and paid for. Since it was only a frame shack, however, and since it held men of desperate character with desperate friends who might try to break in to them, a special force of volunteers began to labor day and night until they had built up a huge wall of stone, fully three feet thick and rising as high as the eaves of the frame shack.

Thus was the outer shell of security provided, and the inner strength was furnished some time later when a series of iron bars like a gigantic net had been run across the top of the building. Thus secured at the top and the sides with impregnable strength, the jail was known as the terror of ill-doers, and more than one desperado who scorned the weaker inclosures in the mountains, and who had broken from more than one, lost heart in this fatal place and ended his own life rather than wait for the surety of the men of the law.

The Duke had reached the rear of the jail itself by the time he finished the picture of the place to his own satisfaction. It had not been altered during his three years in the prison. He stepped to one of the side windows and peered through. All was as he remembered it when, as a boy, he had played at night near the old house and had looked through this same barred window into the dimly lighted interior. It was as dim as ever. Only one light was burning, and by that faint illumination The Duke saw the brother of Sally as the sole occupant of the prison.

They had not put handcuffs on the youth. He sat with his arms folded, reclining on a cot, with his shoulders against the wall and his broad-brimmed sombrero drawn deeply over his face. With the spurs glistening on his boots it seemed for all the world as though he were about to rise and go forth from the jail. The Duke saw old "Greasy" Dowler, so many years cook and general roustabout at the jail. He had brought in the evening meal to Sam. He had waited until the youthful desperado finished the meal, and now he had gathered up the tray and was roaring with laughter at the last story of his own telling.

Now he turned, presenting a bowed, shapeless back, and hobbled out of the big room on his flat feet. The door opened, a deputy looked in with Tom Onion himself behind, then stepped back again. In the front rooms of the jail there was a storm of talk, a great play of lights. The town was gathering here and pouring up and down the steps to celebrate its victory. And it was not the end of this young marauder they were so gay about. It was the death of The Duke which made them rejoice.

He ground his teeth when he thought of that! Before

his career was over they would have double cause to wish that he had died this night!

But how to get at Sam? He might climb to the top of the building and see if it were possible to effect an opening among the bars. So, as he looked up, he instinctively caught strong hold upon the bars of the window before which he was standing, leaning his weight back as he looked up. And as he did so, one of the bars seemed to turn slightly in his hand, with a small, harsh sound of grating.

He could not believe it. He renewed his hold. He wrenched—and there was no doubt that the iron stirred in the mortar in which it was imbedded.

34

◉

Truth Will Out

HE COULD NOT BELIEVE what touch and ear had told him. Yet was it not possible, he wondered, that the jail had existed for so many years on its reputation that it had been allowed to run down? He hastily put this one fact to the proof. He ran back to a pile of junked timbers behind the jail. He picked out a stout two-by-four. He returned, and, inserting this, he pried against that bar which had already seemed weak and, under the great pressure which the lever exerted against it, the bar was torn bodily from the mortar which held it. The lower end thus freed, The Duke was about to try his luck with the upper portion of the rod when the door opened again in the front of the jail. He dropped to his knees.

When he arose again the door had been closed. Apparently they were keeping a mortally vigilant guard upon the captive, opening this door at regular intervals to look in upon him. The moment he found that the door had been closed again, he set his lever in place once more and with a single, hard jerk brought it clear. The heavy iron bar fell, and The Duke caught it in midair. He started to work at once on the nearest adjoining bar. It came away with only a shade more difficulty, and in the midst of his operations he found that Sam had noticed him at last and had risen bolt upright from the cot. The Duke waved him back and down, and he sank slowly into his former position just as the front door was opened again. The Duke fell furiously to work on the third bar. It resisted more stubbornly than the other two, but eventually it was torn out.

"Now!" cried Sam from within the window.

He stood, trembling with eagerness and terror, close to the bars. And The Duke looked up at him and in to him with some astonishment. He had not dreamed that this wild young marauder was capable of fear. But he himself knew what the shadow of a prison could work in the soul of the bravest man.

"Quick!" he called.

But there was no need of his admonition. Sam was already through the aperture. It did not seem possible that he could wriggle through so small an opening. But he managed it as though he were possessed of an oiled skin. His shoulders, his hips, worked through, and now he fell heavily toward the ground—might have crashed head down against the rocks had not The Duke caught the falling body in his arms.

He swung it clear and brought it lightly down without accident. The prisoner stood free, uninjured, but The Duke fell back from the other with a gasp, as though he had received just now a mortal stroke. He had had in his arms the body of a woman, and the truth stunned him. It was Sally herself who stood before him—shrinking now as she saw that her disguise was finally penetrated.

It was Sally who had ridden out to find him at the dictates of the old man of the cave! It was Sally who had brought him down with a shot! It was Sally who, riding closer, perhaps to finish the fallen man, had seen the face of him who had danced with her that night before! It was Sally who had kneeled beside him and bandaged his hurt and brought him back to consciousness! It was Sally, again, who had saved him from the pursuing posse. It was still Sally who had talked to him in the character of a girl one moment, and the next instant had rushed out at him like a fury in the guise of her pseudo-brother.

He could not believe it. It overwhelmed him! This was the daring outlaw, the wild rider, the marauder—this girl who now trembled before him, more disarmed because he had pierced her disguise than by the danger of half a dozen guns.

In the prison a voice was crying: "Where the— Hey, Tom—Tom Onion! He's disappeared!"

And mad tumult suddenly filled the jail from end to end. The Duke caught her by the arm.

"Sally!" he said. "We've got to run for it. You first. Straight through the trees ahead there. I'm right behind you."

Run? He could barely keep up with her. She reached the barbed-wire fence. She hurdled it like a great racer. And The Duke floundered over it in turn. She darted on with a long, swift, easy stride. They leaped into the dark of the trees safely before the pursuit came boiling through the front door of the jail and spilled across into the open space which surrounded the old building.

And while the posse, maddened by this sudden trick of chance which had defeated them, scurried here and there, shouting, shooting at shadows, raising a thunder of disappointment and rage, The Duke guided his companion straight to the old barn where he had left the bay and Monday. They jumped into the saddles. But when they had ridden outside The Duke paused close to the barn, and he said: "Here's the place for us. They're going to send out riders in every direction. They're going to sweep the hills clean all around Wheeler City. But they ain't going to look this close in. When they've tired themselves out in about five minutes, we'll start!"

She made no answer. All the spirit had departed from her. She sat the saddle with head bowed.

"Sally!" he said suddenly. And he reined Monday, so that the head of the gray came close to the bay. The Duke was at the elbow of the girl. "Sally," he said again, "you're sort of sick thinking of what happened in the cave? Because he's dead?"

"Because he's dead?" echoed Sally. "Do you think I care for that? He wasn't a man, he was a devil. Sorry for his death? Oh, I only wish it had happened years ago before—"

"Before what, Sally?"

"Before—before I met you, John Morrow!"

"Why?"

"Because you'll despise me now!"

"I, Sally?"

"Oh, I wish I were dead!" moaned Sally.

And suddenly she dropped her head in her arms and wept. The Duke could not have been more amazed had the ground split open at his feet.

"Sally," he pleaded, "don't do it. Don't do that, Sally! What have I done to—"

"You know that I—that I—that I—"

"That what, Sally?"

"That I'm shameless!"

"What?"

"Because I've ridden around in man's clothes and—oh, why didn't you leave me back in the jail?"

Still the two ideas were mingled in his brain. On the one hand, it was pretty Sally whom he had danced with. On the other hand, it was that wily marauder and terrible warrior of the Black Hills who stood before him. But now he drew her hands down.

"Will you let me tell you the straight of it, Sally?"

She stopped trying to hide her face.

"Yes," she whispered, "but what is it, John?"

He could not speak for a moment. That name and the voice in which it was spoken stabbed deeper and deeper in him.

Then he said: "I'm a mighty long ways from despising you, Sally. D'you think I was working to get your brother out of jail? No. All the time I seen with something inside of me that it was you!"

As he spoke, he remembered how he had watched with curious emotion the slender figure of that wild rider who had approached him at the charge with poised revolver that other day in the Black Hills. He touched the bandage around his head, almost hidden by the sombrero. The slight pain made the picture wonderfully vivid. There had been something about that galloping enemy which had un-nerved him at the time. There had been something which made it impossible to shoot straight, and his bullet had gone wandering. He understood why, now, just as he understood why it was that the girl in her masculine dis-guise had never spoken to him even during the flight be-fore the horsemen of Wheeler City. She had known that her voice would betray her.

"I sort of guessed it when you first come at me with a mask and a gun," he said. "And I knew it when you come at me the second time that way. D'you think I'd ever of turned my back and run from any man, Sally?"

She had raised her face to the stars.

"I didn't understand," she whispered, "but I sort of begin to, John."

"Because, from the first minute that I seen you there in the gallery over at Warner's Springs, I loved you, Sally. Do you believe me?"

"I'm trying—not to," stammered the girl. "I'm trying to tell myself that you can't mean it—but, just the same—I can't help feeling—that—that—because I loved you, John, when we were dancing there in the hall and all the other girls were looking at you like you were covered with a cloud of fire!"

"Sally dear!"

And then he had her in his arms, and her head was on his shoulder. He kissed her lips. He kissed the tears from her eyes.

"But, oh, heaven help me!" he groaned suddenly. "What right have I got to touch you, honey? I'm an out-lawed man. They've put a price on me by this time!"

"But I'm an outlawed woman, John. We're just the same!"

"You outlawed? Sally, you don't know nothing about these folks—"

"I know that they've hunted me like I was a sneaking coyote."

"That's because they thought you were a man. But if they knowed that it was a girl, there wouldn't be a man that would lift a hand agin' you. There ain't a one of 'em that wouldn't open his house to you—"

"Do you mean that?"

"On my honor."

"But if they're good people, how could they turn you out, John?"

"They got no fault for that. I made trouble for years and years. Now I'm getting some of it back."

He sighed as he realized how perfectly true were the words he had spoken.

"And if I could do just one thing to prove that I ain't what I used to be, every man jack of 'em would be glad to shake hands with me. But there ain't time to talk about me. It's you that I want to know about. Will you tell me, Sally?"

"It's a long story."

"We've got time. We can't leave here for a while."

"Then I'll begin at the beginning."

35

◎

Sally's Story

"I WAS EIGHT when Dad and Mother came down from Montana and started in trying to farm. But everything went wrong. Mother died a month after we settled on the new place. Dad got to worrying. I remember it all pretty dimly. So much had happened since that it's like words half rubbed out. But I remember that Dad got sick, too, and, finally, he decided he'd move. We started out with all the cows being drove ahead of us, driving a great big wagon that had everything we owned in it, and with the horses behind us—them that we weren't driving. Pretty soon a blizzard blew up, and the cattle started drifting. We tried to follow them, but they were moving too fast. And then the horses broke loose, and they were gone.

"Dad stopped the wagon and tried to make a windshield and a fire, but the snow began to come down in wagonloads. It killed the fire. It got colder and colder. The wagon was buried in the snow. And pretty soon Dad just tried to wrap himself and me up warm enough to sit out the blizzard.

"If he hadn't been sick he would of knowed that there wasn't any chance of that. He had to move to keep the circulation moving. But he just sat there, and he died sitting there with me in his arms—"

Her voice died away. The Duke found her hand and pressed it.

"How I was found, I dunno. Uncle Henry would never tell me. I was nearly frozen myself, so that I went to sleep. And when I woke up I was in that cave back in the Black Hills. There was a roaring fire. And Uncle Henry was working over me—"

"Uncle Henry was that old man?"

"Yes."

"He was a real uncle?"

"No. I'd seen him before. And when I first saw him he was a lot different from the way he was when you saw him. That was eleven years ago."

She was only nineteen, then, thought The Duke.

"And eleven years ago Uncle Henry was as tall as you are, and straight as an arrow. He was over seventy even then, but he was as strong as a man of fifty, I guess. His beard and his hair were white even then. And when he leaned over me I thought it was the face of the devil come to take me. I was right! He was a devil!"

"You mean to say that he was mean to a mite of a kid like you?"

"He wasn't mean. He was just nacheral with me the same's he would have been with a daughter of his own. There wasn't nobody in the world that he cared anything about except himself. And I found it out before I'd been in the cave very long.

"He started me in doing work around the cave. I was big enough to be useful, he said, and he started in to make use of me. I had to learn to do the cooking, mend his clothes, and everything else around the cave that needed to be done. Of course, I hated it and I hated him. I tried three times to run away, and each time he caught me. The first time he told me that it was bad for me to run away, and that I might die in the snow and the cold. I answered him back that I'd rather die of the cold than live here working for him. The second time he caught me he told me that if I ran away again he'd have to punish me. And the third time I ran away he caught me, brought me back to the cave, and whipped me with his quirt until I was bleeding."

"The hound!"

"After that I never dared to disobey him," said Sally. "I had to do what he told me to do, and I had to do it quick. He never asked me more'n once to do a thing. If I forgot, he would whip me and not say a word. He never whipped me as though he was angry. He whipped me as though it was simply something that had to be done. When the whipping was over he would light his pipe and seem to forget what he'd done. And he'd keep on whipping me till I found out what it was about. Of course, it didn't take very long for me to print every word he said in my mind. Every syllable he spoke was written into my memory in such a way that it wouldn't come out.

"That winter came to an end. It was the hardest time in my life. In fact, I don't think anyone could ever have suffered any more than I did. Every day was a whipping for something that had been wrong. Every night I dreamed of being tortured by Uncle Henry.

"But when the spring came things were a little better. He showed me the way out of the cave. He got me a horse. And he started taking me on little rides around through the country—not very far, and usually it was the time of dawn or twilight, when nobody could see us.

"He was better to me in lots of ways. He got me a banjo and taught me how to play. And I had to learn quick. He wouldn't stand for mistakes he'd told me about. He taught me to play and he taught me to sing. He had his mind full of old songs, and he made me learn them and sing them to him. You'd think that that would of been a happy time, but it wasn't. He never told me that he liked to hear me. He never told me when I'd sung well. All he said was when I'd done something he didn't like. And mostly he said that with his quirt."

"The yaller—" began The Duke, then choked with rage and could not finish his imprecation.

"I remember only that first year very clear," said Sally. "That was the terrible time. After that I got used to Uncle Henry. It's pretty hard to keep a girl from being happy one way or another, I guess. I always had a horse. And I sure did love them. Then I got to like the old banjo. I used to play it to myself as much as I had time. And sometimes Uncle Henry would bring me in things from his raids.

"I'd learned the first year that he was an outlaw, and that he'd committed all sorts of terrible crimes. Somehow, he made me feel that if the cave was found I'd be killed by the same people who killed Uncle Henry. I got to thinking that somehow, because I'd used things that had been taken from people he'd robbed, I was just as bad as Uncle Henry that had done the robbing. When he brought things home to me—maybe a book and maybe a dress—he'd wait till he saw that I was fond of it. And then he'd tell me a terrible story about how he done a killing to get it. He'd describe all the horrible details and the way the guns went off—until I was sick. And then he'd tell me never to let the people that was friends of that man find me, because they'd be sure to kill me. And I believed him. Well, when I was thirteen—that was five years after he'd caught me—he gave me a revolver, a little, light-mounted thirty-two. And he taught me how to shoot with it."

"He wasn't afraid that you'd use it on him?"

"No, not at all. He'd told me so much about his fights and the people that he'd killed that I'd as soon have fired at an army as at him. And he knew it. But he taught me how to use that revolver. And I loved to work with it. I had all the cartridges I wanted. And it was the one thing that he was never tired of watching me do. I could start shooting at targets and keep it up for hours at a time, and he'd sit and smoke his pipe and watch and tell me what was wrong about the way I handled the gun.

"Of course, it didn't take long for me to learn to handle it pretty well. And at the same time he began to show me how to walk and run. He showed me how to keep my toes pointing straight ahead. He showed me how to run on my toes. He taught me how to throw straight with stones. He gave me a regular schooling in handling myself the way a man handles himself. And then he took away my girl's clothes and burned them. He made me put on a man's clothes. I felt queer and embarrassed—I didn't know why—at first. But after a while the shame left me, and I was happy about the life I was leading. And I was free in my new clothes—I was freer to walk and ride and run. You see?

"By the time I was fifteen he said that I was worthy of having a good horse, and he told me to go get one. By this time he was getting so old and so feeble that he couldn't move around much. He hardly ever left the cave, and I had to do everything for him. But before that time came he'd taught me everything I needed to know in order to steal enough to live on. He'd taken me all over the country. He'd shown me the nearest ranches and all the hills. He used to draw maps in the dirt beside the fire at night, and he'd make me study them. And then he'd make me draw the same map. He'd ask me all sorts of questions—where I'd ride to if I were cornered here or there—until I knew all about the country near the Black Hills. I can tell you every inch of it! But, though I'd gone with him and watched him steal, I'd never taken anything myself. But he'd taught me to think that I had a right to take what I needed.

" 'Everybody has a right to enough to live on,' he used to say, and I believed him. Besides, it wasn't hard to believe him when he was telling me to go and steal the finest horse I could find.

"I hunted and hunted until I found the pinto in a meadow of fine horses, and simply running away from all the best of them. I roped the pinto that evening and saddled him. There was a hard fight trying to break him, but I finally made him do what I wanted him to do. And I got away back to the cave with him. Oh, that was the happiest night in my life, almost.

"Poor Pinto!" she added suddenly with a broken voice.

"And so the time went on, with Uncle Henry getting weaker and weaker every year. But every year I was more afraid and more afraid of him. Besides, I'd got to like the life we were leading. I liked the danger. And I liked the foraging among the ranches at night, even at the

Guthrie Ranch where they kept guards out trying to catch me!"

She laughed happily at the thought.

"But then, one night, I stole up to the window of a schoolhouse where they were playing music. I looked through the window and I saw that they were dancing. I'd never seen dancing before. And when I watched them swinging around the floor, something began to move in me—I began to swing in the saddle with the rhythm, you know. And when I finally went away my heart was aching. I was lonely. Oh, I was so terribly lonely that I thought I would die! And when I came home I got my banjo and played some of the music I had heard, and started dancing with my banjo just as I'd seen them dancing in the school. When Uncle Henry saw me he only said: 'I see that this is the end!' "

36

◉

Without Heart and Hope

"WHAT DID HE mean by that?" broke in The Duke, but nothing in his voice told whether his question was honest inquiry or a test to find out if Sally really did know.

"I can't tell, unless he guessed that pretty soon I'd be so lonely that I'd have to go out where I could find young people. I used to hunt for the dances after that. Every Saturday night I used to go out and try to find one. I'd watch from a window. Sometimes I couldn't get as close as that on account of the people who'd be all around the schoolhouse, and so I'd sit the saddle a long ways off and watch the shadows of the dancers go spinning and swaying across the window shades with the music blowing them along—"

She caught her breath as though the old pain and the old desire were stirring in her.

"I was seventeen when I began watching the dances. For two years I watched them, and for two years I grew wilder and wilder at the thought that I could never dance. And I used to watch the faces of the girls, with their lips parted and their eyes bright.

"Finally, I decided that I'd steal out to a dance in girl's clothes. I rode all the way to Campton. I went through three houses in that town one night, and finally I found what I wanted—a rose-colored dress that just fitted me and slippers to match. Then I rode back. I went south the next Saturday night to Warner's Springs. Then my courage went out of me. I knew that other girls went there with men, and I had no man with me!

"I'd watched dances in that hall from the gallery before, so I went up there that night—and you remember the rest. I didn't dare stay after that first wonderful dance. I was afraid that someone might guess who I was—I was afraid that someone might know the stolen dress I was wearing—and so I hurried away.

"And then—I couldn't stop thinking of you, John! I rode to Wheeler City that next night. I lurked around among the houses until I'd heard all about what was happening. And I got around to the barn where Monday was kept. When the alarm came I saddled him. I took him out and led him away with Pinto. And so I found you, and—you got away.

"And when I went home that night I was wretched, because I felt that I could never let you know I was not a boy. After you'd come to the cave, I had got back just in time to have Uncle Henry tell me that our cave had been found through the water trap, and that the man who had found it must be killed, so I jumped on Pinto, raced around the hills and found you. I remember how your bullet went wide. I came charging in. It was the first time I had faced a man in a fight, but I wanted to be killed or to kill. I didn't care which, because I was ready to die from loneliness and sadness, John. And then, when you dropped from the saddle as I fired, I rode up close— and I saw that it was you! I thought at first you were dead, and I was going to kill myself if you were—but you lived, John. You lived!"

She threw up her hands to heaven in exultation and thanksgiving as she remembered that great moment.

"That night was the time I went to Wheeler City. That was the night of the escape. The next morning, again, I found you in the hills, and I thought that you liked me, but I thought, too, that when you found out who I was, that I was really the outlaw of the Black Hills, you'd despise me. And, finally, I decided that I could not stand it any more. That was why I came charging out at you on Pinto. I wanted everything to end. I was going to ride in shooting wild and I wanted your bullet to finish my life. I was so terribly unhappy!

"And then it came to tonight. I went in to Uncle Henry, and I told him that the fires were all around the hills, that they were sure to starve us out, and that I wanted to die and end it. He started to tell me to put on woman's clothes, and that I'd be safe from danger in them. But I couldn't wait to listen. I hurried out. And after I was captured and poor Pinto was dead, I heard the explosion, and I knew what had happened. Uncle Henry had arranged a great stock of dynamite at both ends of the cave and in the center among the rocks, and he'd decided that if he were ever hunted into the cave he'd bury himself and the ones who were there with him. But after I left him he knew that he was helpless, and he finished—"

She stopped, shuddering.

"Oh, he was a terrible man, John, but he was a wonderful man, too! And I've thought what a great tiger of a man he must have been when he was younger. But now he's ended! And here I am with you, John—and we're going to be happy together!"

He found her hands again.

"We'll be happy later on," he said. "We'll be happy then, Sally. But just now we've got to wait until I'm no longer an outlaw—"

"Wait?" she echoed.

"Until we can be married, Sally."

"Will that keep me from following you, John?"

"I can't let you come!"

"John!"

"Do you think I can let you throw your life away on me, Sally?"

"Then it was simply talk—you didn't mean a word of it—you don't truly love me!"

"Hush!" he said. And then, striving desperately for the loophole of escape: "Will you wait here for thirty minutes, alone?"

"You'd never come back to me."

"On my sacred word of honor!"

"You swear you will?"

"Ah, yes!"

"Then——" She clung to him suddenly, then thrust herself away, and with a twitch of the reins he sent Monday flying away into the night. Once, before he reached the next cluster of trees, he looked back and gave himself the last sight of her. Then he bowed his head and plunged into the gloom beneath the boughs.

He would never see her again. Of that he was sure. But, in the meantime, he would make his last play. At the Fryer place, by this time, Steve Guthrie and Charlie should have met. Perhaps, indeed, their meeting had already passed and was ended. In that case he had lost his chance of extorting from one of them the confession of guilt which would free him, John Morrow, from the charge of murder which was driving him into outlawry.

He circled around the town. Once, at the approach of hoofbeats, he swung Monday to a halt in the lee of an old shack and waited while ten cursing, fuming men raged past him, swearing instant death for the outlaw of the Black Hills and all those who might have helped in his escape. The miracle had been accomplished, and the famous jail of Wheeler City had been broken. It was like the fall of a famous man!

The Duke saw them out of sight and then went on, running Monday hard, until he came at last in sight of the old Fryer place.

It was far gone with the neglect of man and the steady pressure of the elements. There was not a single unrotted board on the premises. To the side The Duke saw that the huge barn, which had been standing in a broken-backed, knock-kneed fashion three years before, had now fallen and melted toward the earth into a shapeless mass. Other sheds had crushed down under the weight of the years. Only a few small structures had hung together. The house itself was smashed flat at one end and still pushed up to its full height at the other end. It made a figure that reminded The Duke of a horse striving to get up from the ground, his fore-quarters cleared and braced on his legs, his haunch still down.

What had once been a pleasant meadowland around the ranch house had now reverted to a small and bristling, second-growth forest. In the midst of this, John Morrow flung himself from the back of Monday. He had no heart left, and no hope. The black wrecks of the ranch buildings and the utter silence seemed proof enough that Steve and Charlie had already come and gone.

Something bright slid among the trees to his right. It was the moon just pushing up above the eastern horizon, a yellow moon which quickly was shaking herself free from the black horizon.

The Duke ran on more hastily. That pricking of the bright moon into the field of the night in some strange fashion raised his heart. He came in view of the rear of the house, still raised from the ground to its full height. And then he stopped short. For there they were, standing close together and talking vigorously and with many gestures.

To shoot them down was not what he wanted. One of them must speak and tell the world what he knew. How could he be compelled?

37

In the Clear

"COUNT IT OVER before we part, Charlie," the voice of Steve was saying as The Duke drew closer.

"I'll do the counting when I get home alone," said Charlie. "I'm still hearing them hoofbeats in my ear."

"You're dreaming, Charlie. There ain't anyone riding around tonight. They're all back there in the town, shaking hands and getting drunk because they got the kid from the Black Hills. They'll be lynching him for the killings that you done, Charlie!"

"Shut up!" snapped Charlie.

"D'you think somebody'll hear me call you a killer? If they could see your face, wouldn't they know you for 'Irish' Charlie?"

The Duke started. He himself had heard many a time and oft of this notorious bad man. Irish Charlie! He had heard tales of the man in his boyhood. How many killings should be attributed to him, no man could tell.

"No matter what they see or hear, I ain't going to hear it from you, understand?"

"All right. Only I'm telling you that you'd better count that money before you leave me."

"Oh, the money's right enough."

"I want to hear you say that after you've counted. I ain't going to have you leave me and come back tomorrow saying that I gave you short change!"

"Well," growled Charlie, "it sure ain't like you to turn so honest all at once. But—I'll count it."

He drew out a wallet. He opened it. It was stuffed with bills.

"One—two—three—" he began to count.

Steve circled to his left.

"Stop where you are!" snapped Charlie. "Think I'm going to have you behind me while I got this much money in my hands? No, no! I know too much about you, Steve. You'd choke me in them big hands of yours—and then go and collect the reward!"

He laughed at his own horrible joke and went on with the counting. Steve had shrugged his shoulders in acquiescence, and now he leaned back against the standard of what had once been a pump. His right hand touched the handle, now a rust-eaten bar of bent iron which rested against the old standard.

"There's two thousand," said Charlie, putting a certain number of bills to one side. "I sure hate to go on with this. I think I heard hoofbeats a while back. They may mean danger, Steve."

"Sure," said Steve. "You can't always tell. Danger there may be!"

And, as he spoke, he swung up the heavy pump handle behind him, brought it over, and crashed it down with terrible force on the head of Charlie. There was no moan or cry from the outlaw. He sank in a heap and the money fluttered out of his hand. Over him stood Steve for a moment, then he began to laugh. It froze the blood of The Duke to listen to him. And yet laughter it assuredly was, and mirth that came from the heart.

"Honesty is the best policy," said the murderer, still chuckling. And he began to gather up the fallen money. And as he leaned over, The Duke began his approach. He was no great expert on the trail or at woodcraft, but when a man stalks an enemy he stalks with all the instinctive cunning of any beast of prey.

He came as silently as a shadow. He slipped around the corner of the house. And then bad luck struck him. His heel crunched on a bit of half-rotted board, and at the sound the big man whirled. He wheeled with gun drawn, letting the money drop from his hand. And The Duke, snarling like a cornered wildcat, sprang at his throat.

His right fist landed like a hammer on the temple of Guthrie, and the huge rancher let his weapon slide out of his fingers. He gave back one reeling pace, then, with a sort of groan of fury, he lurched in to the attack. No strength of hand could have stopped him. But the long-bodied Colt had slid like water into The Duke's hand. He jammed the muzzle within a yard of Guthrie's thick body.

"I'll blow you to smithereens, Guthrie," he said. "Just—"

Steve could not stop his rush until his chest was touching the chest of The Duke. There he paused with his hands suspended in air, hands capable of breaking The Duke in two as they descended. But the muzzle of the Colt was prodding his ribs. Presently he drew back.

"What's in your head?" he asked. "I s'pose you're out here to try to cut in on the reward? You want to claim part of the credit for killing Irish Charlie?"

"It ain't going to take me long to tell you what I want. Put your hands behind you, Steve. Put the wrists together, and then turn round with your back to me."

The rancher hesitated.

"Don't you think that it'd please me to pump you full of lead? Do what I tell you to do or you're finished, Steve!"

And Steve, his shoulders sagging, obeyed. His wrists were bound behind him. His knees and his heels were tied hard. That done, John Morrow kicked some rotten boards together, piled them in a heap, and in another moment had a fire blazing. He added more wood. The flame leaped.

"You'll have half the town out here," groaned Steve. "They'll lynch you by the light of this fire, you fool!"

"They're welcome to take me," said The Duke. "All I want is five minutes with you."

As he spoke he shoved the end of the old pump handle into the fire which he had kindled. Next he took out a few pieces of paper from his inner coat pocket, and a stub of a pencil.

"Steve," he said, "you're going to write down here the whole truth—that it was Irish Charlie that killed William Guthrie, and that it was you that hired him to do it. You understand?"

"I understand that I'll see you hanged first! What's that?"

"What?"

"I saw something move there among the trees."

"My hoss, I guess," said The Duke without turning his head. "Steve, you're going to write down that truth if I have to brand you with the iron until you do it!"

"What?" groaned the rancher.

"You heard me talk," said The Duke.

He picked up the pump handle by the cool end. He drew the other end, smoking, from the fire and waved it so that the fumes passed into the face of the rancher.

"Will you talk?" he asked.

He dropped the iron back into the fire.

"I'll smear your face into one lump!" he declared.

"Morrow," said Guthrie. "I've got over eight thousand dollars in cash that I can pay you—"

"And then bash my head in like you did with Irish?"

"It's only the beginning of what I'd pay you, Morrow."

"How could I be sure you'd pay?"

"I'll give you any oath you want."

"Don't talk to me about oaths. I seen you murder Charlie."

"What proof do you want?"

"I want you to state the facts and sign what you state."

"So you can blackmail me to death?"

"No, so's I can show the facts to Tom Onion and get cleared."

"And what would I get?"

"A chance to clear out of the country. There's two hosses—your own and Charlie's. You can take 'em both. And you can take this dirty money of yours, too. There ain't any harm in that. I don't want it. You've got eight thousand and two hosses and a chance to run. Ain't that enough for you?"

"And if I don't talk?"

"I'll warm you up with a red hot iron till you change your mind."

"There ain't enough devil in you to let you do that, partner!"

"You don't know me, Guthrie. I'm aching to let drive a couple of slugs through you. Now, talk up quick. Will you write down the plain facts for me?"

"Morrow, I'll pay you half the value of the ranch if you'll let me get off—"

"D'you think that I'll take money for my spoiled reputation?"

"Then gimme the paper—but you're a fool, and as big a fool as ever lived!"

He had taken the paper and the pencil as The Duke freed his right hand. But here a voice spoke from the side.

"There ain't no need to do any writing, Guthrie. We've heard enough and seen enough to hang you for what you've done. And we've heard enough and seen enough, Morrow, to put you in the clear!"

The Duke wheeled upon the speaker, and all he could at first make out was a narrow line of moonlight sliding down the barrel of a leveled rifle. The man was hidden by the shrubs. But his voice was well known. It was Tom Onion. Nor was he alone. There were others behind the bushes. In the last few seconds a dozen men had crawled up within close shooting distance of The Duke and Steve Guthrie.

The Duke raised his hands high above his head.

"Tom," he said, "come out and take me. I'm sure tired of fighting the law!"

"Take you?" echoed Onion, standing up, with his rifle, however, still held ready. "Why should I take you? There ain't nothing agin' you, Morrow. We been fooled. All we owe you now is thanks for winding up this deal. If you'll act as my deputy, you can ride on the far side of Guthrie taking him in!"

He caught the hand of John Morrow and wrung it.

"This ain't all we've found in the last few minutes," he said. "There's a girl that we found back yonder. She's sort of lonely, Duke. And, putting two and two together, I sort of think that she'd be powerful glad to see you, son!"

The Duke answered with a startled exclamation; the next moment he was racing in the direction of Monday.

There was this remarkable thing to be observed—that The Duke had been popular among the ladies and hated among the cowpunchers when he reigned in Wheeler City in the old days. But after the wedding with Sally it was soon discovered that he was better liked by the men, and that the women could not avoid speaking bitter words. They could have forgiven him all of his crimes, but they could never forgive him for bringing in one who eclipsed the very pride of the town.